THE LONG WAY HOME

the long way home

KATHY ALTMAN

AUTHOR'S NOTE

The Long Way Home is the re-release of a Harlequin SuperRomance, and was previously titled *The Other Soldier*.

THE LONG WAY HOME

Copyright © 2023, 2012 Kathy Altman

Cover Design by: Sommer Stein, Perfect Pear Creative

Digital ISBN-13: 978-1-7323580-4-1

Print ISBN-13: 978-1-961992-00-9

This book is a work of fiction. The characters, names, places, and events portrayed in this book are products of the writer's imagination and are not to be construed as real. Any similarity to real persons, living or dead, or actual events, locales, or organizations is entirely coincidental and not intended by the author.

For more information on Kathy Altman and her books, sign up for her newsletter or visit her website: www.kathyaltman.com.

For Mom,

my fellow book fiend.

- 1 -

PARKER PATTED THE SUN-warmed dirt she'd scooped around the young plant, singing along with John Travolta as he bragged about making out under a dock. When Olivia Newton John started trilling her side of the story, Parker's cell phone died.

Darn, darn, darn, darn, *darn*. And how typical. The man gets to finish while the woman barely gets started.

Parker fished the device out of the bib pocket of her overalls and sat back on her boot heels. The screen had gone dark. She'd forgotten to charge the dumb thing. Again.

She tugged the earbuds free with a sigh and stuffed the whole mess into her pocket, ignoring the dirt she should have brushed from her gloves. Just as well. If Harris had walked up on her while she was singing, he'd have demanded hazardous duty pay.

Or not. She pressed her lips together. Harris Briggs knew better than anyone that she couldn't afford even regular wages.

A feisty spring breeze carrying the scent of damp earth and lilacs chased the thought away. She rose to her knees and pulled off her hat, enjoying the rush of air that cooled her sweat-soaked head. Hands on hips, she surveyed the progress she'd made since lunch. A stubby string of bright green plugs stretched away from her. A little compost, a little water, a lot of sun, and next June, Thistle Hill Growers would have its first crop of strawberries.

Parker grunted and snatched up her water bottle. If only a child were that easy to raise.

"Ma'am?"

She jumped. The bottle slipped from her grasp and hit the ground with a sloshing thud. Lukewarm water pooled beneath her right knee. An unfamiliar male voice clipped out an apology and she lifted a hand to shade her eyes. Standing at the edge of the strawberry bed was a tall, well-built man wearing a black beret, tinted sunglasses and a class-A U.S. Army uniform.

Tim.

She blinked, then sat down hard. A swell of grief crowded her lungs and she struggled to catch her breath.

Not Tim. Of course not Tim.

It could never be Tim.

The soldier muttered something and dropped into a crouch in front of her. His sunglasses dangled between his fingers. She lifted her gaze to his face and winced at the grim remorse she saw there.

Don't be so pathetic, Parker Anne.

"Forgive me," he said.

She stared into eyes the color of maple syrup, eyes that looked so much older than the rest of him, and slowly shook her head. Then realized he might take that as a refusal. "No need," she finally murmured. She pushed to her feet, waving away his offer of help. "I'm fine." She stepped back from his spotless uniform and slapped at the mud clinging to her knees. Head bent, she blinked like a madwoman.

"You sure you're okay? You went white there for a second."

"I just—" She swallowed hard and straightened. "I thought you were someone else."

"Yes, ma'am." He removed his beret, revealing dark, close-cropped hair. "Your husband."

"You...served with him?"

For a split second his features went rigid. "No, ma'am. I'm with the 1st Infantry Division out of Fort Knox. But I was deployed to Baghdad, same time as Sergeant First Class Dean." He hesitated, then extended a hand. "Corporal Reid MacFarland."

She peeled off her right glove and took his hand. His grip was strong and confident, and despite the remoteness in his eyes he made her feel...wistful.

And we're back to pathetic. "Parker Dean," she said, and let go. "Kentucky's a long way from Pennsylvania. What brings you to Thistle Hill?"

"I hoped we could talk." He picked up her hat. "Somewhere out of the sun?"

Apparently he'd noticed the whole red hair and freckles thing. And although she should know better, his concern defused her internal I'm-alone-with-a-strange-man alarm. While she debated whether to lead him to the house or to the potting shed that doubled as her office, he slipped on his shades, paused, then pulled them off again. She couldn't help noticing the slight shake in his hand.

The corporal outweighed her by a solid fifty pounds and out...well, out-heighted her by five or six inches. He was a soldier. He'd survived combat. In Iraq.

And *he* was nervous?

Not good. Sudden tremors rippled up and down Parker's legs. Her little family couldn't handle any more bad news.

"Tell me why you're here." *Then go.* Before he could answer, her stomach dropped. "The death gratuity." She'd invested that for Natalie. For college. No way she'd let them —

"No, ma'am. I'm not here in any official capacity."

"But you're..." She gestured, and he glanced down at his crisp class-As.

"I wanted to show my respect."

"I see." Though she didn't. Not at all. She backed away again, fighting the urge to tug that uniform close, to wrap her arms around it and rest her cheek against the familiar green wool. She hadn't seen dress greens since the funeral.

"Might as well spit it out," she said, with a lift of her chin. "Nothing you can say could be worse than what I heard thirteen months ago. Friendly fire, they told me —" She swallowed, and jerked her shoulders up and down. "I doubt you can top that, Corporal

3

MacFarland."

"I'm sorry."

She grimaced and wiped a wrist across her forehead. "No. *I'm* sorry. You have nothing to apologize for."

"Actually, I do." His jaw flexed. "Your husband was killed by a missile fired —"

"From a U.S. drone. A Hellfire, they said." Did she really have to hear this again? "What's that got to do with you?"

"Everything." He straightened shoulders already level enough to make any carpenter proud. "I'm the one who sent the drone."

* * *

WIDE-EYED SILENCE. THEN the distant bark of a dog and a rushing noise as a mass of starlings flew overhead, the sound like rows and rows of clothes-pinned sheets flapping in the wind.

The woman he'd made a widow stared back at him, face rigid, lips parted. Red chased the pallor from her cheeks and her hands clenched at her sides. She seemed to shrink right in front of him, every muscle tightening, clenching, compacting her into a monument to rage.

"You s-sent it? On purpose?" Her voice started out no stronger than a thread and ended up a hallelujah chorus of bitter fury. "Are you saying my husband was collateral *damage?*"

"No. *No.*" Jesus. He'd screwed it up already. "I'm saying it was...my mistake."

"Are you — you — why would you even think you could come here and — my God —" She stumbled back a step and threw out an arm. Her glove sailed away and landed in a distant patch of clover. She pointed toward the gravel driveway, where he'd parked his Jeep, her entire body trembling. "You need to leave. Now."

He wanted to. God knew he wanted to. But he'd be damned if he'd add "coward" to all the other labels he was lugging around.

He'd come to make whatever amends he could. Do something, anything, to ease the loss he'd caused. His counselor had advised against it.

His counselor didn't have nightmares.

"Hear me out. Please." He pulled in a slow breath. "I need to apologize—"

"Apologize?" She made a horrible, strangled sound he figured was meant to be a laugh. She drew a wrist across her face again, but this time it wasn't sweat she was wiping away.

He cleared his throat. "I'm not asking for forgiveness."

"Good. That's good. Because you won't get it. Your 'mistake' cost my husband his life. His *life*." Her voice broke and she jammed the heels of her hands to her eyes. He doubted she noticed she was still wearing one glove. She dropped her arms and glared. "How dare you. To come here like this without... What were you thinking?"

"Ma'am, I can only say—"

"No. *No.* Don't say anything." She was shaking her head at him, eyes shimmering with unutterable grief. "I don't know what you want from me, but you've already taken enough."

He winced. "I only wanted to—"

"No. You don't get to want anything." She choked on a sob. "I can't...I can't do this."

He watched her stalk away, her path not entirely straight. She headed for the nearest of a trio of plastic-wrapped Quonset huts that looked like they'd survived a hurricane—barely. Reid's insides ached, as if he'd taken a knee to the gut. But she hadn't said anything he hadn't already said to himself.

"Parker!" She ignored the shout that came from somewhere behind them. Moments later she disappeared into the greenhouse. A sixty-something man in baggy overalls—must be some kind of uniform—strode around to face Reid, brawny hands on hips, no hair above his neck save for the steel-colored eyebrows that shaded a narrowed gaze.

"What's goin' on? Who're you?"

Reid sized up the other man. Rough, no-nonsense, shoulders like a lumberjack. Carried himself as if anything in his way had better get the hell out of it. Ten to one a former Marine.

Huh. Could be he'd go back to Kentucky sporting a cracked rib or two.

Things were looking up.

"Corporal Reid MacFarland." He hooked his shades in his breast pocket and offered his hand. "I came to see what I could do."

"Harris Briggs." He gestured with his head at the greenhouse where Parker Dean had sought refuge. "You in her husband's unit?"

"No, sir. I'm the one who killed him."

Briggs sucked air and his eyes stretched wide. "I'll be damned," he muttered. He looked down at the ground, scratched his chin, looked back up. "You mean to kill him?"

"No, sir."

"They call that an accident."

"They call that fratricide."

Briggs eyed Reid's stripes. What was left of them. "Got away scot-free, did you?" When Reid didn't answer he pulled a pack of gum from his bib pocket and held it out. Seriously? He'd just admitted to manslaughter and the old guy offers him a stick of gum? Reid's muscles were clamped so tight he couldn't even shake his head. Briggs shrugged and tucked the pack away, unopened.

"Tell me somethin', Corporal. What happened over there?"

"No offense, Mr. Briggs, but you're not the one I came to see."

"Fair enough." He moved past Reid and plucked Parker Dean's water bottle from the strawberry patch, used it to motion toward the greenhouse. "Wouldn't listen to you, huh?"

"Can't say I blame her, sir." Reid nodded once. "I'll be on my way."

"Why is everyone in such a blasted hurry?"

Reid blinked. "With all due respect, shouldn't you be chasing me off the property?"

"Ain't my property." Briggs caught his eye and shrugged. "Been over a year. Talkin' it out might help her move on."

Move on. Right. As hard as it had been for Reid, he couldn't even imagine what the widow had been through. Not to mention her kid.

"You overseas all this time?"

"I came when I could."

"So what now? You headin' back home?"

"I wanted to apologize. It's the least I can do."

"What's the most?"

"Sir?"

"You said apologizin's the least you can do. What's the most?"

Reid shifted. Talking to Briggs was like having a conversation with his own conscience.

"I'm on thirty days' leave. I didn't know what I'd find here, but I'd planned to offer to help. Any way I could. Always supposing — " he eyed the greenhouse " — Mrs. Dean was willing to have me around." Which, clearly, she was not.

Probably figured he'd go after her kid next.

His neck muscles locked. *Suck it up, soldier.* He'd never expected this to be easy. Had counted on the exact opposite, as a matter of fact.

"Good idea, offerin' to help." With a sweep of his muscled arm, Briggs indicated the farmhouse, the garden plots, the greenhouses. "We could use it."

Reid studied the house. Two stories of weathered wood standing in a copse of trees bordered by acres of flatland. A tired-looking Toyota hunkered in the yard, flanked by an oak tree sporting a tire swing and an unruly hedge showing off sunshine-yellow blooms. A pink bicycle with a purple bear duct taped to the handlebars lay on its side in the grass.

In comparison to…everything…his five-year-old Jeep looked brand spanking new.

Beside him Briggs stroked his chin. "Sure does need a paint job."

"Like a desert needs water."

"That mean you're stayin'?"

"That's up to Mrs. Dean." He pulled a folded piece of paper from his breast pocket. "My cell number. Unless Mrs. Dean calls and tells me not to come, I'll be back in the morning."

"Where will you be till then?"

Reid put on his beret. "I'll find a motel."

"We only got one. Joe's not officially open, but I guess he'll put you up." Reid nodded his thanks and Briggs hooked his thumbs in the straps of his overalls. "This mean you won't be coming back if she says she doesn't want you?"

"That's right." Hadn't Reid done enough to this family?

"You, uh, never met Tim Dean, did you?"

"No, sir."

"Neither did I. But I can tell you he'd believe his wife and daughter deserve better than a personal check."

Reid stiffened. Briggs had read his mind. But what choice did he have? Financial help made perfect sense, considering Reid had caused the death of the family's breadwinner. A death that had left a widow and a child to fend for themselves.

He tamped down a surge of regret he'd let play out later. Much later, when it was just him and a bottle of beer. Or three.

Reid didn't have many expenses, and he sure as hell didn't spend much of his pay while deployed. He'd already talked to his bank about a loan. Whether or not she let him pitch in with physical labor, he'd planned to give Mrs. Dean enough money to keep her family solvent. He'd hoped to have a frank discussion with her about that. Given her reaction, it seemed a check in the mail was the best bet.

Yeah, it was guilt money. Didn't matter. Still had to be paid.

He frowned at Briggs. "I'd like to help, but I have to respect Mrs. Dean's wishes."

"Never mind her. I'll talk her around. Woman's too stubborn for her own good. I know what you're thinkin' — she can hire help. Easier said than done here in Thistle Hill. And even if we do find someone, she can't afford to pay what they'd be asking. You gonna walk away from a war widow in dire straits?"

Reid's mouth flattened. "If she wants me to."

Briggs waved a hand. "Now, don't go gettin' your dress over your head." He scratched the back of his neck. "I'll see what I can do. You prepared to work if she takes you up on your offer?"

That was the idea. He'd put her in this position. It was up to him to get her out. And he had a month to do it. Assuming Briggs could talk her into letting him back on the property.

Reid squinted. "Long as you don't expect me to wear overalls."

"You can wear a tutu for all I care. Might even draw some customers."

Reid grunted. Tutu, hell. He should have packed his tactical gear.

A loud, rumbling sound. The two men looked toward the road, and watched a school bus lumber to a stop at the end of the gravel driveway. A black Labrador retriever rounded the far side of the house, tail high, bark impatient, legs a blur. A young girl in bright pink jeans and a matching shirt stepped off the bus. She walked a few feet and dropped her backpack at the same time as she fell to her knees in the grass. Her arms went around the dog and she nestled her face in the shiny jet fur.

Reid's scalp started to prickle. He resisted the urge to tug off his beret.

The dog wriggled free, ran a short distance and stopped, inviting the girl to give chase. She went along with the game, running after the Lab and covering half the distance to the strawberry patch before noticing Reid. She stumbled to a stop, mouth open, russet hair swinging around her face. Briggs called out to her but she ignored him, turned and dashed for the house as if suddenly caught in an icy downpour.

Like mother, like daughter.

The dog, on the other hand, greeted Reid as if he were packing bacon. He pushed his nose at both palms, snuffled up and down both legs, and ran figure eights around both men. When he paused to conduct another inspection Reid stroked his silky head, fighting the urge to hug him just as the girl had.

"What's his name?"

"Chance. Sweet dog, but dumber than chickweed."

"Hey, boy. Hey, Chance." At the sound of his name the dog barked and jumped up onto his hind legs. He braced his front paws against

Reid's dress jacket.

"Careful, now. Don't want to sully that uniform."

Reid's fingers tightened in the Lab's fur and he glanced over at the farmhouse.

Too damned late.

* * *

PARKER'S SHOULDERS ACHED BUT she didn't dare ease up on the scrub brush. Best thing in the world for emotional overload? A bucket of warm soapy water, a flat surface and a set of nylon bristles.

Unless there was something in dropkick range. But she couldn't afford to play soccer with her plants.

Unfortunately the scrubbing thing wasn't really working, either. She could barely breathe, with all that fury blocking her throat. She'd been doing so well, no longer stressing about forgetting to mail her letter to Tim, or wondering if he was using his sunscreen, or when he'd next get the chance to call home. Keeping it together for Nat —

She sucked in a scalding breath and felt it sear all the way up to her eyeballs. *Forgive me,* the corporal had said. Now she knew he'd meant for so much more than startling her.

"You're rubbin' that worktable like you think a genie's gonna pop out."

Parker stopped, stared down at the suds coating the table and slowly relaxed her grip on the brush. Then she whirled and threw the dumb thing at the bucket. The resultant spray of soapy water was nowhere near as satisfying as she'd hoped. She yanked off her lime-green rubber gloves and tossed them after the brush.

"Did he tell you who he was?" She snatched up the hose. "Unbelievable, isn't it? What made him think he could… Why would he even think I would consider —" She squeezed the nozzle too hard and water jetted off the tabletop and ricocheted back into her face. "*Damn* it. What I'd like to know is, why is that man even still in the Army?"

Harris took the hose away. "You need to calm down, my girl." He plucked a handkerchief from his back pocket and held it out. "Nat's home. Why don't you go check in with her and I'll finish up here."

"I can do it." She wiped her face, jammed the handkerchief down into her bib pocket with her phone and grabbed at the hose. Harris held it out of reach and she frowned. "I can *do* it. Why don't you go pester Eugenia?"

He scowled and flushed at the same time. "Don't you think it's time you learned to delegate?"

"Don't you think it's time you learned I'm in charge?"

He raised an eyebrow. Parker felt a gush of mortified heat sweep up through her chest and into her neck. While she struggled to find the words to apologize, Harris tucked the hose nozzle in the crook of his elbow and took his time unwrapping a stick of gum.

"I'm so sorry," she said. "I didn't mean it."

"I know that, Parker Anne. Anyways, Eugenia and I aren't datin' anymore."

When Harris got that look on his face Parker knew better than to push her luck. She collapsed back against the table, palm to her forehead. What she'd give for a handful of ibuprofen and a caffeinated soda. The last thing she needed to do was alienate her strongest ally. Thanks to Harris Briggs, she'd finally come to terms with Tim's death. And Nat's nightmares had only just gone on hiatus. Neither of them should have to deal with an in-the-flesh reminder of what they'd lost.

And how they'd lost him.

Thank God she'd sent the corporal away before Nat got home.

"Nat knows to get started on her homework," she said. "She'll be fine."

"She's bound to have questions."

She left her hand where it was and talked into her wrist. "About what?"

"About your visitor."

She launched upright. Oh, no. Oh, God. "She met him?"

"Not *met*. *Saw*. And as soon as she saw, she ran."

Parker's hands shook. She turned and leaned on the table, palms pressed flat on the soapy surface. "I don't need this. Nat doesn't need this. Not now."

She stared through the plastic sheeting at the row of feathery pine trees that separated the greenhouse from the "garage" that was little more than a leaky barn. "He came a long way for nothing. I don't have the slightest interest in helping to ease that man's conscience. If I were in his position I'd never even presume to—" Emotion backed up into her throat again.

"The man's tryin' to do the right thing."

Parker turned her head sharply. "You're defending him?"

"It was an accident. More than a year ago. He wants to apologize. I think, my girl, you should hear him out."

She shook her head, not believing what she was hearing. "You of all people," she whispered. "You know what we've been through. You've seen—" Wait a minute. She turned, and crossed her arms. "I get it. Marines, wasn't it?"

"That has nothin' to do with it."

Oh, please. Then something he'd said finally registered. "What do you mean, he *wants* to apologize? Isn't he on his way back to Kentucky?"

Harris's expression turned mutinous and Parker was tempted to grab the hose and turn it on him. The last time he'd wanted his way, he'd sulked until Parker had given in and ordered a dozen quince trees. Not one had sold.

And she never did get that jelly he'd promised.

He fingered a leaf on a geranium that sported blooms as red as a male cardinal. "He offered to stay. Help out."

"He what?"

"He wants to make sure you and Nat will be okay."

"We'll be a heck of a lot more okay without him around. I couldn't look at him without thinking of…of Tim." She gulped, wrapped her arms around her waist and held on tight. "I don't want him here."

"He's a soldier and he deserves your respect. No different from your husband."

Her body went slack. "It is different. It's hugely different. Tim never killed anyone." As soon as the words were out of her mouth she recognized the absurdity. She had no way of knowing what Tim had done in theater. She began to pace, shaking her hands as if she'd burned them. "You know what I mean. If he killed anyone it wasn't an allied soldier."

"Probably not. But you don't know that. If he did, wouldn't you want him to have the chance to ask for forgiveness?"

She stopped pacing. "He really got to you, didn't he?" Her fingers dug into her hips. "Where is he, anyway?" So help her, if she found out he was anywhere within even a mile of her property…

Harris carefully set the hose aside. "Listen, my girl. MacFarland may be a soldier, but he's a man first. A man trying to make amends. Remember that five-year-old boy, run down by a drunk driver a few months back? You said then that you didn't know how the driver could ever live with himself after being responsible for something like that."

Parker suddenly had trouble breathing. "Are you actually telling me that if I don't forgive him he'll kill himself?"

"All's I'm sayin' is, think about the consequences of your actions."

"Too bad this…corporal…didn't follow that advice." Harris frowned and she scrubbed her palms on her overalls. "This conversation is over. I don't want to see that man, I don't want to talk to him, I don't want him talking to me."

"What if he goes back to the desert and gets himself killed? You think you might be sorry you didn't give him a listen?"

"This is unbelievable. He makes a mistake that costs a man's life and I'm the one getting the lecture."

"I'm tired, Parker Anne."

"Me, too. So let's drop it. Why don't you go on up to the house and—"

"I mean, I'm *tired.* I can't keep up anymore. For Pete's sake, I'm old."

She looked at him then, really looked at him, at his sunbaked skin and disappointed shoulders. She fought the sudden sting of helpless tears.

"You're not old. But you are right. I work you too hard. I'm sorry, I get so caught up in—" She swallowed. "I'll figure something out. Get you some help. Why don't you take it easy for a few days? I'll handle tomorrow's delivery."

"You think I don't know you can't afford to hire anyone else right now? And you can't run this place by yourself. There's the spring contract orders to fill and more coming in every day. Unless you've found the secret to gettin' by on a few hours' sleep every day, I don't see the harm in lettin' the man help out."

"I thought I'd made myself clear. That's not going to happen."

"It's for your own good."

"I think you're more worried about him than me. Since when did you become so charitable?"

"Since when did you become so selfish?"

Parker stumbled back a step and banged up against the table. Harris looked at her, his eyes sad.

"You need help. He needs to help. Gardening's therapy. You're not the only one suffering, my girl."

"But Nat—"

"Needs to learn not to hightail it every time she sees a man in uniform. She also needs to learn the power of forgiveness. And who's she gonna learn that from, if not you?"

"I can't forgive him. You don't know what you're asking. Even *he* knew better than to ask for that."

"Doesn't mean he doesn't want it." He waited a beat. "All I'm askin' is for you to try."

Parker shook her head. "That's too much. I'm trying to rebuild here. Not just the greenhouses, but our lives. I don't have time for anything—or anyone—that threatens that."

Harris didn't say a word. Not that she'd expected him to. How could he argue with her wanting to put her family first?

R EID SQUINTED THROUGH THE windshield. The motel outside
Thistle Hill looked about as inviting as a trailer park after a
tornado. But according to Harris Briggs, it was his only option.
Unless he wanted to sleep in the Jeep.

Still, the dingy, mildew-coated structure almost made him
homesick for the pitiful piece of real estate he'd been assigned at Al
Asad Air Base—which had included room for his bunk and his
footlocker, and not much else.

Hell, who was he kidding? He'd been homesick for his unit since
stepping off that cargo plane at Godman Army Airfield. Especially
after learning he'd been kicked out of Fort Knox housing. New
regulations—all unmarried soldiers had to find accommodations off-
post. His shoulders tightened, and he rolled them back to shrug off
the tension.

He pulled into the motel's crumbling asphalt lot and parked in
front of a battered metal post turned golden by the afternoon sun. The
pole supported a newly made sign that read Sleep at Joe's.

Clever. And just the kind of place he didn't need. Odds were that
behind the registration desk lurked an attention-starved, big-haired
woman who would set aside her latest diet bible and siphon Reid for
information like she was a '78 Lincoln and he was the last gas pump
for five hundred miles.

The backseat of the Jeep was looking better every second.

Then he thought about his unit over in the sandbox, and how
during missions they had to sleep in trenches dug for protection from

mortar fire. What did he have to complain about? He got out of the Jeep, stepped over a cluster of wilting daffodils and entered the office.

The clerk manning the desk was just that—a man. Despite his stubbly jaw and frayed jeans and T, he didn't seem the casual-conversation type. And the book he set aside when Reid walked in had nothing to do with weight loss. Instead it was a book of paint and fabric samples.

The clerk gave him and his uniform the once-over and leaned forward, elbows on the counter. "Need directions?"

The man's eyes held misplaced respect. Reid lowered his own gaze and pulled his wallet from a back pocket. "Only to an available room." He slid a credit card across the counter. The clerk didn't even glance at it.

"Sorry, man. Not open for business yet."

Damn. "Any recommendations?"

"There's a Motel 6 twenty-five miles east."

"Thanks."

The phone trilled and the man nodded, then turned away. Reid was at the door when the man called after him. "Not one to ask for favors, are you?"

Slowly Reid turned. "Meaning?"

"That was Harris Briggs on the phone. Said he'd told you to mention his name." The clerk shrugged. "I have a room that's clean but postapocalyptic ugly. I just bought the place. The reno's barely started."

"I can handle a lot of ugly."

Another survey of his uniform. "Bet you can." The clerk pushed across a registration form. "Staying long?"

"No idea."

"Just keep me posted."

Reid signed the form and offered his hand. "Reid MacFarland."

"Joe Gallahan." He held out a key card. "Room six. Questions?"

"Yeah. Where can I get something to eat?"

An hour later, on the toaster-size TV—hell, a laptop could have

16

gotten a better picture — James Coburn demonstrated his prowess with a knife in *The Magnificent Seven* while Reid eyed the remains of a pepperoni pizza that had looked a lot better than it tasted. He hadn't wanted to settle for fast food, but neither had he had the energy to take Gallahan's advice and look for something to eat in the next town.

Of course if he had, he'd have missed soaking in the atmosphere of Thistle Hill's only motel. He looked around with a grimace. The place must have been sitting empty for years. Considering what kinds of creatures had probably been hanging out rent-free, he probably shouldn't be making jokes.

Probably shouldn't be breathing without a mask, either.

Gallahan had one hell of a job ahead of him.

If the motel's exterior, with its lime-green paint, scraggly landscaping and crevice-ridden concrete qualified as a horror flick, then the interior had to be every Michael-Myers-on-Halloween-night movie ever made spliced into one gory, never-ending saga.

The cheap paneling on the walls bore twice as many scars as the plastic covering Parker Dean's greenhouses. Cigarette burns decorated the dresser, the table and the nightstand. He suspected that the carpet, which had been repaired many times over with duct tape, hadn't started out that muddy-brown color. And someone had painted the ceiling turquoise, presumably to cover up water stains. Reid muttered a quick prayer that it didn't rain.

But despite the less-than-lovely interior, the room was clean, just as Gallahan had promised. Not a speck of dust in sight. Someone had worshipped the bathroom with a scrub brush, and the fresh scent of lemon lingered just beneath the smell of tomato sauce.

He let the slice of pizza fall back into the box and found himself wondering what kind of meal Parker Dean and her daughter were sitting down to. Something healthy and hearty, no doubt. Like roast beef and mashed potatoes. Or spaghetti with meatballs. He frowned at the grease-laden pizza and closed the lid.

Then again, maybe she didn't have time to cook, since she was a single parent. Thanks to him.

He grabbed the TV remote and stabbed at the power button. Wondered for the hundredth time if he'd done the right thing, coming to Thistle Hill.

No way Harris Briggs would be able to talk Mrs. Dean into letting him help out. And even if he did, was it fair of Reid to do so? What the hell had he been thinking, expecting a grieving family to accommodate the man responsible for their grieving in the first place?

Money was the kinder option. Before he took off in the morning, he'd leave a check with Gallahan.

He finally recognized a far-too-cheerful chirping as his cell phone. The screen displayed an unfamiliar number and for a second or two his lungs went AWOL. Had Harris Briggs managed the impossible?

"That you, Corporal?"

"Mr. Briggs."

A pause. "I'd tell you to call me Harris but I doubt we'll be usin' each other's names much."

Right. "She said no."

"That's puttin' it mildly." When Reid snorted softly, Harris Briggs cleared his throat. "It was a pleasure to meet you, son. We appreciate what you boys are doin' over there."

Reid thanked him and ended the call.

So that was that.

Son. He sat back and mentally sifted through years of memories, scrambled to single out the one where his father had last called him "son." Couldn't find it. And suddenly, desperately, he needed it.

A quick, disgusted shake of his head. Enough with the self-pity.

He should be relieved. Should be grateful he didn't have to spend his leave trying to fix something destined to remain forever broken. He'd tried. And failed. He'd write that check, and when the loan came through he'd write a bigger one. One that would require years of monthly payments.

So why did he feel like he was getting off easy?

No doubt Parker Dean would agree. His mouth relaxed as he pictured her. She'd looked like she'd been digging an underground tunnel to Canada. She'd worn a sweat-soaked T-shirt under an oversize pair of mud-streaked overalls. Dirt marked both cheeks and flecked the cinnamon hair gathered at the back of her head. But despite all that mud he'd registered creamy skin, a curvy figure and eyes that promised sincerity and humor.

And once she'd found out who he was, she hadn't hesitated to tell him to go pound sand.

Tim Dean had been a lucky man. Too bad Reid had no business thinking of Parker Dean as anything other than someone he owed a hellacious obligation to.

Out of the corner of his eye he spotted movement. The stealthy, scampering, wall-hugging movement of a mouse. Squatters. Terrific. They'd have to go. He hadn't signed on for roommates. Not even for one night.

He stood and reached for the phone, intent on petitioning Gallahan for a few traps. A glance at the corner where the mouse had disappeared and he hesitated, let his hand slide off the receiver.

For fifteen months he and thirty other guys had tolerated a family of sand rats in their tent. Certainly he could handle a mouse or two.

Live and let live, and all that.

He collapsed onto the bed, and threw an arm across his face so he wouldn't see the room start to blur.

*   *   *

PARKER CREPT DOWN THE hallway past her daughter's bedroom. Thank goodness for the night-lights Nat had insisted on when they'd moved in. Their eerie green glow helped her reach the attic without breaking a toe. She eased the seldom-used door open, flipped on the light switch and pulled the door shut behind her.

She shivered and hesitated on the bottom step. A short-sleeved tee and flannel pajama bottoms were no match for the attic chill. Why hadn't she thought to grab a sweater? She grunted. Forget the sweater. It was the middle of the night. Why hadn't she stayed in bed, instead of baking muffins and playing safari in her own attic?

She wrapped her arms around her waist and peered up the worn, narrow flight of stairs. But it wasn't the cold or the cobwebs draped along the walls that rooted her in place. She hadn't ventured up there since she'd tucked Tim's things away a year ago.

Don't be such a baby.

She took in a breath, then another, and started to climb. The air smelled thickly of dust, faintly of machine oil and faded roses. But the way her stomach was rebelling, anyone would think a family of skunks had moved in.

Five steps up she snagged a sock on a nail head. She yanked her foot free and kept going. She'd have to come back with a hammer.

If only all of her problems could be solved so easily.

Half an hour later, sitting cross-legged on a comforter she'd scavenged from a cardboard box, she thumbed through the last of the seven photo albums stacked at her hip. She'd had the sudden urge to look through them all — the pictures of her college days in Blacksburg, Virginia, where she'd met Tim; their wedding photos; their first home on post at Fort Bragg in North Carolina; Nat's birth and progression from toddler to second-grader.

Parker closed the album. So many blank pages.

Nat was now in third grade. They'd stopped taking pictures after Tim died.

Guilt settled in. The final picture in the album was one Tim had taken of Nat. She stood beside their car in sneakers and a pink-and-purple-striped bathing suit, her hair in pigtails, her face tearstained and tragic. In her left hand she held what was left of Tim's favorite fishing pole. She'd slammed the car door on it, shearing off the tip. Tim had spent thirty seconds raging, five minutes mourning, and three days laughing. Since Nat already had her swimsuit on he'd taken her to the water park, to show there were no hard feelings.

Her husband had been a forgiving person. Unlike his family.

Parker's parents had been in their late forties when she was born, and neither her mother nor her father had lived past seventy-five.

Which meant that Tim's mother and brother were the only other family Nat had. But they were family in name only. They hadn't spoken to Parker since the falling-out at Tim's funeral. No one would ever describe them as forbearing.

She should be grateful. If not for that she might have backed out of buying this property. She and Nat would never have moved to Thistle Hill. Would never have realized Tim's dream.

And anyway, who was Parker to judge? She hadn't contacted Tim's family, either. Of course, she had no illusions about herself. Forgiveness was beyond her.

Her eyes filled. She hugged herself and began to rock. *I can't do it, Tim. I can't forgive him for taking you away.*

She'd wondered, of course, about the details of the incident that had ended Tim's life. Her calls and emails had netted no information beyond that horrific phrase "friendly fire." She'd always pictured the perpetrators as a group. A featureless squad.

This was worse, having a face—one face—to apply to her imaginings.

The door at the bottom of the stairs squeaked a warning. Parker barely managed to dry her face with the hem of her T-shirt before her daughter's head poked up out of the stairwell. Her hair was flat on one side and tousled on the other and she was knuckling the sleep from her left eye. A series of thumps and some heavy breathing signaled Chance was close behind her.

"Mom?" Nat yawned. "Something's burning."

Oh, God. "The muffins!"

The album slid to the floor with a muffled *whump* as Parker scrambled to her feet. That's what she got for indulging in a one-woman pity party. She hustled down the stairs behind Chance, whose tail wagged with delight at this new game. Parker's foot caught the nail again and this time she left her sock behind. When she hit the first floor the smell of scorched batter was unmistakable. By the time Nat reached the kitchen Parker had pulled the pans out of the oven and both she and Chance were staring at the shriveled, blackened remnants.

All those ingredients, wasted. She sighed and dropped the potholders onto the counter. "Not even Chance would go for these." He barked once, and plopped down onto the braided rug. Parker made a face. "Didn't think so."

Nat peered over her shoulder. "Isn't charcoal supposed to make you hurl?"

"If you can get past the smell long enough to actually take a bite, then yes, I think it's a given you'll puke. And speaking of smell..." Parker heaved open the kitchen window. When she turned back around Nat sat hunched over the kitchen table, chin propped in both hands.

"Hot chocolate?"

Nat nodded, then bit her lower lip. "He made you sad, didn't he?"

"Chance?"

"That soldier."

Parker paused, the two mugs she'd selected from the tree on the counter poised in midair. "What makes you think I'm sad?"

"Mom. Why else get up in the middle of the night to bake muffins?"

"Maybe I was hungry."

Nat rolled her eyes. "You were hanging out in the attic. With a bunch of photo albums. If you were hungry you wouldn't have let the muffins burn."

Busted. Parker set a container of water in the microwave to heat and sat next to her daughter. "All right. Yes, he made me sad. I miss your father, and I know you miss him, too. Seeing someone wear the uniform Daddy used to wear...that was tough." She paused. She'd tried to ask Nat about it earlier, but the little girl had first clamped her lips tight and then, when Parker had gently persisted, she'd scuttled up to her room. Now Parker tried again.

"Harris said you saw him, too. Did it make you sad?"

Nat hung her head. She swallowed, and the sound was loud in the midnight kitchen. Parker reached out and tucked Nat's soft auburn hair behind her ear. "Want to talk about it?"

22

She mumbled something and sniffled. Parker waited, and was about to ask again when suddenly Nat raised her head, and Parker's heart ached at the hurt in her daughter's eyes.

"At first I was so h-happy," Nat whispered. "I thought it was Daddy. I mean, I knew it couldn't be, but then I thought maybe it was a mistake after all, that the bomb had missed him and they couldn't find him but then they did and he wanted to surprise us and—" Her chin trembled, and she swiped at her nose with the heel of her hand. "Then I saw it wasn't him and I ran away because…Daddy always told me to be a little soldier and…and…and I didn't want his friend to see me cry." She squeaked out the last few words and broke into sobs.

"Oh, Nat. Oh, sweetie." Parker gathered Natalie onto her lap and into a hug. She squeezed her daughter hard, fighting and losing the battle against her own tears.

Nat pressed her face into Parker's tee. "Did he leave because of me?"

Were they still talking about their visitor? "You mean—"

"Did he leave because I ran away?"

"No. No, honey. He left because of me." The microwave beeped. Parker ignored it.

"Why?"

"He wanted to stay for a while. And I thought that would be too painful for us."

Silence. Then, "Did he know Daddy?"

Parker shook her head, realized Nat couldn't see her, and leaned away. She smoothed the hair out of Nat's face and shook her head again.

"So why did he come?"

"He'd…heard that Daddy had died."

"And he wanted to help?" Parker nodded. "That was nice." Nat sniffled, and dipped her head. Chance abandoned the rug and pressed against her knee. "So you think he might come back?"

"Not unless I ask him to."

Nat opened her mouth, shut it, frowned. Parker braced herself.

"Maybe he's lonely."

"What?"

Nat slid back into her own chair, tearstained face suddenly animated. "Maybe he was lonely, and he heard about what happened to Daddy, and he figured we must be lonely, too. So he came to keep us company."

Blindly Parker stood and groped for the microwave. "I already told you why he came. He isn't lonely."

"How do you know? Did you ask?"

"Nat, we can't invite every lonely person in the world to stay with us. It's not feasible."

"But I'm not asking about *every* lonely person. I'm asking about him."

"Nat." Parker stirred the powder into the water and set a mug on the table. "Drink your hot chocolate and go to bed. You have school tomorrow."

Her daughter frowned down into her mug. "No marshmallows?"

"Natalie."

"Remember when we took in Chance, Mom?"

Oh, dear Lord.

Nat bent down and hugged the Lab, resting her cheek on top of his head. "You said it was wrong to turn your back on someone in need."

"Chance is a dog."

"Yeah, but he's human like the rest of us."

Parker wanted to laugh but didn't have the energy. "What is it about this man? You never even talked to him."

Nat straightened, and up went the chin she'd inherited from her mother. "What if it was Daddy? What if he didn't have anyone? Would you want a family like us to turn him away?"

It was like facing a nine-year-old Harris Briggs. Parker's fingers curled tight and she fought the urge to kick a table leg.

"He's not your father. And he won't be staying long. He has to go back overseas."

24

"To be a soldier."

"Yes, to be a soldier."

"What if he dies like Daddy?" Her eyes filled again. "And he doesn't think anybody cares?"

It was a conspiracy, that's what it was. Nat didn't even know the whole story but just like Harris, she was determined to make Parker out to be the bad guy. Her fingers started to ache, and she frowned down at the dishrag in her hand. She'd squeezed all the water out onto the floor.

"Mom?"

Parker squatted and scrubbed at the linoleum a lot harder than she had to. Then she jerked to her feet and carefully laid the dishrag over the rim of the sink. "I'll give it some thought. All right? No promises. Now if you don't want your drink you need to get to bed."

Nat heaved a put-upon sigh and carried her mug to the sink. She eyed the ruined muffins. "You making another batch?"

Parker nodded. Might as well. No way she'd get any sleep. Not now.

"Could you add some chocolate chips this time?"

That was how Harris preferred them. "You planning to share?"

"We should do something nice for Harris. He works hard."

Parker's breath snagged. "Yes, he does. Have you—" she swallowed " —noticed he looks more tired than usual lately?"

Nat nodded slowly. "I didn't want to ask him about it 'cause I figured he'd just yell."

Parker gripped the back of the nearest chair. Had she been that blind? She straightened and motioned Nat toward the stairs. "Time for bed, kiddo. And on the way you can tell me all about it."

*   *   *

HARRIS OPENED THE DOOR the following morning and Parker thrust the plate of muffins at him. "You're sick, aren't you?"

He backed away from the doorway, rubbing his stomach where

she'd shoved the plate. "A moment ago I felt fine. That was before the bruised rib."

"Stop it. Talk to me. What's going on?"

"You tell me."

She pushed past him into the living room. "I thought you were scamming me. When you said you were tired. I thought you were trying to play on my sympathies so I'd let MacFarland stay. Then Nat said something and — " She shoved her hands deep into the pockets of her overalls. "It's true, isn't it? You're sick."

"You make it sound like I have TB or cancer or schizophrenia. Something that'll put me in slippers and a hospital gown, eating baby food and watching game shows for the rest of my life."

"You don't have cancer." Thank God. Her knees went weak and she sank down onto the seen-better-days sofa. It went so well with the battered pine coffee table and the over-the-hill leather recliner. "How long will that be?"

"What's that?"

"The rest of your life."

She watched him struggle with a smart-aleck response. Finally he shrugged. "Ten years. Ten days. Same could be said for us all." He set the plate on a side table. Denim *shushed* against leather as he settled into the recliner.

"What is it?"

"Viral cardiomyopathy. Affects the heart muscle."

Parker curled her toes inside her work boots, fighting tears he didn't need to see. First they'd lost Tim and now — "What can they do for it?"

"They got me on some medications. Beta-blockers, they call 'em. And the usual no-sodium bull — uh, crap. Maybe someday a pacemaker."

"Is that where you were last Tuesday? At the doctor's?" He gave her a sheepish nod. "Why didn't you tell me?"

"You have enough on your plate, my girl."

"My God, Harris, how do you think I would have felt if something had happened to you? You've been loading the truck and hauling compost and dragging around hoses. And all this time, any one of those things could have killed you."

"Now don't go mixin' pickles with your peppers. Workin' won't kill me. It's *not* workin' that would take me out. I just have to know my limits."

"And when were you going to let me know about these 'limits'?"

"I'm lettin' you know now."

"Harris Briggs," she whispered, and swiped a palm across her cheek. "How long have you known?"

He slapped his hands to his knees and pushed himself upright. "Coffee?"

"Is this why you're so determined about MacFarland?"

"Partly."

A lengthy pause. "How long is his leave?"

"Thirty days. Give or take."

One month. How would she manage, even for one *day*, to be civil to the man who'd brought the worst kind of tragedy into her life?

She moved to the front window of Harris's small brick house and shifted the drapes aside. But she couldn't see anything other than Tim's face.

She had a right to her anger. Just as she had a right to her grief. No one was going to tell her how she should feel.

But Nat had come downstairs that morning looking more rested than she had in months. Before sitting down to her cereal she'd handed Parker a list of strategies to keep the corporal from feeling lonely. At the top of the list she'd written "spend time with him." Which Parker took to mean that Nat herself was feeling lonely. And no wonder, since Parker spent most of her time in the greenhouses or tending to greenhouse affairs.

But there was no money for extra help. And now Harris had admitted to a heart condition. They should both be spending more time with him.

Slowly she turned from the window. "After thirty days, then what?

He'll be gone and we'll still be short-staffed."

"Let me tell you somethin', Parker Anne." Harris stood behind his recliner, his hands gripping the padded back. "I love you like a daughter. Best thing that happened to me in a good long time was the day you moved up here. I realize it was all arranged before your husband died, but you could've changed your mind. And I thank God every day that you didn't. You're my family now, you and Nat. Don't make me spend the time I have left doin' nothing else but worryin' about you."

Her chest went tight. She smiled, but had a hard time keeping it in place. "You'd worry no matter what."

"I know, I know, and there ain't no use puttin' up an umbrella till it rains." He pushed away from the chair. "How about this. How about we take it one day at a time. With an extra pair of hands around you might actually make payroll."

"Low blow, Briggs." But an accurate one. She rubbed her forehead. She wanted to kick and scream and cry and pack up Nat and spend the next month camping out in the mountains.

Harris had been right to scold her for being selfish. Natalie had suffered enough. Did Parker really want to teach her daughter to be unforgiving?

Still. *Thinking* about forgiving someone wasn't the same thing as actually forgiving them. That bit of wisdom might get Parker through the next thirty days.

She scrubbed her hands over her face, then followed Harris into the kitchen. Enough about her. "Does your heart condition have anything to do with why you're not seeing Eugenia anymore?"

He stiffened but didn't turn away from the coffeepot. "We were finished before then. And it ain't none of your business why."

"Fine." She inhaled. "I don't want you to come in today."

He whirled around so fast it made *her* dizzy. Thank God the mug he held was empty. She held up a hand before he could start bellowing. "It's only one day. Besides, I have a list of things you can pick up at Cooper's for me."

"Errand boy. That's what you're reducin' me to?"

"You know better than that, Harris Briggs. And considering how long you've kept me in the dark about this, you're lucky I don't cut off your muffin supply."

He did his best to look menacing. She refused to flinch, and eventually his shoulders sagged. He swung back to the counter and poured his coffee.

"I'm sorry it didn't work out," she ventured. "Between you and Eugenia. She really seems to like you."

"She doesn't like people so much as she likes doin' for them."

"What does that mean?"

"Never mind." He handed her a mug and scowled. "Guess it's too much for a man to hope you put chocolate chips in those muffins."

Parker sighed. Subject closed. For now. She patted him on the cheek and reached for the napkins.

BACKING UP SLOWLY TO the edge of the sidewalk, Eugenia Blue tipped her head and stared with satisfaction at the window display she'd spent most of the afternoon rearranging. Two mannequins wearing flowery summer dresses and wide-brimmed hats sat in an English garden complete with trellises, fake ivy and climbing roses. The plastic ladies leaned toward each other over a small round table, as if sharing a delicious secret. A porcelain tea set completed the picture.

Not bad. Not bad at all. Less than a year ago she'd been holed up in a ridiculously lavish condo in New York, licking her wounds after a brutal divorce. Now she'd established not only a home but a business in small-town heaven, where no one expected her to host parties for lecherous business associates or threatened to withhold sex if she gained five pounds.

She loved having her own shop. The hours were long but the freedom of being her own boss more than made up for it. Eventually she'd have to hire some help, but not until business picked up. Six sales a day wouldn't pay the bills.

Especially if she continued to raid her own stock. She looked down at her sweater set and gave a mental shrug. Who could resist cashmere? And in lavender, no less? Besides, creating such an eye-catching window display deserved a reward.

"You're looking pleased with yourself."

She turned. Joe Gallahan sauntered toward her, zipping up his light jacket against the late-morning chill. Her lips curved automatically as they always did whenever she saw Joe. With his slow, sexy smile and construction worker muscles, Joe could make any woman brighten. Though every now and then she did catch a hint of something dark in his eyes. Something more than sadness. Something that made her wonder how he'd ended up in Thistle Hill.

Something that was none of her business.

"Hello, Joe. What brings you into town?"

"The usual." His smile turned wry and he nodded across the street at the hardware store. "Seems I spend more time at Cooper's than at the motel these days." He gestured at her window. "Looks great."

"Thank you."

"Still on your own here?"

In more ways than one. "For now."

"Guess that means you don't have a lot of time to spare. I know how it is, trying to run your own business. But I'll ask anyway. How about dinner some night?"

Eugenia's eyebrows went up and her jaw went down. According to the dressing room gossip she couldn't help but overhear, Joe didn't date much. Didn't do much at all, besides work on that motel and play whatever sport was in season.

With all the women in town dying to snag his attention, why ask *her*?

He had to be twenty years younger than she was. If she had to guess, she'd say he was about thirty-five. Flattering, to say the least. But though she liked Joe, and admired him for tackling a project like resuscitating the motel from hell, she had her sights set on someone else. Someone who refused to stand still in the crosshairs, but that was beside the point.

"Are you asking me out?"

An instant's hesitation, followed by a warm smile. "Yeah. I am. You choose the restaurant."

It was a quick recovery. And a smooth one. But still a recovery.

"Okay, so not a date. I don't know what I was thinking, considering I'm old enough to be your mother. What did you really have in mind?"

"Hey." Joe moved in, rested his palms lightly on her upper arms. "I may not have come up with the idea, but I think it's a damned good one. And no way you're old enough to be my mother."

His chivalry would have made her feel worse if she hadn't seen the sincerity in his eyes.

"I appreciate that." She backed up a step. "But I'd have to say no, anyway. I'm...interested in someone."

He lifted broad shoulders in a good-natured shrug. "If it doesn't work out, maybe you'll reconsider."

"Maybe I will."

A boisterous laugh on the other side of the street. They turned to see Harris Briggs shaking hands with an elderly man who'd obviously just come out of the hardware store, the plastic bag he gripped practically brushing the sidewalk, making him lopsided. She watched the genial exchange, watched as Harris made the other man laugh. Belatedly she turned back to Joe. And felt mortification heat her cheeks.

"It's no use," she said, in response to his *gotcha* smile. "He refuses to forgive me."

"What'd you do?" He winced and held up a hand. "Strike that. None of my business."

"It's all right. I bought him something, and he didn't appreciate it."
"He didn't like it?"

"He claimed I insulted him. I think I offended his manhood."

"The gift didn't happen to be blue, did it?"

She frowned. "How did you know?"

"Tiny, and in the shape of a diamond?"

She gasped, and slapped him on the arm. "Not *that*. Don't you need a prescription for—" He was laughing and she flapped a hand. "Never you mind. Point is, I blew it."

"You apologize?"

"For all the good it did. I plan on trying again after closing today."

"No time like the present." He looked back across the street. Eugenia grabbed for his arm but wasn't fast enough.

32

"Hey, Harris!" he called. "Got a minute?"

Eugenia swallowed a tortured moan. Joe lowered his voice. "Tell me I called the right man over. Or is it Mr. Katz you have a crush on?"

"Mr. Katz is ninety years old."

"Yeah, but I hear he takes vitamins."

That he could joke so casually about age after her embarrassing assumption made Eugenia feel better. Until Harris stepped up onto the sidewalk, looking like a lumberjack in his heavy boots, jeans and thermal shirt. Eugenia caught her breath and rubbed her suddenly damp palms against the insides of her sweater pockets.

There was something about his size, his solidity, the strength of purpose and kindness in his eyes. He made her feel ultrafeminine. Safe.

And frustrated as all get-out.

He squinted at Joe, then at Eugenia, then back again. "What's up?"

"Just thought you should see what Eugenia's done here. About time someone brought some style to State Street." Joe beamed a roguish smile at Eugenia. "Guess I should get on over to Cooper's before they sell out of drywall screws. Let me know if you change your mind about dinner. I do have more than tax schedules on my mind." He turned and jogged across the street, leaving an awkward silence behind him.

Harris cleared his throat. "You did a good job on your window there," he said at the same time she said, "I owe you an apology."

He grunted. "Most people say thank you when they get a compliment."

"Most people say thank you when they get a gift. You, however, responded with, 'Guess this is our last date.'"

"Most people don't give the sort of gifts you do."

"I'm sorry. The last thing I wanted was to insult you. I'm a make-it-happen kind of person. I see a need, and I want to fill it."

"That's all well and good, but you can't just go around buyin' trucks for folks."

"But it wasn't just folks. It was you. I never thought you'd be so ungrateful."

"Ungrateful?" He scratched his bald head. "Because I was honest about not wanting something I never asked for? Listen, Genie, no man wants to feel like he's bein' bought." Someone drove by in a mud-streaked pickup and honked, and Harris lifted his arm. Eugenia stared.

"Excuse me?"

"If I need a truck I'll buy it myself. Now I'm done explainin'. Like I said before, you and me, we just wouldn't work out."

"You know what your problem is? You're stubborn and you're scared."

He scowled. "There's no call for insults."

"I wasn't trying to insult you, I was trying to enlighten you."

"Either way I don't appreciate it. Guess I best be movin' along."

"You do that," Eugenia snapped, and gave herself a mental eye roll. Why could she never come up with anything clever to say?

And did it really matter? His anger over the issue meant they'd been dating on borrowed time, anyway. If he ever found out what else she'd done, he'd…well, at the very least he'd never speak to her again.

Damn the man's pride.

He swung away, then turned back and jerked his head toward the hardware store. "You datin' Joe now?"

"Why do you want to know?"

"Just wonderin' if you're planning on buyin' him a new motel."

Eugenia sputtered. Harris marched away down the sidewalk, then when he was almost at the corner he turned back. "By the way," he called. "Heard you turned that pretty truck back in and donated the money to the rescue squad. That was a mighty fine thing to do, Genie." He gave her a nod, then continued walking.

Eugenia stared after him, feeling as though someone had grabbed her by the ankles and swung her upside down.

*   *   *

IN, TWO-THREE-FOUR-five-six-seven. Out, two-three-four-five-six-seven.

Her lungs ached. Parker opened her eyes and stared at the door to room six. Then she looked back, toward the sparse traffic that motored past the motel. People ran errands, visited friends, headed home to their families. A squirrel chittered, and she watched it bounce across the parking lot and disappear under a rather sad-looking azalea.

She should call Joe and offer him some pointers. Happier-looking landscaping would be good for business.

She should also stop procrastinating.

She rolled her shoulders back but the tingling in her chest persisted. The deep breathing hadn't done much for her stress level. Apparently it was effective only for mother-daughter-type challenges.

Raise knuckles. Knock twice. Hold breath. The door handle turned — *oh, God she really did have to talk to him* — and she released her breath in a head-spinning whoosh.

Corporal MacFarland wore nothing but a towel, a pair of flip-flops, and a grim expression. "Mrs. Dean. Sorry, I thought it was —" A harsh exhale. "Stand by."

When he shut the door, Parker thought, *Run.* But she stood where she was, rooted to the sidewalk by the image of the left side of his torso, and the faded red ribbons of puckered skin along his rib cage.

He looked like someone had hacked at him with a sword. Her eyes felt wet but she willed the tears away. Darned if she'd let a little sympathy dilute the resentment she had every right to feel.

When the door opened again he wore jeans and a Go Army T-shirt. He waved her in and shut the door behind her.

She looked around the room, but all she could see was the damage to his muscled body.

"How can I help you?"

She turned to find that he hadn't moved, gaze wary, fingers still on the handle. He didn't want her to feel threatened, she realized. But she'd never considered he'd do anything to harm her. Not physically, anyway.

Striving for calm, cool and collected, she settled into one of the two lawn chairs that flanked the scarred round table.

"Well," she said. "Joe's really done wonders with the place."

The left side of MacFarland's mouth tipped up and Parker found herself staring. She turned away, and noticed the duffel bag atop the neatly made bed.

"You're packed."

"Yes, ma'am." He cocked his head. "Are you here to... Will you allow me to apologize, Mrs. Dean?"

She sat back, and the aluminum chair squeaked out a loud complaint. Her hands clutched at the grooved armrests. "We're not talking about an insult here, or a—a fender bender. You can't apologize for making someone a widow."

"I have to try, ma'am."

"Stop with the 'ma'am,'" she snapped. "You make me feel like I should start paying attention to...to denture commercials." Her breath hitched on a sob. He moved away from the door and disappeared into the bathroom. She heard the sound of running water. Seconds later he placed a cup on the table in front of her and stepped back. She nodded her thanks, but kept her hands in her lap. No way she could drink that water without spilling it. She'd humiliated herself enough for one day, thank you very much.

She motioned with her chin at the other chair. "Would you sit, please?" He hesitated, then did as she asked. He sat with both feet on the floor, hands hanging over the ends of the armrests. She raised her eyes to a face she'd hoped never to see again.

"Harris said you don't have to be back on post for thirty days. Wouldn't you rather spend that time with your family?" Her gaze dropped to his left hand. His fingers flexed.

"I'm not married," he said softly. Softly, but not gently. "No family."

"Friends, then."

"My friends are overseas."

A pause. "Where are you from?"

"San Diego." He angled his head. "I'm here because this is where I'm supposed to be."

"The last thing I want is to accept your offer. But you have me at a disadvantage." He waited. She dug her fingers into her thighs. "Harris is sick and...needs to cut back on his hours. I can't afford to hire someone else. Not yet. This morning I called a supermarket over in the next county. They'd wanted to place a large order with us but I had to turn them down. With help we can manage the order. The extra money will pay the most urgent bills, and allow us to make some repairs. If you could stay that long, I'd —" She faltered. She couldn't say it. Couldn't manage the word *grateful*.

He hadn't moved, but a new tension gripped his muscles. Her mind flashed another image of his scarred torso. Was he in pain?

"You don't want me here."

She fought a laugh. *You think?*

"You need money," he continued. He stood and moved to the bed. "I've written you a check. I planned to leave it with Gallahan." He slid an envelope free of a side pocket and held it out.

Her fingers itched to take it. Whatever the amount, it would be a blessing. But she'd promised Harris.

And her forgiveness wasn't for sale.

She pushed to her feet. "Exactly how much does a dead husband go for these days? Shall I tell you the figure the Army came up with? Or do you already know?"

His fingers tightened around the envelope. "I can't match the death gratuity. But if you give me time, I can come close."

She shoved her hands into her pockets to keep them from reaching out. "That money would make my life easier. It'd be easier for you, too, wouldn't it? If I took it? Which is the very best reason to refuse it."

Slowly he lowered his arm. "Yes, ma'am."

"I don't want anything from you. Not your apology, not your sympathy, not your money. But I owe Harris Briggs everything. And

I made him a promise. So, Corporal, it looks like you're about to get a crash course on being a grower. Tomorrow's not good so I'll see you first thing Saturday morning."

Without a word he opened the door for her. She stepped out onto the sidewalk, then swung back around. "One last thing. I need you to stay away from my daughter."

His head snapped back, like she'd taken a swing at him. Parker put up a hand. "Not because... Listen, I know you wouldn't hurt her physically. But you're a soldier like —" She stuck out her chin. "I don't want her forming any attachments."

His jaw looked hard enough to drive nails into concrete. "You don't need to worry. One look at me and she ran like the boogeyman was after her." He shut the door.

Parker's shoulders slumped. Thank heaven he hadn't asked, because she had no clue to the answer.

How did she know he wouldn't hurt Nat?

*   *   *

PARKER SCRUNCHED UP HER face and struggled to hear what Liz was saying. Outside the potting shed, Chance was barking loud enough to be heard across Lake Erie. *Give it* up, *dog.*

"Hold that thought, all right?" Parker pressed the phone to her shoulder and stomped outside. The Lab was fussing at a pine tree, undoubtedly seeing a squirrel in its branches. "Chance!" she scolded. "Quiet, please!"

He looked at her over his shoulder and plopped down onto his belly. "Good boy." She put the phone back to her ear. "Okay, I'm here."

"I'm sorry, Parker. I know I said I could learn about plants and stuff but I'm getting plenty of hours here. The tips are tight. And I need the cashola. I'm saving up for a car."

"I understand, Liz." No tips earned at a greenhouse, tight or otherwise. Parker dropped her head into her hand. "Thanks anyway."

"Hold on a sec." Over the country music playing in the background, Parker heard Liz talking to Snoozy, the owner of Thistle Hill's most popular bar. The only bar, really, if you didn't include the lunch counter at Hunan's. "No, I'm not quitting. And yes, I see him. Jeez, dude, don't blow a gasket." She came back on the line. "I have to go. Wish I could help."

"I appreciate that. I'll see you around." Parker disconnected the call and tapped the phone against her chin. It was either that or heave it against the wall. She didn't have much left to sell. But the set of Desert Rose china she'd advertised for months had finally reaped a buyer. With the money from that, she could afford part-time help. Hence the call to Liz Early. Which had followed calls to six other people who had at one time or another expressed interest in working for her. She'd hoped to bring one of them on board because it would mean not having to put up with Corporal Reid MacFarland for long.

But it seemed she was stuck with him after all.

She set the phone aside, propped her elbows on the slab of wood that served as a desk and lowered her face into her hands. The biggest risk was to Nat.

"God," she muttered. "What if she ever found out?"

"What if who found out what?" Parker snapped her head up. Nat stood in the doorway of the potting shed, one hand on the doorjamb, the other clutching her backpack. Parker waved her in while scrambling to think of something, anything, to distract her.

"Hi, sweetie. I didn't hear the bus. What sounds good for dinner tonight?"

Totally lame. Nat would see right through—

Her daughter stepped into the shed and Chance scrambled in after her. Parker gasped.

"Natalie! What *happened?*"

Fresh tears dampened the streaks on Nat's face as Parker rushed forward and tipped up her chin. "We were playing basketball during gym," Nat whispered miserably. "I ran into a pole."

"Oh, baby." Parker winced at the magenta-colored splotches

surrounding Nat's right eye. Carefully she smoothed the hair out of her daughter's face. "Why didn't anyone call me?"

"The bell was about to ring. Nurse Brewington put some ice on it, then I had to catch the bus."

Parker frowned. The school should have called. She'd have to look into that. She clucked her tongue and took charge of Nat's backpack. "Come on up to the house. We'll get you an icepack." Once they were on the gravel path she put an arm around Nat's shoulders and drew her in close. Chance seemed to sense something was wrong and pressed against Nat's legs.

"What exactly did the nurse say? Do we need to worry about a concussion?"

Nat wrenched away. "They checked me out for all that. I told you. I didn't hit my head, just my face." She walked faster, tennis shoes digging into the gravel. Each breath she took got thicker and thicker. "I'm never going back to gym class again," she choked out. "They can't make me."

Now was not the time to tell her she was wrong. Parker felt a hot swell of sympathy and pressed her lips together to keep from saying the wrong thing. Kids could be so cruel. And Nat's lack of athletic ability, painfully spotlighted every day in PE, gave them plenty of reason to tease.

Parker had tried to work with her. Harris had tried to work with her. But Nat couldn't contain her frustration long enough to practice whatever game she needed help with. Unfortunately, Parker remembered those days all too well.

She transferred the heavy backpack to her other hand and jogged to catch up. "Can we talk about it? How about I make us some pancakes and —"

"I don't want any dinner." Nat's pace quickened to a near-run, the Lab jogging along beside her. "Just leave me alone!"

She dashed the rest of the way to the house, thundered up the porch steps and banged through the front door.

Parker trailed along in her wake. More than a year later and Nat still hadn't come to terms with her father's death. The resulting lack of sleep was ruining her ability to focus. Which explained today's accident. On top of her usual sports-related challenges at school, Nat would never live this down.

And now Reid MacFarland was determined to insinuate himself into their lives.

Another soldier. Another deployment to a war zone.

Another possible heartbreak for Nat.

Parker drew in a quivering breath. How much more could one little girl take?

4

THERE WASN'T A HELL of a lot to do in a motel room at five o'clock in the morning. Especially for a man without the benefit of female company. And he had a whole damned day to twiddle his thumbs before reporting for work tomorrow. After one hundred push-ups, a shower and a chapter of a spy thriller, Reid knew he either had to go out or go crazy. If he were on post he'd be headed to the mess hall for breakfast before reporting for platoon formation and weapons training.

But the slice of pizza from the night before sat heavy in his stomach, so food was the last thing he needed. And he was tired of lying in bed and staring up at that damned turquoise ceiling, replaying the scene where Parker Dean's little girl scurried away from him. He exchanged his bath towel for a pair of shorts and a tee, and headed out for a run.

He couldn't see the lake but he could smell it. Fresh water, decaying fish, seaweed. And though he couldn't hear the surf, he could hear the distant drone of a motorboat. Some early riser on the hunt for lake perch.

Between the smell of fish and the image of fried perch leaking grease onto a plate, his stomach threatened to put an early end to his run. He planned on taking it slow, which was just as well because that's what the citizens of Thistle Hill had in mind, too.

Four times he was stopped. Once by a pair of white-haired ladies in a powder-blue Buick wondering if he'd seen a salt-and-pepper schnauzer and by the way wasn't Thistle Hill a lovely place to visit and which lucky resident had he come to see? — twice by fellow exercisers: one a young man, the other not so young—who'd interpreted his Army tee as an invitation to debate the advantages of the M110 sniper rifle. The last time he was stopped was by a guy in a pickup who wanted to know if he'd spotted a deer carcass that needed scooping up.

By the time he got back to the motel Reid figured he'd already met half the population of Thistle Hill. He wondered if the other half was just as unconventional.

Gallahan was out front admiring the sole bloom on a trio of bushes. "Enjoy your run?"

Reid swiped at his face with the hem of his shirt. "Not much of a run. More like several rounds of dodgeball."

Gallahan nodded wisely. "The people of Thistle Hill like to know who their visitors are."

"A woman just crossed lanes to block me. Wanted to know if I preferred my burgers with or without cheese."

"Audrey Tweedy. If you're vegetarian don't admit it. She'll make it her life's work to win you back into the fold of the flesh eaters."

"I'll remember that." He dug his key card out of his pocket. "Maybe I should stick to a treadmill. There a gym around here?"

Gallahan hesitated, then seemed to come to some decision. "Follow me."

He led the way down the sidewalk to the end unit. Room ten, four doors from Reid. Gallahan produced a key card, pushed open the door and motioned Reid inside.

Just like Reid's room, the paneled walls were a scratched-up, puncture-ridden mess. The water-stained ceiling wasn't much better. There the resemblance ended.

The carpet had been replaced with an oatmeal-colored remnant that almost reached to the baseboards. In one corner stood an industrial-size fan, in the opposite corner a flat-screen television. Rectangular mirrors mounted side by side covered the wall in between. A water cooler and a shelf stacked with folded towels completed the picture of a home gym.

But the equipment was the most impressive feature of the room. A state-of-the-art treadmill, elliptical machine and pulley-based weight system, plus a stand of free weights, all gleamed an unexpected, polished welcome.

Reid whistled his approval. "This is some setup."

"It's convenient." Gallahan held out the key card. "Use it whenever you like. I'm here early most mornings, but I don't mind company."

"Appreciate it. You been in Thistle Hill long?"

"About four months."

"How'd you decide on the place?" Shit. Now he was starting to sound like the little old ladies in the Buick.

"Long story." Gallahan frowned, and Reid knew he wouldn't be hearing it. Fair enough. "Beer?"

"Got a cooler in here, too?"

He laughed. "That could be arranged, but I was thinking more along the lines of Snoozy's. Beer's cold, cheese plate's free, pool table's mostly level."

"Beats staring at that butt-ugly turquoise ceiling. But it's eight in the morning."

"So we'll give it a few hours. Hang out in here if you want." Gallahan tipped his head. "You been in Iraq?"

Damn. Payback was a bitch. "Baghdad."

"Tough job. Thanks for doing what you do, man." He held up his fist and Reid gritted his teeth as they bumped knuckles.

Now he really did need that beer.

They waited until eleven to head to Snoozy's, which was everything a small-town bar should be. Easy to find and open for business. Besides the standard neon signs, wooden bar stools and lighting dim enough to guarantee permanent eyestrain, Snoozy's had something...extra.

Gallahan caught him looking. "Yeah, I know. I forget it's weird until someone like you comes in and looks at it like that." He tipped his chin at the man behind the bar. "It belonged to his wife."

"A sort of tribute?" Reid stared doubtfully at the front corner of the room, where a hot-pink salon chair faced a full-length, gilt-framed mirror draped with leopard-print garlands.

"More like a warning. She took everything he had, except for this place."

Ouch. Reid followed Gallahan to the bar. Behind the scarred wooden counter a tired-looking man with a droopy mustache and purple half-moons under his eyes arranged cubes of cheese on a plastic platter.

Had to be Snoozy.

They ordered two brews. A man the size of an upright freezer with white-blond hair down to his shoulders and scabbed-over knuckles slapped the bar. The wood trembled.

"How about that chili I ordered?" he demanded. He pivoted to his left and caught Reid staring. "Something I can do for you, Sport?"

"Depends." Reid swigged his beer. "Know anything about geraniums?"

The bar went quiet. Behind him Gallahan made a strangled noise. The blond behemoth narrowed his eyes and opened his mouth. Reid tensed, waiting for either an invitation to step outside or a punch to the kidney. The behemoth leaned in. Maybe a head-butt.

"Storksbills or cranesbills?"

Reid stared. Gallahan laughed and thumped him on the back. "Corporal Reid MacFarland, meet Noble Johnson, Thistle Hill's award-winning librarian. You should stop in sometime, listen to him read *The Velveteen Rabbit* to the kiddies. It'll make you weep into your whiskey."

"Kiss my ass, Gallahan." Noble frowned at Reid. "You serious about geraniums?"

Reid's lungs started working again. "For the next several weeks, I will be. Parker Dean's putting me to work."

Noble eyed Reid's haircut. "Knew her husband, did you?" Luckily he didn't wait for an answer. "You want my help, there's three things you gotta do. Make a donation to the library, buy me a beer — " Snoozy slid a bowl of chili in front of Noble, who picked up his spoon and jabbed it at Reid " — and pay attention."

*   *   *

"MA'AM? MA'AM. YOU ALL right, ma'am?"

With a start Parker realized she'd drifted away at the deli counter. She straightened out of her slouch and smiled blankly at the woman with the hair net and the curious stare. Dorothy? Delia. Parker pointed at random. "A pound of that, please, Delia."

Delia frowned. "But you don't like pastrami."

Parker blinked. "Of course." She felt a sudden swell of affection for the small community she lived in and gave Delia a grateful smile. "I'll take the usual, please." Three minutes later she was accepting two pounds of smoked turkey and a pound of provolone cheese. The warm-and-fuzzies lasted until she guided her cart toward the produce section and one of the wheels bumped a cardboard stand. An entire row of flower seed packets rustled and slapped to the floor. With a quiet sigh, Parker bent to scoop them up.

Maybe she'd better save the shopping for another day.

She set the last packet in place and turned to find one of Thistle Hill's newest residents hovering at her elbow. Eugenia Blue smiled warmly, and tucked her short blond hair behind her ears.

"Parker, how nice. I don't see you in town very often."

Parker pasted on an answering smile and scrambled for the energy to be polite. "How're things at the shop?"

"A little slow, but you know how it is. I've only been open a few months." She gestured at Parker's cart. "Harris was running errands just yesterday morning. You should have asked him to do your shopping."

Parker fumbled her smile. Harris would be doing a lot less for her in the future. "I was in town anyway. An appointment with the principal."

Eugenia looked doubtfully at Parker's jeans and polo shirt. "Everything all right?"

"As right as it can be."

The older woman's gaze dropped to her own basket. Carefully she studied each item, as if checking for holes or dents or bruises. "How is Harris?" she asked in a too-careless voice, and Parker's heart went south. Harris and Eugenia had dated a few times but then Harris had announced they'd stopped.

Apparently it hadn't been a mutual decision.

"He's okay," Parker said. But of course Eugenia wouldn't be satisfied with that. Since Harris's news wasn't Parker's to share, she gambled on a distraction.

She backed up and made a show of admiring the sweater set and gray pencil skirt that hugged the older woman's trim figure. "You always look so elegant." She nodded at Eugenia's outfit. "One of yours?"

Cheeks flushed with pride, Eugenia nodded. "You should come by. I'm holding my first sale next week. Trying to get people to come inside instead of peering through the windows." She plucked at her skirt. "I have something similar in sage. It'd go perfectly with your coloring."

"I'll try to make that sale. I don't remember the last time I didn't wear denim."

Eugenia looked like she was floundering for something tactful to say when Hazel Catlett click-clacked up in her low-heeled sandals.

"Parker Dean." Hazel was a white-haired, bright-eyed woman in her seventies who wore lipstick the color of Cheetos. She pointed with a skinny eggplant. "You look fit as a fiddle. Just like that guest of yours."

"I'm sorry?"

"June and I—we saw your soldier out running this morning and stopped to introduce ourselves." Hazel winked. "We couldn't help admiring his…stride."

Eugenia chuckled while Parker curled her fingers around the handle of her shopping cart and squeezed. Hard.

So much for small-town bliss. Yes, Thistle Hill's residents

considered looking out for each other a privilege and a duty. But they also considered gossip a competitive sport.

"He's not *my* soldier, Hazel. And how is June, by the way?"

"She dragged me away from Glenn Ford and Hope Lange just to look for a special kind of noodle she needs for some Thai recipe." She leaned closer, and Parker could see that some of her bright orange lipstick had wandered off into the wrinkles around her lips. "And this is the woman who thinks almond butter is exotic." Hazel straightened. "So, are you two an item?"

Parker was tempted to put her arm around Eugenia and smile an affirmative. But that wouldn't be fair to Eugenia. Darn it.

"Not an item," she said, and just the thought did unpleasant things to her stomach. "Barely friends," she added.

If "barely" meant "when hell freezes over."

"Don't give up, honey." Hazel patted her arm, then frowned at Parker's hair, which she'd gathered at the back of her head and fastened with a big plastic clip. "Speaking of honey —"

"Isn't that June?" Eugenia cocked her head. "Hazel, I think your sister's calling."

"Thank you, hon. My hearing's not what it used to be." She tucked the eggplant in her basket and took off for the pasta aisle.

Eugenia shook her head. "What a pair. Harris calls them Hazel and Nut."

"Today Hazel's the nut. Why is everyone trying to set me up?"

Eugenia shrugged. "It's spring."

Parker's cell rang and she checked the ID. Harris. The knots in her stomach tightened. Something was wrong, she just knew it. She'd wanted to make the delivery herself, but that stubborn so-and-so had thrown a fit when she'd suggested it.

Please let him be okay. "What's up, Harris?"

"I got halfway to Cherry Point before the truck broke down."

Parker closed her eyes.

"Parker? Is everything all right?"

She opened her eyes to find Eugenia watching her anxiously.

Meanwhile Harris's gruff voice was advising her that unless they wanted to pay to have the truck towed all the way to the store, they'd better find another way to get the plants delivered. And soon. Because the supermarket only accepted deliveries until eight.

And if Thistle Hill Growers didn't meet that deadline, they'd be in breach of contract. Which meant they wouldn't be paid. Which meant Parker wouldn't be able to afford the groceries she'd already plunked into her cart.

"I'll bring Pete," she said into the phone. "Where exactly are you?"

Once she disconnected Eugenia shook her head. "Parker, you can't take Pete. Today's Friday. The garage closes early."

Parker choked out a laugh. "Of course it does. Guess I'll just have to go by his house." Which would take her fifteen minutes longer. Each way.

"Why don't you check Snoozy's first? His pickup's usually there when I drive by in the evenings."

"Thanks, I will."

Parker jammed her phone back into her purse. How the heck would she manage if Pete couldn't fix her truck?

*　　*　　*

WHEN PARKER PUSHED INTO the bar's dim interior, Snoozy had Glenn Miller playing. Normally that would have delighted her, but the current situation demanded the most plaintive of country songs. Stress goaded her heart rate into a faster pace as she narrowed her eyes and scanned the room. A lot of familiar faces, but no — oh, Lord. What was *he* doing here?

Corporal Reid MacFarland shared a table with Joe Gallahan and Noble Johnson. Noble was saying something in his I-snack-on-thumbtacks voice and Joe laughed out loud, while MacFarland showed his approval by tipping his beer. Parker felt that now-familiar surge of resentment, the one that set off sparks behind her breastbone. How dare he party — and with her *neighbors* — after taking away her husband's ability to drink, to smile, to laugh?

After taking away his *life*.

Her breath hitched and she turned away before the trio could spot her. *Not fair, Parker Anne.* She'd been struggling to move on for thirteen months. Of course he would be, too. Which was why he'd come looking for her in Thistle Hill.

Not fair, no. But no one had ever accused grief of being rational. And right now she cared about rational as much as she cared about facials and high heels.

"Parker."

She cringed. She hadn't turned away quickly enough.

She swung around. Joe was crossing the room toward her. Behind him Noble remained seated, while the corporal stood beside the table, his expression wary.

"Everything all right?" Joe asked.

"I'm looking for Pete Lowry. Have you seen him?"

"He left about an hour ago. Said something about visiting his folks in Harrisburg. Why?"

Parker clamped her teeth together. "Nothing, I—I just need a mechanic."

"Can we give you a lift somewhere?" Joe asked, as MacFarland came up behind him.

"Mrs. Dean." He looked so different out of uniform. In his jeans and long-sleeved thermal shirt he looked like one of the guys. Like someone who might have hung out with Tim.

Annoyed at the direction of her thoughts, she focused her attention on Joe, who looked amused.

"What's with the formality? I thought you two were friends."

Parker stiffened. Yeah. And Elvis was alive and selling cheesecakes in the Bronx.

MacFarland's gaze flickered, then he raised an eyebrow. "Anything I can help with?"

"She has car problems," Joe said.

"Truck problems, actually."

"Briggs is out on a delivery?" She nodded, surprised, and MacFarland turned to Joe. "Anyone around here have a box truck we could borrow?"

So now he was trying to be a hero? Parker shook her head. "Don't bother. I'll figure something out."

"You may not have to." MacFarland gave Joe an elbow. "Anyone?"

"Pete."

"The same Pete who's out of town? There's got to be someone else."

With a yawn, Snoozy leaned on the bar. "Beanie Watson drives a chip truck. But he's still out making deliveries."

MacFarland looked at Parker. "You on a timeline?"

She spoke through lips that felt like hardening concrete. "Store closes at eight."

"Then we'd better get a move on. We'll start with my Jeep." He turned to face the room and raised his voice. "Anyone here with an SUV or a closed-bed truck willing to help us transport some greenery? Parker Dean here's got a truck out of commission and a delivery due to—" he looked at her and she mumbled a response " —Cherry Point by eight o'clock. We can meet back here afterward and the next two rounds are on me. Any takers?"

A swell of chatter. Joe held up a hand. "Let's rephrase that. Any takers who are *reasonably sober?*"

A few customers stood and the despair holding Parker hostage gave way to hope. At the same time she wished the person responsible for that hope had been anybody, *anybody* other than Corporal Reid MacFarland.

Noble Johnson pushed to his feet and hitched up his pants. "I know where we can get hold of a minivan," he said. Everyone turned to stare and he flushed bright red. "What? Not like it's *mine.*"

*   *   *

REID COULD SEE IT WAS killing her, having to accept his help. Which didn't bode well for what he had in mind over the next several weeks.

He got the impression, though, that it wasn't just him. Parker didn't want to be indebted to anyone, just as Briggs had said. And she sure has hell wished she'd never set foot inside the bar. But if they could save her delivery she'd see that getting help didn't always have to suck.

Two hours and one sprawling, mismatched caravan later, Parker, Briggs, Gallahan, Noble, a man with graying, close-cut black hair wearing a black polo shirt and smelling like French fries, a skinny kid who looked barely twenty-one and favored light beer, and Reid all stood in the parking lot of the supermarket that, despite its ultimatum, had allowed Thistle Hill Growers to make a late delivery. Parker stood in the middle of the cart-strewn parking lot, arms crossed against the night chill, and thanked her hastily assembled league of laborers.

"I don't know what to say. You all have been so generous with your time. And your gas."

"That was Noble," someone called out. "He had the chili."

Laughter, and a few choice words from Noble himself. Parker thanked everyone again, and only the tension in her jaw betrayed what her indebtedness cost her.

"Don't forget the beer," the same voice pleaded.

Reid assured them he'd honor his promise, then hunted down Briggs. "What about the truck?"

"I already arranged a tow. But I'm not sure why we're botherin'."

"I can take a look at it tomorrow."

"You know engines?"

Reid shrugged. "I know moving parts. I'm a machinist."

Briggs grinned and slapped him on the shoulder. "I knew you'd come in handy." Parker walked up and Briggs stopped grinning. "I know, I know. You want me to go home and tuck myself in. Maybe I'll heat myself some milk before I change my diaper and go night-night." He stomped off. Reid expected Parker to take off after him but she hesitated. In the dim glow cast by the light post he could see the conflicting expressions on her face. She wanted to thank him, and at the same time she wanted to tell him to go to hell.

What else did he expect? Yeah, the Army had decided not to court-martial him, or charge him with homicide, since he'd believed he was firing at enemy soldiers. He still felt like a criminal.

So he couldn't blame her for thinking he was one.

Which meant he really didn't want to hear her stumble through a thank-you.

"I'm heading back to Snoozy's," he said, and dug in his pocket for his key fob.

She moved a few steps back, toward her Camry. "I, uh, I need to get home."

She'd asked a neighbor to stay with her daughter while they finished the delivery. He didn't know Parker well, but he did know she'd want to keep that favor short.

"Thank you." She licked her lips. "For—"

"No big deal." She looked surprised that he'd cut her off, and annoyed, but mostly relieved. He hadn't done it for her. Damned if he'd stand there and listen to her tone waver between courteous and contemptuous.

"I'll see you in the morning," she said. She looked as excited as a soldier tapped for patrol after a whopping two hours' sleep. He couldn't help watching the determined rhythm of her stride as she walked away.

Reid gritted his teeth. *What the hell have you gotten yourself into, soldier?*

5

THE SAUSAGE-AND-EGG biscuit Reid had eaten for breakfast never quite managed to make friends with his stomach. He parked the Jeep—this time in the weed-infested gravel lot on the far side of the third Quonset hut—and took a swig of ginger ale. He'd have to start eating better, and make sure he took advantage of Gallahan's gym, or else he'd be in a world of hurt when he got back to his unit.

The soda helped. Another hefty swallow and he set off in search of his temporary employer. The one who'd had all night to change her mind. He'd stashed the envelope containing the check in his glove compartment, just in case.

It had rained sometime during the night, and his boots squeaked over the damp grass. Over by the tree line a gaggle of frogs chorused their good mornings. In the predawn dimness Reid checked out the first greenhouse, breathed in the smell of flowers, of dirt, the sweet, sharp scent of wet gravel. No Parker Dean.

He found her in the next hut, which looked just like the first. Gently whirring fans hung suspended from the structure's metal ribs. Racks inside the door held rakes and hoes and shovels. Rows of scarred plastic and metal tables and benches brimmed with container after container of ruffled, rainbow-colored blooms.

He shifted his gaze from the greenery and zeroed in on Parker. She worked at the other end of the shelter, back toward him, head bent in concentration, nimble fingers plucking brown leaves out of the bright pool that rippled along each side of the concrete path.

"Mornin'."

Reid jumped. Damn, when was the last time he'd let someone sneak up on him like that? He turned, and automatically reached for the mug of coffee Briggs offered. "Good morning. You always up this early?"

"Didn't want to miss the show."

Reid's gaze returned to Parker, who hadn't acknowledged either of them. Briggs gestured with his own mug.

"She's got them earbud thingies in. Likes to start off her day with some kind of self-help recordin'."

Reid took a sip of coffee and it was all he could do not to spit it back out. Briggs chuckled. "You'll get used to it." He nodded at Parker, who'd worked her way closer. "This should be interesting."

"Why's that?" Reid set his mug on a table. He'd find someplace to dump it later. Like a barrel marked Hazardous Waste.

"She's not happy you're here but she'll want to show you the ropes yourself. Girl's not good at handin' over the reins."

At that moment, Parker turned and spotted Reid. Her backbone snapped straight. He waited, settling his gaze on a face even more hostile than the one he'd seen yesterday at the motel. Still it was a nice face, with smooth, pale skin, light brown freckles and bright hazel eyes. And a pair of nicely shaped lips, currently pressed in an unfriendly line.

He'd bet money at least one of those ropes she'd be showing him came equipped with a noose.

*   *   *

PARKER HAD A PLAN. A plan to avoid Corporal MacFarland. It involved...well, avoiding Corporal MacFarland.

Which would help keep her from being arrested for assault with a pitchfork.

But as easy as her plan sounded, she'd stayed awake most of the night coming up with it. At least she'd had plenty of practice over the years, operating on little to no sleep—before Tim deployed, during his deployment and after his death.

No way she'd let dealing with the corporal throw her off track.

Except, it already had. Just not in the expected way. Those scars... He could have played them up, used them to gain an advantage. Instead he'd scrambled for a shirt. And what he'd done for her in the bar—without his organizing that caravan, her business would have lost much-needed revenue.

Part of her appreciated his resourcefulness. A very small, tiny, minuscule part. The rest of her nurtured an all-consuming resentment.

Though her conscience kept reminding her that the resentment wasn't entirely justified. Even her earbuds couldn't drown out the voice of her conscience. She shoved the useless things into her pocket and forced her legs into motion.

"Morning," she said stiffly. "Saturdays are busy around here so I don't have a lot of time to spare. Harris, can you please show the corporal what to do?"

Briggs coughed. "Sorry, but no can do."

"You all right?"

"Didn't get much sleep last night." He paid sudden fierce attention to a rip in his long-sleeved shirt. "I came over to let you know I need a few more hours."

Uh-huh. She crossed her arms. "You got out of bed, got dressed and drove all the way over here to tell me you're going back to bed? You could have called."

"Guess I was hopin' by the time I got here I'd be feelin' better."

He did sound tired. Suspicion gave way to worry and she dropped her arms. "Anything I can do?"

"Not a thing, but thanks for askin'. I'll just go home and catch a few more winks. Be back after lunch."

"Call me first. If you're not feeling better I want you to stay home."

"What're you packing for lunch today?"

"Chicken salad and carrot cake."

He winked at MacFarland. "Then I'll be back before lunch." He turned and strolled away, cut himself off mid-whistle and ducked out the door.

Parker watched him go, wishing she didn't feel like she was the only solo guest at a dinner party because her two-timing date had just bailed on her.

MacFarland cleared his throat. "Mind if I ask a question?" Without looking around she made a don't-let-me-stop-you gesture. "Can I get in on some of that chicken salad and carrot cake action?"

She resented the heck out of the involuntary pleasure his words sparked. She put on a frown before she turned, and it deepened on its own accord. The man knew how to wear jeans and a sweatshirt.

And why should she care? She slapped her gloves together, impatient with the ridiculous turn of her thoughts. "You work here, you get lunch. Want some coffee before we get started?"

"Not if it's from the pot Briggs made."

She supposed she should give him credit for trying. But she didn't have the time or the energy for banter.

"Follow me," she snapped, and wondered if he'd salute behind her back. She led him inside the first Quonset hut and made a point of closing the door firmly behind them.

"Always make sure the door is shut tight. If Chance gets in and sees anything move, even if it's just a leaf, he'll chase it. Which means something will get broken. Someone's delivery will be shorted, and I'll lose money I can't spare."

"Understood."

With a brisk nod, she launched into her spiel. "We have three greenhouses. Hut One for geraniums, Hut Two for petunias and pansies, Hut Three for seed propagation." He opened his mouth and she held up a hand. "No football jokes."

"Wouldn't think of it." She shot him a look but his expression remained neutral. He followed her inside. "Seed propagation?"

"We save money by collecting seeds from existing plants to grow new ones. Actually, we only use seed propagation for the pansies. For the petunias and geraniums we do what's called vegetative propagation, which is basically taking cuttings to grow new plants."

"Kind of like cloning."

"Exactly like that."

She walked him up the aisle, breathing in the scent of the geranium leaves. He noticed it, too.

"I smell apples."

"It's the foliage. You'll also notice nutmeg and lemon." Usually the scents calmed her. This morning she was fighting a headache.

He stopped to finger one of the thin black tubes inserted into the soil in each flower pot. "These deliver water?"

"It's called drip irrigation. We use recycled water and also rainwater. I'm only using it indoors, though. Sun exposure reduces the life cycle of the rubber." She pointed at the plants hanging over their heads. "We use it for the hanging baskets, too. We have the assemblies on a timer so it's all automatic. Hut Three has a different system. For the seedlings we use overhead misters." An orange glow radiating through the plastic walls of the hut alerted her to the sunrise. Soon she'd have to get back to the house and arrange some breakfast for Nat.

And let out Chance, who was no doubt draped across the foot of Nat's bed despite orders that he sleep in the laundry room.

"Ready to move on?"

She didn't bother walking him through Hut Two. He stood at the entrance and stared at the expanse of flowers — on the benches, in midair and even on the floor. Those awaited delivery, Parker told him. His gaze lingered, she noticed, on the section of black pansies. They'd always fascinated her, too. But his question had nothing to do with flowers.

"You've already watered this morning?" He was eyeing the floor.

"We keep the concrete damp on purpose. Cuts back on spider mites and powdery mildew." And in that instant, an idea was born. She bit back a smile and led the way to Hut Three.

"So the buildings aren't heated?"

"What? Oh. No. When we're ready to expand we'll consider it. It'll take some money to install the convection tubes but obviously it'll let us grow year-round."

"What do you do during the winter?"

"Produce seedling plant and rooted plugs for other greenhouses." She gave a half shrug. "That's the plan, anyway. We didn't get many buyers this past winter. We'll do better this year."

There wasn't much to see in the last hut. She walked him around the property and showed him the potting shed/office/coffee mess, the garage and the compost bin. They walked past a grove of lilacs and the heady scent, combined with the cheerful songs of the robins hunting worms in the dew-damp grass around them, cheered her.

Silence. She turned to find him watching her. "You love this place," he said.

"I do. So you can see why…" She trailed off.

"Why you'd put up with having me around?" He nodded once. "So, what can I do to help?"

"Follow me."

After leading him to the storage end of Hut Three she selected a bucket, a soft-bristled scrub brush and a container of bleach. She pushed them at him and said, "Garden hose is just outside."

He accepted the items as though they were a pile of dirty diapers. "What are these for?"

"Remember that mildew I mentioned?" She waved a hand at the nearest wall. "Don't scrub too hard or you'll tear the plastic."

* * *

REID STRAIGHTENED, AND WINCED as the stiffness in his back reminded him he'd been hunched over for hours. He peeled back a latex glove and glanced at his watch. Okay, maybe not hours. Still, ninety minutes was a long time to be bent over a bucket of bleach.

His wince graduated to a grimace. Normally he wasn't much of a complainer. This morning he had two good reasons. One, he never did get a decent cup of coffee. And two, he'd spent way too much time last night worrying when he should have been sleeping.

Worrying about whether he'd be able to make a difference. And if Parker would break her promise to Briggs. Seemed she planned to keep it after all. But for how long?

The breeze was back, and it carried the scent of spring through the greenhouse. He drew in an approving breath. All in all he'd rather smell flowers than a platoon of sweaty men any day. Not to mention bleach. He peeled off the gloves, pushed his hands into the small of his back and stretched. Time to see if he could get away with making his own pot of coffee.

A clearing of a throat. A young, female-type throat.

Aw, hell. Reid squeezed his eyes shut and slowly lowered his hands to his sides. He hadn't expected to have to deal with her so soon. Even as he opened his eyes and turned, he told himself he should just ignore her. Show her he was someone she didn't want to be around.

Green eyes watched him warily. At least he assumed they were both green. One was nearly swollen shut. Damn. All that black and blue had to smart.

After a few awkward seconds he managed to find his voice. "Something I can do for you?"

She shook her head. Silence. He sighed, and gestured with his chin. "What's with the eye?"

She shrugged. Still not a word. Reid knew he'd lost his charm a long time ago but this was ridiculous. Had she come just to stare? He was tempted to turn around but something in her one-eyed gaze stopped him.

"Name's Reid. I'm helping out."

"Why?"

Aha. Not his favorite word in the world, but at least it was a word. "I'm on leave for a month. Needed something to do."

Her mouth twisted and she eyed the plastic he'd scrubbed.

"You haven't gotten very far. You spend that much time on every section and as soon as you're done you'll have to start all over again."

Okay, *why* had he wanted her to speak to him? He gave a lazy shrug, and he could tell by the breathy, indignant noise she made that she didn't appreciate his response.

"Do you even *know* what a chrysanthemum looks like?"

He tried not to laugh. She sounded like a teenager. "All right, kid, I admit it. I know squat about plants." Except what Noble Johnson had tried to teach him. And he didn't remember much of that, since the more beer the big man drank, the more Latin he spouted. "But that's what Google's for."

"Whatever. You got a girlfriend?"

Now why was that question a kick to his gut? "No." Then before he could stop himself he added, "Not anymore." Damn, soldier. Shut *up*.

"What happened to her?"

"We just...didn't get along anymore." Not that he blamed her. There was a time he could barely get along with himself.

"'Cause you're grumpy?"

Takes grumpy to know grumpy, kid. "Maybe."

She fiddled with the bracelets on her wrist. "My mom said you came to help 'cause my dad died."

He didn't say anything. There was nothing he *could* say.

"And you didn't even know him." She tucked her hands into the back pockets of her bright pink jeans. "I could tell you about him, if you want. Whenever he came home from being deployed he always had to have my mom's banana muffins. And her meat loaf. He'd ask her to make tons of it and we'd have it with mashed potatoes and peas. I never ate the peas. If she tried to make me I'd feed 'em to Chance. Anyways she'd make him meat loaf sandwiches with ketchup and cheese for when he went fishing. Sometimes she'd put hard-boiled eggs inside to surprise him. Daddy didn't like to fish with worms, he used these squiggly, feathery, funny-looking things called flies and—"

Reid closed his eyes. He was in hell. Forget the searing flames and writhing bodies and agonized screaming. This was true damnation, having to listen to a lonely little girl chatter on and on about the father she'd worshipped.

" —and when I'd forget to shut it he'd get reeeeally super annoyed and—"

"I'm a little busy here, kid," he said, and barely recognized his own voice. "Maybe you could tell me some other time." He braced himself for the tears. But her eyes filled with annoyance instead.

"That was rude," she said. "And my name is Natalie." She turned and marched away with her nose in the air.

Reid blinked. Guilt pressed down on him like a hundred-pound weight. Now he *really* needed a coffee. In fact he'd make it a double.

He headed for the potting shed. No sense in pretending he'd only been following her mother's orders. Truth was, it hurt too much to talk to her. Besides, that kid had more attitude than the desert had scorpions. No way Parker needed to worry about her bonding with Reid.

No longer willing to wait for a new pot to brew, he poured himself a cup of what Briggs called coffee and stared down into the depths. Black. Like Natalie's eye. Where'd a little girl get a shiner like that?

"I asked you to stay away from her."

Reid turned. Parker stood in the doorway to the shed, arms crossed over the bib of her overalls. He allowed himself a mad, crazy moment of wondering how she'd look in something other than denim.

"What happened to her eye?"

Parker pressed her lips together, watched him sip his coffee— damn, that was bitter—and shrugged. "An accident during gym. What did you say to her? She's upset."

"She tried to strike up a conversation. I told her I was busy. She left." He peered at her over his cup. "Just following your orders." *Like a good soldier.*

She let her arms fall to her sides. "I'm sorry she bothered you."

He wished he could say she hadn't. "She's lonely," he said instead.

"She's stubborn. I asked her to leave you alone, but I should have known better. For her that's practically a direct order to stick to you like glue."

"If you're worried, why don't you send her to stay with a friend? Briggs mentioned next week is spring break."

She frowned. "She doesn't enjoy that. Staying over."

"Camp?"

"Refuses to consider it."

Her tone was heavy, and the skin under her eyes looked shadowed. "Why don't you get yourself some full-time help? The death gratuity—"

"Is for Nat. For college."

"It's also for you. I understand you're reluctant to benefit from your husband's death, but—"

"You don't understand anything. And I'm not having this conversation. Not with you." A sudden furious pink bloomed in her cheeks. "You can't march in here and think you can fix all of our problems just so you can march back out again without a guilty conscience. We were doing fine before you showed up."

Like hell. Neither Parker Dean nor her kid was getting enough sleep and according to Briggs the business was on the hairy edge of going under. She had the money to ease her circumstances but refused to use it. Because doing so meant accepting her husband's death?

He wanted to say all of that. But if he did she might kick his ass out. And he needed the twenty-six days he had left to help fix all those problems.

She glared at him, and he figured she was waiting to hear the standard "Yes, ma'am." He kept his mouth shut. She huffed an aggravated sigh.

"Please, just…do your best to discourage my daughter."

She backed out of the doorway and disappeared. Reid dumped his coffee into the sink in the corner.

He could see things Parker Dean couldn't. And damned if he'd ignore them. He was there to help, to ease their load. If easing that load meant doing things Parker Dean didn't like, so be it.

63

She couldn't despise him any more than she already did.

*   *   *

REID STEPPED OUT OF THE shed just as Briggs sidled around the corner. The disappointment on the former Marine's face was a dead giveaway he'd been listening in.

Briggs shook his head and stared in the direction Parker had gone. "It's gonna be a long month."

"Doubt she'll let me stay that long."

Briggs looked at him and sniffed. "You smell like bleach."

"I was waging war against mildew."

"You ready for some real work?"

"I'm ready for some real coffee." Briggs ignored him. "You feeling better, by the way?"

The old man harrumphed and made a show of slapping his pockets in search of his gloves. "Got some outbuildings that need to be emptied. Figured I'd show you what needed to be done so we could get the stuff hauled away. Otherwise those buildings will stay a breedin' ground for rats and snakes."

Rats and snakes. He couldn't wait.

Two hours later Read was swigging water and actually looking forward to lunch. He'd had no idea how much land or how many outbuildings were involved in Parker Dean's operation. Or how much junk was stashed in those outbuildings. Her tour that morning had included only the nearest structures. No wonder she was desperate for help.

Just like the buildings. And paint jobs were the least of the problems.

He stood with Briggs at the bottom of the gravel driveway, facing away from the farmhouse. Sweat slid down his spine. The sun was bright, and the cooling spring breeze had taken off for parts unknown.

His gaze swept the vivid green of the farmland across the road. That thin, hazy streak of blue in the distance had to be the lake. He should take a picture of all that green and blue, cart it back with him to the sandbox.

He swiped the back of a hand across his mouth. "How bad is it, Briggs?"

"Not blind, are you, son? And call me Harris. Anyways, you can see for yourself the place is fallin' down around our ears. Plastic needs to be replaced, tables and benches are rickety as all get-out, and you know as well as I do that truck over there needs an overhaul."

"Cosmetics. Except for the truck." What that needed was a new engine. Next on Reid's list for the day was to see if he could get the damned thing running again. He'd asked about it earlier, but Harris said Parker was trying to get Pete Lowry to come out and take a look at it.

If the mechanic didn't show up in the next half hour, then Reid was going in.

Harris continued to fuss. "You have any idea how much plastic sheeting costs? And I didn't even mention that car of hers. That's a whole nother set of troubles, right there."

"Can I ask you something?"

"Ask away."

"How sick are you?"

"Too sick to skydive, not sick enough to die."

"In other words, mind my own business." Reid resisted the urge to chuckle. "So it'll take money," he said. "I can provide some." Especially if it meant new plastic. New plastic wouldn't need scrubbing. "Tell me what you need."

"You're not worried you'll be throwin' good money after bad?"

"You think that's what I'll be doing?" Harris just looked at him. "All right, yes, I've wondered that. Mostly because—she works so damned hard. She doesn't sleep, she doesn't spend any money on herself—I can't believe he'd have wanted this for her."

"Didn't take you long to figure all that out."

"Wouldn't take anyone long."

Harris grunted. "If I make you a list, you gonna run it by Parker?"

"If I run it by Parker, she gonna let me pay for what's on it?"

"That's about as likely as one of those cows across the way there sproutin' wings."

"Then so is showing her the list."

*   *   *

SHWUP, SHWUP, SHWUP, SHWUP. Parker concentrated on the noise her boots made as she moved through grass in desperate need of mowing. A rowdy crowd of annoying thoughts struggled for attention and she forced herself to focus on the chill of the night air, the glow of the flashlight beam, the lush scent of the distant lake. Was it too much to ask for a little mental vacation?

Her flashlight lit the path to the barn. Overhead a butter-colored half-moon peered through strips of clouds, casting enough light to keep the deeper shadows around her at bay. A leaf trailed along her cheek as she passed under a low-hanging branch and she shivered. She hugged her waist, her sweatshirt bunching beneath her arms.

She stopped at the door to the barn, thought about the truck inside and sighed. Vacation over.

During his first day on the job Corporal Reid MacFarland had done three days' worth of work. He'd scrubbed half the plastic in Hut Three, helped Harris build a more than respectable pile of metal to haul to the scrap yard and another pile destined for the landfill, fixed the leaky spigot in Hut Two and the faulty outlet in the potting shed.

And on top of that he'd managed to breathe life back into her twenty-eight-year-old truck. He'd had to rebuild the carburetor, Harris had told her. Which meant driving thirty miles to the nearest auto parts store. And back. And then several hours of labor. But MacFarland hadn't said a word to her about it because he'd known she wanted to see as little of him as possible.

He hadn't even said goodbye at the end of his very long day. She knew when he left, because she'd heard his Jeep start up and drive away. She didn't know what she'd expected when she'd agreed to let him help out. But she certainly hadn't expected him to work a fifteen-hour day.

She swung open the barn door and hit the light switch. There was a rustling sound, in the far left corner, which she had no intention of investigating. She shuddered again, set her flashlight on the workbench inside the door, and patted the rust-speckled hood of the delivery truck on her way to the driver's side. *Hang in there, baby.*

She climbed up into the seat and found a note propped against the instrument panel.

Mrs. Dean,
Problem with the carburetor. Should be good
to go.
Thank you for lunch.

Something squeezed in her chest. He hadn't signed it. As if he didn't want to remind her of who he was. Because he didn't want her to send him away.

The man carried as much stubborn as she did.

She collapsed against the seat back and winced when her hairclip collided with the headrest, biting into her scalp. Dumb thing. She yanked it out and rubbed her head. The note was still in her hand and the paper crackled.

Her gaze dropped to the keys in the ignition. One flick of the wrist and the engine rumbled to life. She sighed and sent up a prayer of thanks she knew darned well should be directed elsewhere. MacFarland had made the repair sound so simple. But Harris had made sure she'd known the truth. The corporal had gone out of his way — literally — to make sure she'd be able to make the next delivery. After last night he couldn't help but know how important that was.

She turned off the engine, and listened to the muffled *tick-tick-tick* as it cooled. Darn it, she'd rather he hadn't helped at all. It made it harder to hate him.

She leaned forward and rested her head on the steering wheel. Not only had he fixed her truck, he'd saved her the mechanic's bill. When Reid showed up in the morning she'd make it a point to thank him. She didn't want to talk to him, but she had no right to treat him like a third-class citizen.

She sat up, and reread the now-crumpled note. *Should be good to go.* Had he intended the double meaning? She fisted her hand around the paper and moved stiffly as she got out of the truck. She didn't care. Didn't care if he had a sense of humor, or a temper, or a mouthful of cavities, or seven older sisters, or a set of drums in the back of his Jeep.

She already knew everything she needed to know about him.

6

EUGENIA PULLED INTO WHAT Harris called the "staff parking lot". The space, which was separated from the farmhouse by the three Quonset huts, was actually half gravel, half field and if someone didn't start getting serious with the weed killer, the field part would soon take over. Harris and another man—a tall, dark-haired hottie who had to be the jogging soldier everyone was talking about—were unloading what looked like PVC piping and boxes of plumbing parts from the back of a forest-green Jeep. Harris frowned over at her and Eugenia smiled brightly through her windshield. It was either that or burst into tears and no way she'd give him the satisfaction. All right, so, maybe he wouldn't feel *satisfied*. But she refused to humiliate herself by letting him see how much she missed him.

The rat. Her palm was slick, making it a challenge to put her Volvo in Park.

Once she got out of the car she adjusted her sunglasses, smoothed the front of her navy sheath and stepped carefully toward the Jeep. Harris scowled at her over his shoulder. When his partner lifted one of the boxes from Harris's arms, it was his turn to receive a scowl. They exchanged a few growls and then Harris turned back to Eugenia, his load lighter and his expression heavier.

"It's Monday. Why aren't you at the store?"

"Nice to see you, too."

"I'm a little busy here, Genie."

"I can see that." She turned to the younger man and sweetened her smile. "I'm Eugenia Blue. You must be Parker's soldier."

She thrust out a hand, pretending she hadn't noticed his wince. *Not* Parker's soldier, then. Too bad. She'd hoped to indulge in a little matchmaking. He and Parker would look good together. With one or two adjustments, anyway. Probably Parker's sense of fashion — or lack thereof, bless her heart — had contributed to that wince.

Eugenia could fix that.

She tipped her head. "Welcome to Thistle Hill."

"Reid MacFarland. Pleasure to meet you, ma'am."

"Corporal, isn't it?"

"Yes, ma'am."

"Such a gentleman. How refreshing." She waited a beat for Harris to grunt. She wasn't disappointed. Maybe the moody old thing missed her, after all. She spoke through her smile. "I have a dress shop over on State Street. I'd invite you to stop by but I'm guessing that's not your thing."

"You'd be right, ma'am."

"How long will you be with us, Corporal?"

"Give the man his hand back," Harris muttered. She let go with a wink. Reid MacFarland looked from her to Harris and back again, and one side of his mouth tipped up.

"I'm heading back to Kentucky in a few weeks."

"Sorry to hear that." She gestured at the supplies they'd been unloading. "You two are working awfully hard. What are you up to?"

They exchanged a look. "If Parker asks, we're repairing the sprinkler system in Hut Three."

"Repairing? Looks to me like you have enough bits and pieces to replace the whole thing." The men didn't respond. Eugenia clapped her hands together. "All righty, then. Enjoy your stay in Thistle Hill, Corporal. I hope I get a chance to see you again. Make sure Parker and Natalie take you out on the lake at least once. Bye, now." She offered Harris a stiff nod and, mindful that high heels and gravel didn't mix, tiptoed back to her car.

She was reaching for the passenger door when Harris opened it for

70

her. She hesitated, staring down at his strong, tanned arm, then averted her head, leaned in and retrieved the gift basket from the passenger seat. When she turned around, Harris's expression had soured. All her fantasies involving that muscled arm dissolved like sugar in water.

"Enough with the gifts, Genie. When will you learn you can't buy someone's affection?"

"As soon as you learn not to embarrass yourself by jumping to conclusions," she said briskly. Meanwhile, inside her chest, her heart curled into a cold ball of misery. So much for her decision to come clean. Just as well. The man wouldn't know a good deed if it sashayed up and swung him into a two-step.

"The basket is for Parker and Natalie. And I didn't buy these cookies, I made them."

"You made them?" He peered doubtfully into the basket. "Are those supposed to be chocolate?"

"They're singed." She shrugged. "So sue me."

He crossed his arms. "Why are you really here?"

"I'm Parker's friend. That's reason enough."

"If you were truly Parker's friend you wouldn't have baked her cookies."

"Ha ha." God. How witty. She really needed to start watching the Comedy Channel.

"I know that look in your eyes. You here to give Parker money?"

"That's none of your business."

"Which means yes. Damn it, Eugenia—"

"Hey, it's what I do. You know how we rich people are. Splurging is part of my routine. You know, take my vitamins, check my email, spend a few thousand dollars on something I don't need."

His expression remained fierce and she drew herself up. "I repeat, none of this is your business. But let me put your mind at ease. I'm not here to give money. I'm here to loan it."

"'Cause you want to help her? Or 'cause you want to impress me?"

That stung. "I don't think I could impress you if I stripped naked and juggled five flaming torches while reciting the entire Gettysburg Address. In French."

Harris scrubbed his palm over his bald head. "You're addicted, that's what you are. You're like your own personal Publisher's Clearinghouse."

"What is your problem? It's my money. I'll do what I want with it."

"Wanna bet?"

"What are you talking about? Do I want to bet that it's my own money? I'm fairly certain I'd win that bet."

"What I mean is, I'll bet you that you can't stop yourself from offering money to someone or buying somethin' for someone for, say, thirty days."

"That's not fair. Pete Lowry's daughter is having her baby shower. I can't go without a gift."

Harris held up a hand. "We won't count the baby shower gift."

"Exactly what is this supposed to prove? And why do you care, anyway?"

"You afraid you won't be able to do it?"

"I'm *afraid* I've had enough of your nonsense. I'll let you two get back to what you were doing. Don't work too hard, you hear?" She sidestepped Harris, waved goodbye to the corporal, and gave her hips an extra swing as she followed the path to the farmhouse.

*   *   *

BOTH MEN WATCHED HER go. When she disappeared around a corner Reid turned to Harris, eyebrows lifted. "That naked juggling thing? That would impress me."

"No one asked you."

"Think she might hire herself out?"

"I think you better stop flappin' your jaw before you get something wedged in there. Like my fist."

Reid considered, then turned back to the Jeep. "You were pretty rough on her about that loan thing. How do you know Parker wouldn't be interested?"

"You know as well as I do that girl's too proud for that. Holds on to her independence like Chance holds on to a steak bone. Two reasons she's accepting help from you. One, between you and me we didn't give her a choice. And two, she doesn't know half of what you're up to. We both know she'd rather eat dandelions for a week than ask for help."

"Can you do that?"

"What?"

"Eat dandelions?"

"Hell if I know."

Reid snatched up a receipt that had fluttered to the ground, and examined it far too closely. "That what you think I'm doing? Trying to buy Parker's forgiveness?"

"No, son. I think you're trying to make amends and ease your conscience at the same time." He propped his arm on a box Reid had maneuvered onto the bumper. "Genie's not feeling guilty, she's just a little confused about how you make friends."

"And keep lovers?"

The top of Harris's head turned red and at first Reid thought he wouldn't answer. "Never got that far," he said gruffly.

"She thanked me, you know."

"Eugenia?"

"Parker. For fixing the truck."

"Why wouldn't she?"

"You know as well as I do she can barely stand the sight of me." He hefted a box to the ground and straightened, ran his hand over his hair. "That next morning she made a point of coming to see me. To thank me." Parker Dean had grit. And class. Reid knew she'd rather toss her overalls onto a bonfire than go out of her way to thank him. He hadn't done what he had to make her grateful, but the fact that she was felt like a big step forward in his quest for absolution.

He gave Harris a look. "She made a big deal of it, as a matter of fact. Seemed she'd heard all the details from someone." Harris grunted, and Reid poked his tongue into his cheek. "Made me a cake."

"Mighty nice of her." Harris froze, then swung around, eyes narrowed. "Carrot cake?"

"What do you think?"

"Any left?"

Reid chuckled. "What do you think?"

"That's plain rotten."

Reid kept smiling. Gallahan had just about wept with joy when Reid had offered him half his prize. "Does Eugenia bake?"

Harris grunted. "Not well enough so's you'd actually want to eat anything she makes."

"What'd she do that was so bad you can't forgive her for it?"

"I know what you're thinkin', but the situation's different."

"How?"

"What she did was worse than—"

"Manslaughter?"

Harris opened his mouth, closed it, reached for his pack of gum. "When you put it that way…" He paused while opening the pack, and jabbed his chin at the sky. "Smell that?"

Reid inhaled automatically. Copper. And the sky looked—

"Gonna rain."

Reid leaned against the liftgate, shaking his head at Harris's pathetic attempt to distract him. "What did she *do?*" The older man mumbled something before shoving a stick of gum in his mouth and Reid leaned in. "Didn't catch that. She did what?"

"For Pete's sake, she bought me a *truck.*"

Reid was sorry he asked. In a sad, perverted kind of way he'd wished Eugenia Blue had actually done something worthy of Harris's contempt. If Harris refused to forgive Eugenia for buying him a gift, what the hell kind of chance did Reid have with Parker?

He gave himself a mental shake and hissed in an exaggerated breath. "A truck, huh? I'm surprised you didn't call the cops."

Harris continued to make bodily threats Reid paid little attention to. He stared in the direction of the farmhouse.

Seemed to him Eugenia Blue was lonely. Who could blame her for trying to change that?

*   *   *

PARKER WAS BALANCING A stack of plates and bowls still warm from the dishwasher when someone knocked at the back door. She called for her visitor to come in, almost fumbled the dishes when she realized it might be MacFarland, and turned from the cabinet with a belly gone haywire. Her breath left her lungs in a relieved whoosh when she saw who it was. Eugenia, who looked as elegant as ever in a navy sheath and pearls, carried a gift basket topped with a sunshine-yellow bow. Parker accepted it with a wide smile while trying not to wish she'd at least put on her frilly apron to cover her ratty jeans.

Darn it, she didn't have time to care about her appearance. Though lately she'd taken to wondering how she might fit some primping in. But only because she had a daughter to set an example for.

She pulled Eugenia into a one-armed hug. "What a nice surprise. What's the occasion?"

"I'm celebrating closing the store early today. Although I shouldn't. Celebrate, I mean. I closed because I had a sum total of one customer this morning. Maybe since the kids are out of school this week everyone's on the road. Anyway, I wanted to cheer you up."

"Cheer me up?"

"You know. That thing with the delivery truck and all."

"Oh. Well. The important thing is that Harris is all right."

Eugenia frowned. "Why wouldn't he be all right?"

Oh, Lord. Parker busied herself peeling the cellophane away from the basket. "Well, I mean, the engine could have caught fire. Or someone could have come along and...robbed him while he was waiting for a tow."

"Wow. Things really are bad. I've never known you to be so negative."

Parker gave herself a mental kick. "Forget I said that. And I'm *positive* these cookies will be perfect with a cup of tea." She lifted the paper plate out of the basket and stared. Were those scorch marks?

Eugenia laughed and waved a hand. "Those aren't for eating. I suppose they're not even really for show. While I was wrapping those babies up I was hoping you'd be one of those people who believes it's the thought that counts."

"I do believe that. And I happen to have a chocolate cake that will go just as well with our tea. And you—" she patted Eugenia on the shoulder and pointed her to a chair "—get an extra big serving." Parker sliced the cake and poured the tea and settled herself opposite her guest.

Eugenia picked up her fork. "Nat must not be home. Otherwise she'd already be bargaining for a second piece of cake."

Parker laughed, struggling to drag her thoughts away from the long list of chores begging for her attention. "You know my daughter well. Actually, Ivy Millbrook invited all of the third-graders on a tour of her dairy farm. I think it was the promise of a picnic that cinched the deal for Nat." Which had shocked Parker, considering how sensitive Nat was about her black eye. She'd changed her mind at the last minute, of course, as Ivy hovered on the doorstep, the borrowed school bus idling at the bottom of the driveway. When Ivy had assured Nat she'd get special treatment because of her injury— including a private introduction to a newborn calf—Nat had hurried back inside to get her jacket. Relieved, Parker had hugged Ivy—a little too tightly, judging by how quickly she'd backed away once Parker had let go.

She smiled at the memory, lifted her mug and focused on Eugenia. "You wanted to talk with me about something?"

"What I said before, about things being bad? I'd heard you were having a hard time."

Carefully Parker set her mug back down. "What exactly did you hear?"

"That your greenhouse venture isn't doing as well as you'd hoped."

Okay, *that* conversation she could handle. "It's true things are a little challenging right now. But every start-up business has growing pains. We just have to be patient."

"In case you need more than patience, I'm here to offer you a loan. Wait, I take that back." She grimaced. "Initially I came to offer you a loan, but then I ran into Harris outside and he bet me I couldn't stop offering people money."

"He did what?"

"It sounds terrible, doesn't it? But he might actually have a point." She hesitated, then shook her head. "Nope, he's wrong. It's my money and I can do what I like with it. But I'd still like to win that bet." She gave Parker a sly smile. "Although I can't *officially* offer you a no-strings-attached, no-interest, straight-up loan to put you in the black, if you were to *ask* for one I'd be more than happy to say yes."

"That's very generous. And I appreciate it, Eugenia. I really do. But I can't take advantage of you like that."

"It's not taking advantage if it's something I want to do."

It was tempting. Very tempting. Parker had nothing left to sell. No time for a second job. No hope for any income except what she got from the business. From the *struggling* business. A loan from Eugenia would make paying off her debts so easy. She indulged in a brief fantasy where the mail didn't include overdue notices, a brand-new dishwasher did the after-dinner chores and she and Nat ate in a restaurant more often than once every few months.

The bubble popped. What if she couldn't pay the money back? Eugenia might insist she didn't care, but Parker did. If defaulting didn't cost her Eugenia's friendship it would certainly mean the loss of the other woman's respect. And it would mean dipping into Nat's college fund.

Then Parker really would hate herself.

She covered Eugenia's hand with hers. "Thank you. So much. But I can't take your money."

"Why not? I promise you I have no ulterior motive, no dastardly master plan. I don't understand why no one will let me help."

"What if something happened and I couldn't pay you back? I'd feel terrible if I had to default on the loan and so would you. I can't tell you how much I appreciate the thought, but I don't think it's a good idea to mix finances and friendship."

Eugenia sat back. "I realize we don't know each other that well. It hasn't even been a year since I moved here and most of our get-togethers included Harris." She shifted forward again. "You've never said much about your family. Harris once told me you moved here right after Tim's funeral, but he's never met any of your relatives. Can you count on any of them for help?"

"It's a long story. The short answer is no. They can't help." They wouldn't even think to offer.

"I see." Eugenia sighed and stabbed her fork into her cake. "Well, what good is having money if I can't spend it on my friends?"

Something clicked for Parker. "Did you try to spend it on Harris?"

Eugenia's fork clattered to the plate. "Now you're going to tell me the same thing he did. That you can't buy affection."

"Actually, I was going to ask why you'd try to buy affection you already have? That's like demanding to pay full price at a fire sale."

Her smile was lost on Eugenia. "If you're trying to tell me Harris is interested, you're wrong. He has about as much romantic interest in me as he has in his garbage disposal."

"I'm sorry, I shouldn't have said anything. Let's talk about something else."

Eugenia's shoulders slumped. "I'm sorry, too. It's just...it's nice to be needed, you know?"

Parker nodded, and watched as her guest took a bite of her cake. It *was* nice to be needed. Or at least, it had been. She hadn't been needed as anything other than a mother since Tim died.

She had one friend now. Harris. And he didn't like to ask for help any more than she did. As much as she loved him, she missed having a female friend to laugh with, be herself with, confide in. Once they'd moved to Thistle Hill she'd isolated herself and Nat from her former friends. Not intentionally. There was just so much to *do*. And precious little time for a visit, let alone a chatty phone call.

People had offered to help. Thistle Hill was a friendly place. But once you started to depend on people, once you started to *care…*

She traced the raised pattern on her napkin and thought about what Nat had said, about Reid MacFarland being lonely, and suddenly her cake tasted less like chocolate and a whole lot more like regret.

*   *   *

REID SHUT THE DOOR TO the hut, took five steps and hesitated. Was that snuffling he'd heard? He turned back and held his breath. Oh, yeah. No mistaking the sound of a dog rooting around for trouble.

He'd shut Chance inside the greenhouse.

Shit. How the hell had the dog gotten in without Reid noticing? He yanked open the door and startled the Lab just as he was lifting his leg in the corner. "Whoa! Hold on there, boy." He hustled over and bent down to grab hold of the collar and caught air instead. Chance dove under the nearest table. Damned dog wanted to play. Reid grabbed for the Lab's tail and missed. Chance scampered halfway down the concrete path, looked back at Reid and pissed on the nearest table leg.

"All right," Reid growled. "Game on."

Ten minutes later he dragged the panting Lab back outside, almost catching them both in the door in his rush to secure the hut. When he let go of Chance the Lab wagged his tail and barked once, as if to say, *Well, that was fun,* then took off toward the house. Reid followed more slowly. He'd almost blown it, big-time. And here it was only Wednesday. Only his fifth full day on the job.

Parker had discouraged him from coming in on Sunday but of course he'd insisted. He was there to work, not read the paper. But if Chance trashed the greenhouse, no amount of overtime would save Reid's ass.

He pictured Parker's face as she heard his confession that he'd let her dog destroy some of her precious plants. She didn't look happy.

Then he indulged himself and pictured the rest of her. Which made *him* happy. He sighed, and imagined her expression if she found out he was fantasizing about her. Huh. Just as well he hadn't already eaten his lunch because the bloodlust on her face was enough to turn a man's stomach.

Not that they were bonafide fantasies. More like…imaginings. He couldn't help himself. It was driving him crazy. Day after day after day she wore another pair of those damned overalls. How long before he got a chance to see her in something other than that blasted Farmer Brown getup?

And how many pairs of those things did she own, anyway?

With her baggy, sweat-stained clothes, tight-lipped glares and mulish independence — not to mention the horrific circumstances that had brought them together — he should have no personal interest whatsoever in Parker Dean.

Try telling that to his whacked-out libido.

He rounded the house and settled on the front steps, resting his elbows on the worn plank floor of Parker Dean's porch. He distracted himself with an exercise he and his squad members often relied on when they needed to center themselves — the mental cleaning of their weapon. He closed his eyes and imagined the breakdown, heard the click and snap as parts came away, felt the polished sheen of metal, smelled the — okay, that wasn't gun oil he was smelling. It was a calming, flowery scent, one he recognized from the yard behind the house where he grew up. He opened his eyes and turned his head, spotted the familiar purple, cone-shaped blooms on a bush almost as tall as he was.

A bush he could never remember the name of.

"How come you're not eating lunch at the picnic table?"

Another sneak attack. Jesus. Once his heart settled back down to a normal rhythm he looked over his shoulder. Parker's daughter stood just outside the front door, a plastic bottle of purple juice in one hand, a paperback in the other. And a pair of flamingo-pink high-tops on her feet.

He hid a smile. She'd get a kick out of that chair at Snoozy's. Too bad she'd have to wait a dozen years or so to check it out.

He got to his feet. He had errands to run, and Parker had made it clear she didn't want him chitchatting with her daughter. But as he turned to say goodbye, he caught a lip tremble that could only mean he'd hurt her feelings.

Hell.

He hesitated, and gripped the railing with his left hand. So he wasn't into making kids cry. So he'd take a few minutes to convince her she hadn't chased him away, even though she had.

So sue him. "It's Wednesday. How come you're not in school?"

"I asked my question first. How come you're up here?"

"Not hungry," he said, and gave her a look. The look he'd perfected for wayward squad members. The quit-while-you're-ahead-and-I-won't-make-you-cry-out-for-your-mama-look.

Didn't even faze her. Instead of trembling in her boots or fainting dead away she held out her wrist. "I got this for my birthday."

She wore a watch with a bright pink band. The oversize face was painted with the black outline of a cat's head, topped with a hair bow. Pink, of course.

The kid sure did like pink.

"Nice," he said.

His reaction obviously disappointed her. "Hello Kitty," she prompted.

She had to be kidding. "No way I'm talking to your watch." He shouldn't even be talking to *her*.

"No, it's...never mind." She leaned against the opposite railing and tipped her head. "You must be a good soldier."

The "suck" part of "sucker punch" was having to pretend the blow didn't hurt. Reid held back a grimace. Yeah, he was a good soldier. Had been. Past tense. He watched her spin the watch around her wrist.

"Why do you think I'm a good soldier?"

"'Cause you suck at gardening."

He choked out a laugh. "Yeah, but I'm learning. Now it's your turn. No school today?"

"Spring break."

A hurt silence. Because he hadn't noticed she'd been home from school Monday and Tuesday? He banged the flat of his hand against the railing.

"Look. I have errands to run." He started to back away.

"Can I come?"

He froze, then gestured at her paperback. "Don't you have homework?"

She shook her head. "This is my treat book."

"Your what?"

"My treat book. It's what I read in between book report books."

He tipped his head and read the title. Lifted an eyebrow. "Aren't you a little young for Agatha Christie?"

"Aren't you a little old?"

"For what?"

"For anything."

He blinked. "You're a real charmer, kid." A glance at the house behind her had him shaking his head. "I doubt your mom would appreciate you coming with me. You'd be bored anyway. I'm only going—"

"If you don't want me to come along, just say so. 'No' takes a lot less breath."

The sass in her words was absent from her river-green eyes. Reid rubbed his fingers over his chin. The hell with it. Let Parker be the one to say no. That's what moms were for.

Besides, maybe Nat would put in a good word for him. Reid needed all the help he could get.

"Tell you what, kid. If your mom says it's okay, I'd be happy to have you ride shotgun."

"Really?"

He checked a watch he wasn't wearing. "You have three minutes."

She moved almost as fast as the day she first caught sight of him.

Five minutes later they were on their way to the lumberyard. He didn't have to strain for a conversation opener. "Ever read Dorothy Gilman?"

She had a hank of hair curled around one finger when she shook her head. "What's she write?"

"She wrote the Mrs. Pollifax series, about a feisty old lady who works for the CIA. Kind of like a modern Miss Marple."

"Cool. You like mysteries, too?"

"Yeah, I do. But I prefer authors like Ed McBain, Patricia Cornwell, Robert Ludlum. I like my books to have some grit."

"Blood and guts, you mean." That superior tone again. Then she threw a right hook. "My dad liked to read."

"Yeah?" He managed the word despite the feeling that someone had grabbed him by the throat.

"Classics, mostly," she continued, as if he'd asked. "He really liked Hemingway."

The wistfulness in her voice was creating chaos in his gut. He cleared his throat. "I'm sorry about your dad." She'd never know how sorry. His fingers tightened on the wheel.

She gave him a look, like she was evaluating him for something. "Sorry enough to buy me an ice cream?"

"Oh, you're good."

"Well, are you?"

Sorry enough to get you a lifetime supply, kid. He started to say, "We'll see," but remembered how much he'd hated those words when he was a kid. "We'll see how big a help you are," he said instead. She nodded, and he hustled for a subject other than her father. "Got any hobbies other than reading?"

She shrugged. "I like to ride my bike. And Mom's teaching me how to bake. How about you?"

"Your mom has never offered to teach me how to bake." He wrenched his mind away from the image of Parker Dean in a frilly apron. And not much else.

Nat snorted. "You know what I meant."

"I like to play pool," he said. "Run. Lift weights."

"You like sports?"

"Yes, ma'am."

"Any good at softball?"

"Some. When I'm not deployed I pitch for an Army team. Why? You like to play?"

"I'm not very good at it." She dipped her head. "We're going to be playing in gym."

Uh-oh. He knew what was coming. Hell, he wouldn't mind giving the kid a few pointers. But Parker had told him in no uncertain terms to give her little girl a wide berth.

So why agree to let Nat run errands with him?

His stomach muscles tightened, and he looked over at his passenger. "Tell me the truth. Your mother really give you permission to come with me?"

She blinked at him, chin tucked, eyes wide, face turned to give him the maximum effect of that shiner, and he knew.

Damn it to hell. Didn't matter what else he achieved that day. When he and Nat got back to the house, Parker would be pissed with a capital P.

Any points he'd earned with Parker Dean had just turned into, as his fellow squad members would say, a big bag of dicks.

*   *   *

PARKER STOMPED UP TO the picnic table, hoping that the one infinitesimal portion of her brain that wasn't quivering with fury would remember later to ask MacFarland to cut the grass. Which just made her madder. When the heck had she started to depend on that interfering interloper?

Harris didn't even look up from his clipboard when she stopped in front of him, her hands on her hips, her breathing as ragged as the cuffs on her overalls.

"Where is he?"

"Wanna be more specific?"

"Don't play games with me, Harris Briggs." She shook a piece of paper under his nose. "What is this?"

"Looks like a receipt."

"For forty rolls of polyvinyl. I don't buy polyvinyl. I buy polyethylene."

"Which is why we already need more plastic."

If he weren't a sick old man, she'd kick the bench right out from under him. "On top of this I got a call from Pete Lowry. He wanted to let us know that the engine for the delivery truck should be in tomorrow, and was MacFarland still willing to pay extra to make sure he had it installed by the weekend."

"Sounds like a man with a deadline."

"More like a man with a death wish. How am I supposed to pay for all this? I told him I wasn't going to touch the money we got for…from the Army."

"I believe he has it covered."

"He knows about the extra delivery, but there's no way that'll —" She stared at Harris. "What do you mean, he has it covered?"

"I mean he's paying for it."

"That's ridiculous." She gestured with the paper. "We're talking thousands of dollars."

Harris went back to his clipboard, and Parker sank down onto the nearest bench. "This isn't right. This isn't what I agreed to."

Harris chuckled, and Parker turned on him with renewed fury. "You think it's funny? That he's running up debts I can't possibly repay?"

"Now you know how he feels."

Suddenly it was as if someone had yanked a plug and all of her energy had drained out of her. There was no comparing a man's life to money, but there was also no sense in arguing. MacFarland was determined to fix something that could never be fixed. Did he even care that he might break himself in the process?

Slowly she got to her feet and stuffed the receipt into her pocket. "Where is he now?"

"Out buying lumber."

Just like that, she snapped back into fighting form. Enough was enough. "That's it. That is *it*. Who on God's green earth does he think he is, coming in here and taking over and making decisions without even *pretending* to care what I think?" She marched away, came to an abrupt halt, marched back.

"Why are you here, by the way? I thought you had errands to run. And where's Nat?" The look on his face gave it away and she gave a closemouthed scream of fury.

"Now, don't go puttin' your blooms in a blender. She said you'd given her permission."

"To go with *you*."

Harris shrugged. "He offered to run my errands for me."

"Harris Briggs, one of these days I'm going to lace your carrot cake with rat poison and bury you in the compost heap."

He patted his pockets, no doubt looking for a pack of gum. "And my middle name is Marion."

"Am I the only one who sees what he's trying to do here?"

"Make life easier for you?"

"First you, and now my daughter. I'm living with a bunch of...of pod people."

"Come on in." Harris grinned and mimed the backstroke. "The water's fine."

* * *

AN HOUR LATER, PARKER was at the far end of Hut Three checking on seedlings, singing Carrie Underwood under her breath and fantasizing about Louisville Sluggers, when Nat exploded through the greenhouse door.

"Mom! Guess what, Mom?"

Parker straightened. And couldn't help smiling when she saw clear evidence of what her daughter had been up to.

"Hot-fudge sundae," she said. The child seemed to have a knack for finagling ice-cream treats.

Nat scrubbed a hand over her mouth. "Something better."

Parker clutched at her chest melodramatically. "Better than ice cream?"

She looked up then, saw MacFarland approaching and felt her smile fade. She couldn't read his expression, and that kicked off a twister in her stomach.

"We saw Joe Gallahan at the lumberyard. He was buying some stuff for the motel. Anyway, Reid and Joe were talking, and they didn't know I could hear, and Reid said I'd asked him about softball, and Joe said me and Reid could practice with his team. Anytime we wanted. Isn't that great? Maybe they could teach me to play good enough so the kids at school won't laugh."

"'Well enough,'" Parker corrected automatically. A stark coldness began to creep into her heart at the worship on Nat's face when she talked about MacFarland.

"Mom? You're gonna let me play, aren't you? When Joe asks if I can join the team you'll say yes, right?"

She tore her gaze away from Corporal Inscrutable. "Nat, I'd like to get some more details from the corporal. Why don't you go on in the house and wash your face and hands."

Nat hesitated, then nodded. "Should I set the table?" she asked, and it was all Parker could do to keep from howling.

"Sure, sweetie. That would be nice." After she'd gone — a little too energetically for someone who usually shunned soap and water and never set the table without being asked at least half a dozen times — Parker turned back to MacFarland, her hands clenched into fists, her arms stick-straight at her sides.

"I don't even know where to begin."

7

MACFARLAND HELD OUT A placating hand. "I didn't know she was listening when Gallahan and I were talking. But I do think it's a great opportunity."

"Do you."

"The team meets Tuesdays and Thursdays. Next practice is tomorrow night. Gallahan and I thought Nat might want to come along and get some pointers. We never meant to arrange it without your permission."

"That's the problem, isn't it?" Parker gritted her teeth. "I *have* to give permission. Otherwise I'm the bad guy."

MacFarland said nothing. What could he say? He and Nat had Parker right where they wanted her. Intentional or not.

"You knew I didn't want you hanging around her."

He sighed. "When was the last time she spent a day with someone besides you? And I don't mean her teachers."

"That is not your concern."

"No. But it should be yours. You're independent. Do you realize you're raising your daughter to be the opposite?"

Parker wanted nothing better than to smack that know-it-all look off the corporal's face and send him packing. But she had a daughter who was desperate to succeed in a sport, any sport. And a whole team of men willing to help. She also had a truckload of materials — literally — that needed installing.

But between softball and doing father-daughter things like getting ice cream, it wouldn't be long before Nat started to depend on having MacFarland around. With her business at stake, Parker didn't think she'd be far behind.

And how about that big fat elephant in the room? The reason why Nat's own father wasn't around to buy her ice cream? Then the child had to turn around and ask *MacFarland* for help. Parker resented the heck out of that. She hadn't counted on the corporal morphing from public enemy number one to concerned acquaintance.

Or maybe "extortionist" would be more accurate.

"The plastic was delivered today," she practically snarled.

"Roger that."

"That's it? *Roger that?*"

He cocked an eyebrow. "You want to high-five?"

Parker sputtered, and his other eyebrow went up. Cocky son of a —

"You are not in charge here," she said through gritted teeth. She folded her arms across her chest, her movements so forceful she nearly pulled a muscle. "You placed an order without my approval. Several orders. If you're going to humiliate me by paying my bills then the least you can do is pretend to care what I think."

"In the immortal words of Captain Hawkeye Pierce, 'Never let it be said I didn't do the least I could do.'"

"Not. Funny," she growled.

He gestured with his key fob. "Look. I'm not trying to humiliate you. I'm trying to help you. And you're right. I should have consulted you. I didn't because I knew you'd say no."

"You could have blamed Harris," she muttered.

"I'm sorry?"

"I have a feeling you had a partner in crime. This has Harris's grubby little fingerprints all over it." A sharp exhale. "What you're doing is helpful. I admit it. You're taking care of things I don't have the time or the money for. But I resent having to accept help, and I resent it even more when — "

"When I'm the one giving it."

"I was going to say, when I'm not allowed input, but that works as well."

"If things are so tight why don't you pack it in? Give up the greenhouse gig for something more dependable?"

"No," she said quietly. "I won't give it up. Tim and I bought this place before we knew he was being deployed. The plan was to come up on the weekends, make repairs a little at a time. Then once he was out of the Army, we'd turn it into a full-fledged business. He wanted this for us. I need to make it work. I will make it work."

She congratulated herself on sounding more confident than she felt. Especially considering the utility bill she'd received in the mail that morning. Hundreds of dollars overdue and she had no idea how she'd pay it.

"But would he have wanted you to work so hard?"

"I think he'd understand why I need to."

MacFarland grunted, then turned sideways and leaned back against the nearest bench. "So where do we go from here?"

"You could leave."

"I could."

And if he did, Nat would hate her. But it wouldn't be the first time, and it wouldn't be the last.

"We had an agreement," MacFarland said.

She'd been thinking about where he'd go when he left, since he was still on leave. And she realized he *had* no place to go. "This…whatever this is…this isn't about making amends. This isn't about me, it's about you."

"Explain."

"You're lonely. You said you have no family. If you died in Iraq you wouldn't have anyone mourning you like Nat and I mourn Tim. That's what this is about. You want us to be your family."

He gripped the edge of the bench so hard his knuckles turned white. "If I needed to find a family to adopt, I could have found one on post. I sure as hell wouldn't have driven five hundred miles."

"You had an excuse to take us on. You had an in. You *owed* us. We couldn't say no."

His jaw flexed and with rigid motions he pushed to his feet. "My unit is my family. The men I train and eat and fight and struggle and bleed beside, they're my family. They understand me."

"But that's not enough for you, is it?" She glared at him, the only noise in the hut her sharp, shuddering gasps of breath.

"All right. Yeah. This is about me. About how I can't live with myself. About how I need to help you in order to help myself."

Parker thought about Harris, about the work they had lined up, and her shoulders sagged. There were advantages to letting MacFarland stay. But how could she stand it?

She shook her head. "I can't have you spending any more of your own money."

"I'm not a kid. I know what I can afford. But let's not pretend that's what's bothering you. It's not the money. It's that it's not *your* money."

"What's that supposed to mean?"

"Like I said before. You're independent."

"And I plan to stay that way."

"I'm not trying to take away your independence, Mrs. Dean. I'm trying to restore it." He made a quick, pointed survey of the greenhouse and cocked his head. "Let me know when you've made a decision."

He shoved the fob into his pocket and headed for the door. Parker curled her fingers into her palms. A good exit line, but she wasn't buying it.

"I'm not buying it," she called after him.

He stopped. Didn't turn around.

"You're not here to give independence. You're here to take absolution."

He did turn then. "I'm not here to take anything. But yes, I'd accept forgiveness if it were offered."

She didn't have to say what she was thinking. No way she could keep the scorn out of her face. His hands clenched at his sides as anger sparked in his eyes.

"You're not even willing to consider it, are you? Because you think forgiving me betrays your husband? Because you don't want to let me off the hook? Maybe your resentment keeps you company. Or you're afraid I'll go back to the desert free to pull another blue on blue. Hell, maybe next time I can wipe out an entire unit."

"That's a hideous thing to say."

"Know what I think? I think you don't want to forgive me because it just might mean you'd have to forgive yourself."

"For what?"

"For whatever it is that keeps you digging in the dirt all day, every day. For whatever keeps you from using even the smallest portion of the death benefit to make your life easier." He jabbed a finger. "For whatever just put that flare of regret in your eyes."

"Regret?" She stomped toward him. "It's called grief, Corporal. Don't you dare suggest I should be ashamed of it."

"No. This isn't grief. Grief is natural. Healing. This is punishment. You don't think I can recognize when someone's raking their own ass over the coals?"

Parker was shaking so hard it was a wonder her bones weren't rattling. She threw her arms wide. "What? What do you want me to say? That I cheated on my husband? That he cheated on me? That he beat me on Thursdays? That I'm glad he's dead because now I can send Nat to college?" Tears flooded her throat and she swallowed twice. "That's what you want, isn't it? You want to hear something that'll make you believe I didn't love him. Haven't missed him. Something that'll make you feel better about blowing him up." She choked and bent forward at the waist, the humiliation of tears nothing next to the very real possibility of throwing up at his feet.

He dragged in a long breath.

"Jesus. I'm sorry. Parker, I'm sorry." His hands were at her shoulders, then her back, rubbing, soothing, desperate to help. He tried to guide her to the bench in the corner but she gathered what little energy she had left and shoved at his arms.

"You've no right to judge me," she whispered. "If you'd managed to forgive yourself you wouldn't even be here."

His hands stilled, and he stepped away. "You're right," he said tonelessly. He hesitated, then retraced his steps to the greenhouse door.

She waited for the crunch of gravel signaling his retreat before sagging against the nearest bench. What in God's name was she going to do? She could keep her business, or she could keep her grudge. Sell, or sell out.

The decision was hers alone.

* * *

THE ALARM ON HIS watch. His turn at sentry duty. Already?

Move it, soldier. No riding the bed. He pushed himself up and around so his feet hit the carpet.

Carpet. Not sand-covered plywood. Reid scrubbed a hand over his face. The ringing continued. Not his watch. His cell. He grabbed it.

"MacFarland," he mumbled.

"We need to talk."

He snapped awake. Turned on the light. Parker sounded upset.

And why the hell wouldn't she be? He glanced around the room. At least it wouldn't take long to pack.

"I'm listening," he said.

"I can't leave Nat. Can you come here?"

"You want me to drive over." He squinted at the clock on the nightstand. "At one-fifteen in the morning."

"I'd like to get this settled."

Huh. "Ten minutes." He stood and reached for his jeans.

His headlights spotlighted her as he pulled into the driveway. She'd been waiting in the dark. She leaned against a post at the top of the porch steps, wearing jeans and a gray sweatshirt that hung to her knees. Her arms were wrapped around her middle, and even from a distance he could see her shivering.

He climbed the first two steps, then noticed her feet were bare. No wonder she was vibrating. He wanted to wrap his arms around her, pull her into his body heat and keep her there until she stopped shaking. But that was the last thing *she'd* want. So he kept his distance, and gestured at the door.

"How about we go inside?"

He gritted his teeth when she shook her head. She'd rather freeze than let him inside her house?

"Nat," she said, and he understood. But the kid's window was right overhead.

"You don't think she'll hear you chew me out here on the porch?" When she didn't answer he swallowed an impatient grunt. "How about we sit in the Jeep? I'll turn on the heat." She looked at the Jeep, and back at him, and this time he let loose a growl. "At least go put something on your feet. I can't just stand by and watch your toes drop off."

She went in. When she came back out several minutes later she wore a thick pair of socks and carried two mugs of steaming coffee. Which made him feel guilty all over again.

"Thank you," he muttered, and sank down onto the top step. Surprisingly, she did the same. He breathed in her sweet, summery scent — honeysuckle? — felt his pulse rev, and decided he'd better hold his breath.

They sat without speaking, sipping coffee. Night sounds surrounded them — the drone of insects, the muffled squawk of a roosting bird, the sigh of a breeze. Gradually Parker's trembling eased.

"Your parents," she said suddenly. "They're not...living?"

He clenched his teeth against a sigh. Why did women always have to know this shit? But this wasn't just any woman. He blew on his coffee, taking his time.

"My dad died when I was four. Lung cancer. I was a junior in high school when my mom died. Heart attack."

"What did you do?"

"Moved in with my uncle."

"Is he in San Diego?"

"Six feet under."

She shifted and stared down into her mug. "That's a lot of death."

A brutal silence, while they both considered the one particular death they had in common. She swallowed. "Is that why you joined the Army? Because you had no family left?"

"I joined because my dad was a soldier. Infantry. Sort of a tribute."

"A way to get to know him."

"That's right." He heard the surprise in his own voice and grunted. "Mom wouldn't have approved."

She sipped at her coffee, made a small sound as though she found it too hot. "I've made plenty of mistakes," she said slowly. "Hurt people. Made poor decisions. But I loved my husband. And he loved me. I couldn't sleep, letting you think it might have been otherwise." She turned her head. It was too dark to see her features, but his gaze followed the pale outline of her profile. "I'm not punishing myself, but even if I were it wouldn't be over my marriage. That has nothing to do with how I feel about you. About this…situation."

"Before you say anything else—" *before you tell me to leave you the hell alone* "—let me apologize. I shouldn't have said what I did. I'm sorry."

A soft sigh in the darkness. "I overreacted."

"You're overstressed and overworked."

"You're the reason I'm stressed. And I work as hard as I have to."

"I can help lower the bar."

She wrapped both hands around her mug. "No more psychoanalyzing?"

"No, ma'am."

She set aside her coffee and propped her elbows on her knees. "Nat cried herself to sleep tonight. Because I told her I hadn't made a decision about softball practice. And she said I'm mean to you." She didn't give him a chance to respond. "We both know I need you to stay."

Reid blinked. A few weeks away from his unit and he must be getting soft. Just one ambush after another.

"As a matter of fact, you're holding up your end of the bargain with a lot more grace than I'm holding up mine. But I can't help it," she said, her voice husky. "Or maybe I can, and I'm simply choosing not to." She turned a bit, and leaned her back against the railing. "I think part of what's bothering me about this...arrangement...is that I can't help feeling I'm letting Tim down. That I'm somehow dishonoring his memory. Though Tim was a forgiving man. Which makes everything I just said an excuse."

He couldn't help admiring her frankness even as she was twisting a steak knife in his gut. "You don't need an excuse. I'm invading your territory."

"Yes. You are."

That steel in her voice again. Honeysuckle and steel. A hell of a combination. And he wanted it, he realized. Wanted her compassion and sincerity and candor. Wanted her to feel about him even a fraction of the way she'd felt about her husband.

A hot, heavy ache slammed into his chest. It took his breath, and he clenched his jaw so hard he wouldn't be able to chew without hurting for a week.

Corporal Reid MacFarland, you are one sorry asshole.

"All that said, I have one condition. I want to know how it happened."

And there it was. The reason she'd summoned him. He jerked to his feet, and hot coffee splashed his jeans.

Son of a bitch.

He'd known she'd ask. Of course she'd ask. His counselor had said that getting it out in the open would help them both. Still he figured he'd enjoy this conversation about as much he'd enjoy finding a camel spider in his rack.

He tossed the rest of his coffee in the grass, set the mug down on the nearest step and faced her, square on, just as he'd faced the panel at his hearing.

"My platoon was called in to help defend an outpost in the Erbil province. Another unit was holed up there, with major casualties. We'd barely arrived when dozens of insurgents attacked. We were under intense mortar fire and we countered, but the assault was hot and heavy. On the north side of the outpost a squad took orders to flank the attack with an M270. A rocket launcher. One of those men was your husband."

She hadn't moved. Sat so still, in fact, that she seemed to have become part of the post. His fingers had worked their way into a rigid clench. He forced them to unfurl and they started to tingle.

"I was watching streaming video of the attack," he continued. "Infrared images relayed from a Predator overhead. Somehow Sergeant First Class Dean got separated from his unit. On my monitor I spotted a mass of hotspots corresponding with the enemy's location and...called in the drone. Less than ninety seconds later the missile found its target." His throat felt gritty, as it did after a desert recon. "I found out later one of those hotspots was one of our own."

A moment of horror he'd relive forever.

Parker lurched to her feet, and he braced himself. After a few moments, she bent down and gathered up both mugs. "Good night," she said. She crossed the porch and disappeared inside.

*   *   *

REID CAUGHT ONLY GLIMPSES of Parker during working hours the following day. He saw her first thing in the morning, as she left the potting shed after laying out a fresh supply of homemade granola bars. Then three hours later, as he maneuvered the tractor around the huts, he caught sight of her bending over her seedlings. And finally at noon, as he headed toward the picnic table and fifty yards away she waylaid Harris and handed him their coolers.

No surprise she was avoiding him. He'd avoid himself if he could. The surprise was that she'd made him lunch. Business as usual. When there probably wasn't too much more he could do to add to her misery.

That first day on the job, despite all the talk about chicken salad and homemade cake, he figured with Parker Dean making him lunch he was lucky to get bread and water. Moldy bread, and water straight from a rusty tap. Yet he'd never enjoyed his noontime meals more. Today she'd packed them roast beef roll-ups, homemade coleslaw with pineapple, deviled eggs, a banana, and miniature pecan tarts — her own version of an MRE. Only edible. More than edible. He'd taken to eating a light breakfast — fruit and store-bought protein shakes — just so he wouldn't end up with Chance — or Harris — begging him for what he hadn't managed to finish.

For dinner he usually hit the soup and salad bar at the local grocery. Which was where he finally caught up with Parker. He came up behind her in the produce section and angled his cart to block her exit. She selected a bag of carrots and nearly dropped them on the floor when she saw him. She looked down at the bag, hefted it a few times, and he had a feeling she'd like nothing better than to heave it at him.

"Corporal." She glanced around, as if checking for witnesses.

"Mrs. Dean." He nodded at the bag she clutched. "You gonna throw it or what?"

She considered. "Maybe next time." She added the carrots to the other vegetables in her cart and made a show of consulting her list.

"Harris talk you into making another cake?"

"They're for stew."

A woman wearing fuzzy blue bedroom slippers coughed loudly as she steered her cart around them. Parker must have realized Reid wasn't going to move because she gripped the cart's handle with both hands and leaned forward, as if ready to ram him.

"Don't let me keep you from your shopping," she said.

"You okay?"

"Excuse me?"

"You didn't get much sleep last night."

"I — I'm fine. Thank you."

"Good." She wasn't fine. But maybe if he pulled his head out of his ass and said his piece she'd get home at a decent hour and could turn in early. "I wanted to let you know that Gallahan and Noble Johnson are coming over tomorrow to help replace the plastic on Hut One.

Also, I talked to Harris and from now on we're not making any decisions without consulting you. Anything comes up, we'll follow the chain of command." He held out a hand. "Truce?"

After a brief hesitation she clasped his hand, her own warm, strong and firm. While the rest of his body craved that same warm and purposeful contact, he remembered the first time he'd offered his hand to her. And how she hadn't known she should have refused it.

She remembered it, too. He could see it in her eyes. Then she blinked the memory away and let go.

"By the way," she said, a small catch in her voice, "the spring festival is this weekend." When he gave her a blank look she raised her eyebrows. "Thistle Hill's annual Welcome Spring Festival? You haven't noticed the banners hanging over the streets downtown?"

"Oh. Right. Those."

"I could use you Saturday, if you're free. It's a long day, and a bit chaotic, but since home owners are anxious to start working on their flower gardens, we'll be able to move a lot of merchandise."

He stared. Had she just asked for his help?

"It means setting up a canopy and tables, and waiting on customers. A lot of standing, and...dealing with the public." She bit her lip, and some distant part of him realized she was warning him there'd be questions. Or maybe warning herself. "I'll provide all your meals."

Was she going to give him ice-cream money, too? *Suck it up, soldier.* Wasn't the lady's fault he was falling for her.

Or that he could never have her.

She tipped her head. "Think you might be willing to give us a hand?"

"Whatever you need," he said gruffly.

"Thank you." She swallowed, and from her expression the taste was bitter. "I'd better get back. Harris agreed to stay with Nat, but only if I brought back a half-gallon of his favorite ice cream." She offered an awkward wave, then took off so fast her cart nearly popped a wheelie.

*   *   *

EVERY SPRING, THISTLE HILL'S business owners gathered together to transform the elementary school's football field into a fairground. Only once in fifty-two years had the festival been canceled — and it wasn't because of bad weather. According to Harris, the county's unofficial mayor had been implicated in a scheme to rig the Miss Lilac election. It seemed His not-very-honorable Honor had promised eighteen-year-old Bonnie Ehrlicher the coveted purple crown, the position of spokesperson for U Drive It U Buy It Used Cars, and a publicity tour that stopped at every lakefront bed-and-breakfast within a hundred miles.

All the other contestants announced they would boycott the festival. As did their families, their friends and the owners of U Drive It U Buy It, who preferred to hire someone who didn't mind being paid in oil changes.

Then the unofficial mayor's wife paid a dairy farmer to transport his cows to the school and allow them to graze on the football field. She also paid him not to clean up afterward. Which is when the county decided to cancel that year's festival. And forever changed the name from Spring Fling.

Parker never tired of hearing that story.

This year she and Nat would participate in the Welcome Spring Festival for the first time, since neither had been feeling festive enough to attend last year. Parker resolved to make the most of it, for Nat's sake especially.

She was up at five that Saturday morning, packing the cakes and pies she'd baked Friday, and pulling the last of the muffins from the oven. The night before MacFarland had loaded the canopy and tables and other supplies they'd need into the truck. Once Parker finished up in the kitchen, she'd do the same with the plants, and finally the baked goods. Hopefully Harris would show up in time to help. He'd agreed to stay behind with Nat and bring her to the festival later.

No sense in dragging the poor kid out of bed this early.

She heard a noise at the back door. Had Chance been out all night? She glanced at the clock. Or maybe Harris had arrived. Before she could cross the kitchen, MacFarland stepped inside. Parker's heart gave a funny little flutter and she pressed a hand to her chest.

Things had been awkward between them since their late-night meeting on her front porch. Although, when had things not been awkward between them? But no way she could miss that MacFarland had been working harder than ever. Hut One looked fetching in its new coat of plastic and Hut Two was next on the list. The grass had been mowed, the staff parking lot had been weeded and raked, and her Camry had received a long-overdue oil change. Which meant she wasn't all that surprised to see him, though she did wonder how he operated on so little sleep.

"It's five-thirty in the morning," she said. "And come on in, by the way."

"Thank you. And I'm sorry." But he looked far from contrite. "Thought you could use some help. And I smelled muffins."

"From all the way over at the motel?" She batted the hair out her eyes with the back of her wrist. "I thought you were going to meet us at the school."

"Couldn't sleep." He pointed his thumb over his shoulder at the coffeepot behind him. "May I?"

"Of course." She fetched a mug for him, then returned to the kitchen table to finish wrapping individual muffins. She glanced up and saw him watching her, and couldn't help a laugh. "You look like Chance, hoping I'll drop something." She held out a muffin.

He accepted it with a hum of appreciation. "I pay no attention to insults before I've had my breakfast."

"And after?" When she found herself staring as his long, tanned fingers peeled away the liner, she averted her gaze.

"Depends on who's doing the insulting."

Parker continued to wrap while MacFarland ate and sipped at his coffee. But her fingers had turned fat and clumsy, and she ended up wasting several lengths of plastic wrap. The presence of a man in the kitchen — even this man — had made the quiet dark suddenly intimate. She scrambled for something to say, but her throat had closed and she was finding it difficult to breathe.

He finished his muffin, washed his hands and turned from the sink, one eyebrow lifted. "How can I help?"

She couldn't answer for a moment, taken aback by the pleasure his question sparked. Seemed her usual resentment toward him had decided to sleep in that morning.

"You could start loading that first bench of plants in Hut One. Harris should be here soon to help."

"Anything else need to go in the truck first?" She shook her head. "Keys in the ignition?" She nodded. "Okay if I take this with me?" He lifted his mug. Another nod. He poured more coffee and left.

Parker stared after him. MacFarland's presence had given the kitchen warmth, and a sense of companionship. His offer to help had made her feel as if she didn't have to go it alone, after all. But of course she did. He wasn't staying. Even if he wanted to, she couldn't allow it. And in the end, that's how she preferred it.

Half an hour later he came back into the kitchen, an odd look on his face. He'd brought the sunrise with him — the kitchen window she'd had her back to was filled with the reddish-orange glow of a new day — and when he opened the door she heard the robins singing. He set his mug in the sink then faced her, hands on his hips. "We did this wrong," he said.

She caught her breath. "I'm sorry?"

"We're setting up the canopy first, right? Then the tables? Then unloading all the plants and — " he waved at the boxes on the table " — goodies?"

She blinked, and her shoulders slumped. "Darn."

He nodded solemnly. "Double darn. I should have loaded the tent and the tables last."

"It's not your fault. You were only doing what I asked."

"This is your first spring fling. Next year you'll know."

She wasn't sure why she flinched. "It's a festival," she said carefully. "Not a fling."

A beat of silence while he held her gaze. "Roger that." But though his tone was grave, one side of his mouth had tipped up. He motioned with his chin at her overalls. "You're not going to wear something more...festive?"

She should feel insulted. So why did she have to fight to keep her mouth from curving? "Don't think of them as overalls. Think of them as a wise business decision. It's all about image. People see you looking like a farmer, they assume you grow things. They see overalls, they get that I have a green thumb."

"Or they're waiting to hear banjos in the background."

She dusted crumbs off her hands. "I show up in a dress and heels and they figure my staff does the dirty work. That gives me less credibility."

"Forget credibility. You show up in a dress and heels and I'll give you fifty bucks."

She froze. Instantly his expression sobered. "That was inappropriate. I apologize." He pointed at the boxes on the table. "These ready to go?"

For the second time that morning, she stared at the door after he'd gone. And hated herself for conducting a frantic mental inventory of her wardrobe.

*   *   *

AN HOUR LATER, THEY'D unloaded the truck. Flats and pots and hanging baskets spilling over with flowers littered far more than Parker's share of the football field. Luckily they had helpers, lured by the promise of a muffin or a bag of cookies as payment. The tables went up and the plants were put on display, but when MacFarland pulled out the canopy, their help disappeared.

All but Liz Early, the bubbly twenty-something who waited tables at Snoozy's. She hovered in the background with her fabulous shoulders and long, crinkly jet hair, pretending an interest in Parker's baked goods when all the time she was scoping out MacFarland. Either that or she was fascinated with the canopy he was unrolling.

MacFarland stood over the bundle of canvas and the stack of poles and raised an eyebrow at Parker. "You have an expectant look on your face. You do realize this in no way resembles the tents the Army erects?"

That was when Liz strutted into view, her smile sassy, her dark eyes wide. "Oh, please." She checked him out, top to bottom. "You expect us to believe you can't manage an erection?"

Parker sucked in a breath. Definitely not the canopy Liz was interested in. Too bad the woman was as friendly as she was feisty. It made it so much harder to hate her.

MacFarland's mouth seemed to be having a seizure. Liz thrust out a hand. "You're Corporal Reid MacFarland. I'm Liz Early."

"I've seen you at the bar. We could use a hand, if you'd like to help us out."

She leaned in, and spoke in a loud whisper. "You already have one."

"So I do." He grinned, and let go. "I guess you already know Parker Dean."

The women exchanged greetings and MacFarland made assignments. Liz hefted the mallet and sidled next to Parker.

"Mmm, mmm, mmm." She sounded like Nat, the moment before diving into a stack of chocolate-chip pancakes. "Looks like I should have taken you up on that job offer."

Parker managed a smile. "He's only here a few weeks."

"And what a few weeks it could be."

Someone hollered Liz's name. She lifted a hand to shade her eyes, and waved. "Be right there," she yelled back. She surrendered the mallet to MacFarland, her mouth turned down in a pout. "Duty calls. I volunteered to help with the face-painting booth." He tugged at the mallet and she held on. "Why don't you stop by? I'll think of something creative to paint on your —" her gaze dipped " —cheek."

"Interesting offer," he said. "But I'll be busy all day with Parker."

She let go of the mallet. "Lucky Parker," she said with a wink, and Parker's face went hot.

After Liz left, MacFarland turned to Parker and raised an eyebrow. "Ready to get busy?" Her cheeks flared hotter. Grinning, he handed her the mallet.

It was the heat. *Had* to be the heat that was making her feel light-headed and completely off-kilter. Never mind that the temperature couldn't be above seventy.

Four times she found herself far too close to him, as she steadied each of the canopy's corner poles while he fastened eight lengths of nylon rope and drove eight stakes into the ground. Which meant she had to remind herself four times to breathe through her mouth so she wouldn't inhale the scent that had teased her in the truck—his soap smelled clean, subtle and spicy.

She'd be a lot more comfortable if he smelled like compost.

Once they finished setting up and MacFarland moved the truck to the parking lot, it seemed the entire Thistle Hill community appeared. Finally Parker noticed what she'd been too busy to take in—both sides of the field were now lined with tables and booths and canopies similar to theirs, a DJ had set up his equipment on a wooden platform in the center of the field and was playing soft rock, and someone was frying chicken. Considering breakfast had consisted of a cup of coffee and a spoonful of muffin batter, it was no wonder her stomach sat up and took notice.

"Smells great, doesn't it?" MacFarland handed over the truck keys and Parker got another whiff of him. *It certainly does.* She was instantly disgusted with herself and shifted to the side while MacFarland checked his cell. "Ten o'clock. Guess it's too early to hope we could get a drumstick or two." He caught her look. "What?"

She shook her head and turned away. Something had changed. She'd actually been pleased to see him that morning. And the thought of his being around for another three weeks didn't fill her with the usual crippling dread.

She didn't know what to think. She wasn't ready to forgive him.

She wasn't even ready to like him. And she didn't want him to think he was off the hook.

She sighed, and gave MacFarland a sidelong glance. He was crouched under one of the tables, trying to fix a wobble. His shirt stretched over hard-earned muscles and she looked quickly away. The man was working his butt off for her. For himself, actually, since he was trying to pay down what he saw as an obligation, but still. Her business was benefiting. And it took a lot of energy to hold a grudge. And wouldn't it be better for Nat — and prevent a heck of a lot of questions from their neighbors — if she and the corporal pretended to get along?

So when he stood, said her name and looked concerned, she adopted a pleasant expression. Made a noncommittal comment and turned to answer a question about a hanging basket.

*   *   *

EYES NARROWED, REID STUDIED Parker. Something had changed between them. Since that morning she'd actually been halfway relaxed. He cocked his head, watching as she accepted a customer's money, and wondered if he'd ever be on the receiving end of that smile. Maybe she'd find it in herself to forgive him, after all. As long as he didn't do anything stupid. Like give in to the urge to taste her.

"Sorry we're late." Harris greeted Reid with a handshake and looked back over his shoulder at Nat, who trudged a good twenty steps behind. When she finally looked up, Reid winced. Her expression was one big scowl. He raised an eyebrow at Harris.

"She wanted to bring Chance."

Ah.

Nat schlepped around behind the canopy and dropped to the grass, facing away from the field. She plucked a paperback from her back pocket and bent over it, head practically between her knees. Reid scratched his chin. "Think I'll give her a minute or two. To settle in."

Harris winked. "Good idea."

Parker finished with her customer and went behind the canopy to greet Natalie. Harris stiffened, and Reid wondered whether the old man thought they might have to break up a mother-daughter brawl. Then Eugenia Blue walked up to the booth. When she said her good-mornings, she avoided looking directly at Harris. And vice versa.

Reid was just about to make an asinine comment about the weather when Parker came up to join them. "Don't go back there unless you've had a Valium," she warned. Harris snickered and Eugenia made a sympathetic noise. Reid resisted the sudden need to put his arm around Parker and pull her close.

From the stage came the opening notes of Whitney Houston's "I Will Always Love You" and Harris slapped a hand on the counter. "Gotta go, folks. Promised to help out with the hot dog stand but I'll be back to check in. Get a chance, wander on over and get yourself a chili dog. Joe makes the best in town."

Reid blinked. "Gallahan? Isn't he vegetarian?"

Harris grinned, but it looked forced. "He won't eat 'em, but he sure can grill 'em."

Eugenia watched him as he headed downfield, toward the concessions. "I heard Harris is in charge of the lemonade."

Parker made a strangled noise and Reid swung around. But she wasn't choking, she was laughing. He exchanged a mystified glance with Eugenia, and Parker laughed harder. She stood with one hand on her belly, the other over her mouth, hazel eyes crinkled as she struggled for breath, and something loosened in Reid's chest.

Eugenia huddled over the counter, as if expecting Parker to reveal a juicy piece of gossip. "The lemonade. Is it that bad?"

Parker dropped her hands and pulled in a breath. "Only when you taste it."

Frowning, Eugenia straightened. "What does he do to it?"

"No idea. He refuses to reveal the recipe. Which is probably just as well. But it's a recipe he swears by."

Reid gave a quiet snort. "Sounds like it's a recipe he should swear *off*."

Parker giggled and pressed her palm to his arm, leaning in, as if in agreement. But almost as soon as she made contact, she yanked her hand away, and the amusement on her face twisted into dismay.

He blinked and looked down at his arm. The hell of it was, it had happened so fast he hadn't even had time to enjoy it. How pathetic was he, that one fleeting touch made his freaking week?

And why the hell did she have to act as if he were contagious?

8

PARKER MUTTERED WHAT SOUNDED like an apology and turned away, busied herself rearranging pots. Belatedly Reid remembered Eugenia, who stood as if in formation, watching them with a speculative gleam in her eye. She met his gaze and smiled brightly. "I'll be back later," she chirped. She patted Parker's wrist. "You, I have a surprise for. Don't disappear on me."

She left. Reid watched the back of Parker's head for a while, then pretended interest in a group of kids on the DJ's stage doing some kind of line dance to a Taylor Swift song. He should probably say something, but what?

When the music stopped Reid recognized a distant, tinny sound. Nat was playing a game on her mother's cell. He could have kicked himself. For the past several minutes he hadn't spared one thought for the kid.

Maybe by now she'd gotten over her grumps.

He wandered to her side and stood over her, marveling at the nonstop motion of her thumbs. A texting champ in the making. When she relaxed her fingers and the music indicated she'd moved up a level, he crouched down beside her. "You're pretty good."

"Whatever."

He grinned. Yeah, she was a grump, but she was a cute grump.

"What's the deal?" he asked. "It's a beautiful day, you've had a nice break from school and you have an entire festival to explore. What more could you want?"

"Chance."

"You're smart enough to know why bringing him here isn't a good idea. Why don't you look around, find something to take to him when we're done?"

She dropped her hands, still holding the phone, looked straight ahead and heaved a loud sigh. "Like what?"

Good question. "How about a hamburger? Or a ball or something." He snapped his fingers. "I heard someone say something about an insurance guy down at the other end handing out Frisbees."

She looked at him then, and the spark of interest in her eyes belied her careless shrug. He got that she wanted to save face — there was no way to come out of a pout gracefully — but he wondered if something else was going on. He stood and grabbed a couple of bottles of water from the cooler.

"I'll walk down with you. Hold on while I tell your mom we're going."

Two minutes later they'd joined the throngs of people trekking along the sidelines, eyeing the tables and booths. Nat trudged beside him, her head bent and her hair shielding her face, the bottle of water cradled against her belly. Reid opened his and took a swig. "Want to tell me what's bothering you?"

She shook her head.

"I'll buy you that Frisbee."

She stopped short and an elderly couple behind them nearly tripped. Reid apologized while Nat glowered. "You said he was giving them away."

"He charges extra if you're not wearing a smile."

She stared, and her chin started to quiver. Reid cursed himself. "Hey. I was teasing." Tears pooled in her eyes. *Nice work, asshole.*

She gave him her green-and-yellow-tinged poor-pitiful-me look. "I missed softball practice," she said.

And there it was. "Yeah. You did."

"Joe's going to think I don't really want to play."

The way she said his name… She had a crush. *I know how you feel, kid.* Reid kept his expression carefully neutral. "He knows your mom needed time to make a decision about that."

"You could have talked to her. You could have made her understand."

Reid took her water bottle from her, unscrewed the cap and handed it back. "I did. She did. You'll be at practice on Tuesday." He started walking again. Nat hurried to catch up.

"But I wanted to go Thursday."

This time he was the one to stop, and almost got clipped by a motorized wheelchair. "I think you're playing me, kid. You expect me to say something along the lines of 'You should be more grateful' or 'Being a team player is more than about playing sports.' But like I said before, you're smart, so you already know how hard your mom works to keep you safe and happy. So I'll say this instead — sometimes you have to wait for what you want. And sometimes the waiting sucks. We have a saying in the Army. 'Embrace the suck.'"

"What's that supposed to mean?"

He shrugged. "It sucks, you can't change it, may as well accept it with grace and soldier on." He tapped her bottle with his and took a drink, relaxing when she did the same. He almost choked in his rush to swallow. "Look." He pointed to a kid smacking another kid on the butt with a bright orange Frisbee. He raised his eyebrows and gave Nat a *what do we have here?* look. "Think we can get one in pink?"

* * *

PARKER'S BOOTH WAS AS popular as she'd hoped it would be. But it wasn't her geraniums or her cheerful ceramic planters or even the generous slices of chocolate amaretto cake drawing the crowds.

It was Corporal Reid MacFarland.

The women ogled him, the men shook his hand, the teens and twenty-somethings — male and female alike — grilled him about the Army, and the grandmotherly types watched him, and then they watched Parker, and then they watched him and Parker together. Parker felt like an exhibit at a museum. By noon she was ready to pack up and go home. She could tell MacFarland was, too. And no wonder,

111

considering they'd both been awake before dawn.

Behind Parker, Nat giggled. Parker gave the customer her change — the woman had bought the last of the muffins, thank goodness — and turned. At the back of the canopy MacFarland was rearranging plants and throwing dead leaves at Nat while Nat tried to balance her freebie Frisbee on her elbow. Parker rolled her eyes.

"You two have had too way much sugar. Forget the baked goods. How about some lunch?"

Nat raised a palm and MacFarland gave her a high five. Parker bit her lip and reached for the cooler. MacFarland left Nat to help Parker drag it out from under the table.

"I want to thank you," she said quietly. "For whatever you did to coax Nat out of her mood."

"She really loves that dog."

"We found him on the side of the road just after we moved here. He's not supposed to spend the night in her room but I don't fuss too much since she...doesn't sleep well." She finished the sentence reluctantly. They both knew why Nat had trouble sleeping.

"The proverbial minefield," MacFarland muttered.

A woman wearing English riding gear and a preoccupied expression walked past the booth. It took Parker a few seconds to register who she was, since instead of swinging loose the woman's white-blond hair had been gathered into an elegant French braid. Parker ignored a prickling of shame — if she hadn't so desperately needed the distraction she'd have allowed the poor woman to go on about her business — leaned over the counter, and called out.

"Ivy. Ivy Millbrook."

The woman looked over her shoulder, and her pale face lit with a smile. "Parker." Her eyes scanned the stall and its contents as she retraced her steps. "Nice job with the booth. I'm sorry I didn't see you there. Guess I was too busy thinking about putting Cabana Boy through his paces."

"You're giving a riding demonstration today?"

Ivy passed her helmet from one hand to the other and nodded. "We set up a small course next to the playground." Her curious gaze rested on MacFarland and she offered him a dry smile. "Cabana Boy's a stallion, by the way."

MacFarland grinned. "Is he? How nice for you."

Ivy laughed and Parker hurried to make introductions. "Ivy Millbrook, this is Corporal Reid MacFarland. He's, uh, a friend. Helping us out while on leave from the Army." She licked suddenly dry lips and avoided MacFarland's gaze. "Ivy owns the dairy farm down the road. Last Monday she took the third-graders on a tour. Nat's still talking about it."

MacFarland shook Ivy's hand, wished her luck with her riding demonstration, and excused himself with a wink. Ivy watched him go, and Parker suddenly realized she was still holding her sandwich. She set it aside and cleared her throat.

"Speaking of the tour…" She reached under the counter and hefted the box she'd stuffed with muffins, gourmet coffee beans and a striped ceramic pot holding hot-pink pansies. "I put this together as a thank-you."

Ivy's smile faltered. "You didn't have to do that."

"I wanted to show how much I appreciate that you included Nat with the tour." Ivy didn't respond, and Parker bit her lip. Had she said the wrong thing?

When Ivy looked up after studying the contents of the box, her smile was back in place. "Mind if I leave this here and come back to fetch it later?" Parker shook her head and Ivy started to back away. "Great. So. Have you given any more thought to joining our investment club?"

"I've thought about it," Parker said slowly. "Though things are kind of tight right now."

"Believe me, I understand. Just to let you know, we meet once a month. We learn a little, mix a little — it's a great chance for you to get to know some of the women in the community. Even if you decide not to join, we'd love to have you sit in on a meeting."

"Thanks, Ivy. I'll let you know."

The other woman's nod was sharp. She turned and continued on her way to the playground, holding her body a little more stiffly than when she'd first come over.

"I'm ba-ack." Eugenia plopped her handbag on the counter. "Was that Ivy?"

"I don't know how I managed it, but I think I hurt her feelings."

"Did she ask you about the club again?" When Parker turned to look at her, she shrugged. "I'm a member."

"Why the push for me to join?"

"No push. We'd just like to include you."

"Why?"

"Parker. You're a single mother with a struggling business. You're trying to increase commerce in Thistle Hill and even the notorious grump Harris Briggs speaks highly of you. People want to show their support. I get that you value your independence but you also have a responsibility to your community."

Parker narrowed her eyes and flung out a hand to indicate her booth. "Doesn't this qualify as participation?"

"It's a start. But how many other stalls have you visited today? Which is why I'm here." She looked over Parker's shoulder. "You don't mind if I steal her away for an hour, do you, Corporal?"

"Call me Reid. And no, ma'am, I don't."

Parker flushed. How long had he been standing there? She made a halfhearted gesture toward the turkey sandwich she'd left on the counter and Eugenia shook her head.

"You can eat that later. Just make sure your people don't sell it."

"But I can't leave."

MacFarland frowned. "Why not?"

Nat came looking for her sandwich. "What's going on?"

"Cooper's Hardware is sponsoring makeovers and I signed your mother up. Hair, makeup, the works."

Oh, Lord. Parker enjoyed feeling girly now and then as much as the next woman. But her current lifestyle left no time for primping. And who would she primp for, anyway? The dog?

114

She shook her head, and at the same time fought to shake off the urge to sulk. Must be catching. "I think I'll pass."

"Cooper's?" Nat looked intrigued. "Would they use real paint?"

"Thanks a lot, kiddo." Parker reached out and gave Nat's hair a gentle tug. "How much help do you think my face needs?"

"None."

Three pairs of eyes swung to MacFarland. He froze, then drew his brows together. "It's an important lesson," he said solemnly, and turned to Nat. "Don't you think your mom is pretty, just as she is?"

Nat nodded.

Parker wrenched her fascinated gaze from the color in MacFarland's cheeks. She knew an out when she heard one. "He's right, Eugenia. It's an important teaching…thing."

"I'll do it. I'll go with you."

Eugenia laughed at Nat's eager offer. "You just want to watch them use the spackle and putty knife on me. Thank you, Natalie, but I'm determined to talk your mother into it. She might not need much makeup but her hair's a disaster. You're welcome to come and watch, though."

Nat shrugged and turned away, toward the cooler. Eugenia crooked her finger at Parker. "C'mon, neighbor. Follow me."

"You do need a break." MacFarland handed her sandwich to Nat. "So go."

Parker scowled, tempted to snap a salute. "I thought you were on my side."

"Always," he said, his voice suddenly grave. Parker stared into his eyes, and her chest tightened. Maybe it was a good idea to take a break, after all.

Halfway to the Cooper's Hardware booth she was still thinking about MacFarland's sideways compliment. She glanced at Eugenia, elegant in her fawn-colored casual pants and blouse, then glanced down at her own overalls, which she'd defended so righteously to MacFarland. It wasn't that she didn't have any pride. She just didn't have any time. And no one she wanted to impress.

Truly.

She slowed, and stopped. But Eugenia cut her off at the pass. "Once they're done with you, the good corporal won't be able to tear his eyes away."

Not that again. "That is not going to happen. Even if he didn't live in Kentucky. Even if he weren't about to spend the next year and a half in a war zone. Even if he won the lottery and offered me three million dollars, it wouldn't happen. I am not interested in Corporal MacFarland. Okay?"

"Really? Even if he won the lottery?"

"Eugenia…"

"All right, fine. I get the message. He said something similar so I guess it's not meant to be."

"What did he say?"

"Oh. Do I detect some interest after all?"

Parker made a sound of frustration. "Talking to you is like talking to Harris." Eugenia's smile faded and Parker bit her lip. "I'm sorry. I didn't think."

Eugenia tucked Parker's arm through hers. "Now you owe me. I'm thinking…bikini wax."

*　　*　　*

AN HOUR LATER, PARKER returned to her booth, her hair clip in her pocket, her newly trimmed hair bouncing on her shoulders. The stylist hadn't done much more than shaping and adding a few bangs, but after a session with the eyebrow tweezers, and a little mascara and lip gloss, even Parker had to admit the result was worth the trouble. She felt pampered. Feminine.

And exceedingly grateful that Eugenia had been kidding about the wax.

As much as she hated to admit it, she also couldn't wait to find out what MacFarland thought about her makeover. Which meant it was just as well she'd never be able to re-create the look.

Nat stood behind the counter, stacking quarters, while MacFarland wiped down one of the now-empty display tables. When Nat spotted Parker her eyes went wide and the tower of quarters toppled. "Mom, you look awesome." She rushed around the counter and peered up at Parker's face. "Are you wearing *lipstick?*"

"I certainly am."

"Can I have some, too?"

But Parker's attention had shifted to the back of the booth where MacFarland stood, a rag in his hand and an arrested expression on his face. He tossed aside the rag and started toward them.

"Mom?"

"Yes?"

"Lipstick?"

She forced herself to focus on her daughter. Guilt swelled, and she tucked Nat's hair behind her ear. "You're nine. You know what I'm going to say."

"When you're ooooold-er." Nat's voice was so high-pitched and prissy that Parker couldn't help laughing. MacFarland reached them, and the laugh caught in her throat.

She wanted to kick herself. What the heck was she doing, caring what this man — this *soldier* — thought about her?

Okay, wait. The real question was, when had she stopped thinking about him as *that man* and started thinking of him as a man, period?

He studied her carefully, soberly, and she had to fight to resist jamming her hair back into her clip. She felt her face tighten into a scowl. He raised a hand, as if to touch her, then let it fall back to his side.

"You have beautiful hair."

She exhaled. For heaven's sake, had she actually hoped he'd touch her? "You're just jealous," she managed. "Because you have so little of your own."

"At least I have more than Harris."

"I heard that." Harris strolled toward them, an ice-cream cone in each hand. "No ice cream for the corporal." He turned to Parker. "I'd

117

give you my spare but I have no idea who you are. Which leaves —"

"Me!" Nat bounced up to claim her treat. "Thank you."

"You're welcome."

Nat twirled the cone, licking the drips before they reached her hand. "Eugenia bought Mom a makeover."

"I can see that." His narrowed gaze traveled from Parker to MacFarland. "Either of you good people need a break?" When they both declined, he nodded and ate half his ice cream with one satisfied slurp. "Guess I'll just mosey on back to my lemonade."

He left. Without asking about Eugenia.

Nat reclaimed her mom's cell phone and settled with her ice cream and her game in the grass. Parker turned to find MacFarland wearing a half grin. "You really wanted that cone, didn't you?" Without waiting for an answer, he patted his pocket, as if checking for his wallet. "Be right back." And he was, with a cone identical to the one Harris had given Nat.

Parker murmured her thanks. "You didn't want one?"

He shook his head, and at that moment several people walked up to the booth. "Go enjoy your ice cream. I've got this."

She settled in a chair at the back of the booth, feeling decadent. And charmed. Heavens, it was only an ice-cream cone. But when was the last time someone had gone out of his way to indulge her when she had a craving, let alone recognize that she had one in the first place?

Her thoughts veered toward the erotic, and she shifted in her chair. MacFarland's jeans stretched tight over his butt as he bent over to pick up an empty box. She licked her cone and swallowed a whimper.

MacFarland took care of a spate of customers, then started breaking down empty tables. Parker finished her cone and stood to help. Two boys Nat's age wandered by, heads bent over one of those expensive new handheld game devices. The taller one, whose shaggy, crow-black hair gleamed in the sun, heard the strains of Nat's game and raised his head. He elbowed his friend, a skinny blond wearing camouflage pants and a red knit skullcap. The blond raised his eyebrows. He moved closer, his eyes on Parker's smart phone.

"That's like, ancient," he said.

Nat glanced up, shrugged, and went back to her game.

"Whoa," he said. "What happened to your eye?"

"Didn't you hear?" Crow-hair laughed. "Dude, she head-butted a pole during gym." He moved closer and stood over Nat. "You oughta just bring a book to class and sit it out. You got about as much athletic ability as that pole you clocked."

"Hey, hey, hey." MacFarland swung around at the same time Parker jerked forward. One look at his face and she slowly backed away. He managed to iron most of the fury out of his expression before rounding the counter.

"Being an athlete isn't all there is to life, you know," he said. Crow-hair shot him a "whatever" look but MacFarland didn't react. "You ever think about offering to show her a few pointers? 'Cause that would make you a class act."

"You mean it would make me a dork."

"Yeah," Skullcap said. "'Cause like, you can't teach a penguin how to fly." Crow-hair had to think about that, then they both sniggered and high-fived.

MacFarland was shaking his head and Parker knew he was trying not to pay too much attention to Nat. Somehow he sensed that one look of sympathy was all it would take to push her to tears. "Nice, guys. Real nice. Nat, cross these two off your list for the cookout. They probably don't care about rappelling anyway."

Crow-hair and Skullcap exchanged glances that held more than a little suspicion. And no wonder, since Nat was staring at MacFarland as if he'd just announced that Chance had given birth to a litter of kittens. MacFarland ignored both her and the boys, going about his business, organizing the plants they had left. Parker would have applauded, except she had a sneaking suspicion she knew where he was going with that rappelling thing. Blast his hide.

Finally Crow-hair took the bait. "You that Army guy everyone's talking about?"

"Yeah, what are you, like a SEAL?"

"SEALs are Navy, you moron." Crow-hair pushed at Skullcap while keeping his gaze locked on MacFarland. "Got any medals?"

Skullcap pushed back. "What's rappelling?"

"C'mon, guys." MacFarland snorted. "You don't know what rappelling is?" They shook their heads. "It's the second fastest way to get down a cliff."

"What's the first?"

"Falling."

They all laughed. All but Parker, who could have cheerfully kicked MacFarland over said cliff.

She appreciated his standing up for her daughter, but she *really* didn't like where he was going with this. Descending the side of a mountain with one thin rope for support? Did he really think she'd allow that? But one look at the delight dawning on Nat's face and she didn't have the heart to step in. Not yet.

"How about this. Ever see the first *Mission: Impossible* with Tom Cruise?" Both boys nodded. "Remember that scene at the beginning, when he lowers himself into a bank vault? That's rappelling. He's doing what's called front facing."

"Cooooool." They said it together.

"The regular, feet-first kind of rappelling is what you usually see and it's a requirement for every soldier. In order to graduate BCT, every recruit has to rappel off the jump tower."

"What's BCT?"

"Basic Cadet Training."

"How high's the tower?"

"Fifty feet."

Crow-hair blew air through his lips, signaling disdain. "That's not so high."

"That's what they all say. Until they're standing on that platform looking down."

Crow-hair pointed at Nat. "And you're teaching *her?* To rappel?"

"Yeah. And she's a natural."

Crow-hair shook his head. "This I gotta see."

"That's up to Nat."

"Where do you rappel?" Skullcap was all over it. "Like, off the side of your house?"

Parker gritted her teeth. Heaven forbid.

"A stout tree does the trick."

"Tight. So when's the cookout?"

Finally MacFarland met Parker's gaze, and she raised her eyebrows as if to say, *Yes, when?*

"If Nat decides to invite you, we'll let you know."

"Whatever." Crow-hair looked ready to move on, but Skullcap was still staring in awe at MacFarland. "You a colonel or something?"

MacFarland fought a smile. "Corporal."

"Where's your gun?"

"My 'gun' is called a rifle. It's in the weapons locker back at the barracks, where it belongs."

"Oh." Skullcap scratched his head under his hat. "Ever kill anyone?"

9

PARKER'S STOMACH DROPPED TO her toes. This time when MacFarland looked up, his eyes were empty of humor. His face was tight, his gaze bleak. Parker started forward, intending to chase the boys off. Then a trio of elderly ladies wandered up and the boys took off on their own. Parker let loose a grateful breath. Then she took a closer look.

Hazel and June Catlett. And Audrey Tweedy.

Oh, dear Lord. When Parker reached the group Hazel already had her hand on MacFarland's wrist. "If you want to make some serious money," she was saying, "you should go back to that motel and put your uniform on. Or better yet, your jogging shorts." She leaned in. "And don't bother with a shirt."

"Don't you listen to her," June said. She wore eye shadow the color of a grape Nehi. "If you're going to lose the shirt you might as well lose the shorts, too."

"Leave the man alone." Audrey was heavier than June and Hazel put together but her voice was whisper-thin. "He's a hero. He needs protein." She rummaged in a handbag large enough to tote a small child and came up with a fistful of snacks. She thrust them at MacFarland. "Jerky?"

During all of this, MacFarland had stood rigid. Parker suspected it wasn't manners, but shock, that kept him from running. His hands were relaxed, but she could have bounced a quarter off his shoulders

Then again, she could probably have done that when he *wasn't* on edge. She tugged on his free arm. "Ladies, I'm sorry, but you'll have to excuse him. He has work to do."

Hazel ignored her and patted MacFarland's bicep. "I bet you haven't said one word about your exploits, have you, young man? You soldiers are all alike. As modest as you are handsome."

"We'd like to hear." June batted her eyes. "Wouldn't we, girls?"

A chorus of yeses. Hazel beamed up at him. "Go ahead," she said. "Impress us. Impress our Parker here."

Time for Plan B. Parker let go of MacFarland's arm and swung away, toward the table that held the plants and baskets they hadn't sold. "Before we get into all that, ladies, let me show you what we have over here. You picked a good time to stop by. Everything on this table is half price."

The trio scurried over, made their selections and turned to show them off. But MacFarland had disappeared.

* * *

EUGENIA EYED THE RICKETY-looking booth advertising Burgers, Dogs, and Fresh Lemonade. Calvin Ames, the owner of the diner and a man she'd rarely seen in anything other than a black polo shirt and khaki trousers, worked the grill while Harris conducted what looked like a scientific experiment. Tongue sticking out of the corner of his mouth, he consulted a notebook and used a turkey baster to squeeze a clear liquid into a gallon jug.

A turkey baster. Had he cleaned it since Thanksgiving? If not she may have just solved the mystery of his lemonade's reputedly odd taste.

She looked around, adjusted her purse strap and went back to watching him. He wrung the juice out of a lemon and she felt an answering squeeze in her chest. The man was adorable.

Too bad he was also a rat.

She wandered up to the stand and tried not to feel smug when Harris took one look and dropped his lemon. While he scooped it up off the grass she studied the menu someone had taped to the counter. Harris popped back up and she tapped a finger to her chin.

"I'm curious."

"'Bout what?"

"Your lemonade. I've heard things."

He beamed. "Best lemonade in town."

"That's not what I've heard."

His smile went the way of that last lemon. With a scowl he snatched up a cup and poured from the gallon jug. Shoved it across the counter and folded his arms. A young boy, maybe six or seven, came up to the counter and gave Eugenia a quizzical look. Seconds later a teenage girl ran up, pressed some bills into the boy's hand, muttered, "Hot dog only, no lemonade," and hurried off again. Eugenia toasted the boy with her cup and took a sip.

And promptly spit it out. The kid laughed so hard he lost his balance and staggered backward. Calvin shook his head. Harris looked outraged.

Eugenia swiped a hand across her mouth. "Noble Johnson told me your lemonade was sour enough to shrivel a man's—" her gaze bounced off the boy's face "—taste buds." She turned the cup upside down, spilling the contents onto the grass. "He was right."

With a mournful expression Calvin offered a cup of water. "Need a chaser?"

Eugenia chugged the water.

"Now you're bein' dramatic." Harris sounded petulant.

When she finished the water she resolved to buy a roll of mints to keep in her purse. "Excuse me, gentlemen. I have to go brush my teeth."

Harris came out of the booth. "I'll go with you."

"Why?"

"I nearly poisoned you. Let me make it up to you."

"Don't bother."

"Genie. It's the spring festival. Your first in Thistle Hill. And you couldn't find a more savvy tour guide if you tried. Can't we call a truce for a day?"

She hesitated. When he put it like that...

From the moment he'd spotted her at the stand and realized she'd sought him out, there'd been something in his eyes. Something hopeful. Was he regretting his decision to break things off?

Only one way to find out. "What did you have in mind?"

"They got some games over there." He pointed across the field, at a section that had been cordoned off from the rest of the festival. Two people stood outside the ropes, and it looked like they were recruiting participants. "Win one and you win a lifetime supply of chewing gum."

"Really?"

"Yeah. And my middle name is Marion."

"Don't you get that women don't like to be scoffed at?"

He took her hand, which surprised her so much she stared down at their linked fingers. Harris squeezed. "C'mon, it'll be fun."

"For the contestants or the audience?"

"It's an unspoken rule. Your first festival you have to embarrass yourself in front of witnesses at least once."

"Exactly what is it you expect me to do?" She was as game as the next girl. But if his idea of fun had anything to do with sitting over a tank of water or letting small children hurl dye-filled balloons in her direction, he could just forget it.

"Let's see. Over there they give you a blindfold and a pair of leather gloves and you gotta put on a pair of panty hose —"

"No, thanks."

" — and over there you line up and pass a clothespin attached to a spool of string up through one person's clothes and down through the next —"

"In your dreams."

"And — hey, how about the pillowcase-stuffing competition?"

"I thought the objective was my humiliation, not yours."

His gaze was teasing. "What, your maid show you how to make a bed?"

"I don't have a maid. And I'm not a moron." She made a face. "At least I wasn't, till I let you drag me over here."

For better or worse, they'd arrived just in time to participate. Eugenia recognized the woman running the game—she'd come into the store the week before and bought a dress to wear to a wedding. Eugenia gave her a pained smile.

"Do I really want to do this?" she asked her.

The woman grinned and handed her a pair of suede gloves. "Not without these."

Oh, for God's sake. What was it with the gloves?

She lined up with twelve other contestants, one of them the boy who'd laughed at her at the lemonade stand. He gave her a thumbs-up. She smiled at him. Then, very slowly, he turned his thumb upside down. She blinked, then glared.

Bring it on, small child.

The woman in charge reviewed the rules. Run to the other end of your lane, put the pillowcase on your pillow, return to your starting position, run back and take the pillow out of the case. First one to make it back to the starting position with the empty pillowcase wins.

But Eugenia was stuck on the woman's first word. "We have to run?" Suddenly, she realized she was missing the other half of that "we." She looked around for Harris and spied him fussing at Noble Johnson.

The jerk had bailed on her.

The woman raised a whistle to her lips. Ramming her hands into the suede gloves, Eugenia kicked off her shoes and bent at the knees.

Screeeeech. "Go!"

She hustled to the end of her lane. If she fell and got grass stains on her brand-new Escada wide-leg pants then, by God, Harris would pay. Literally. Dry cleaners were not cheap.

She reached the end of her lane, huffing, bent over and spread the pillowcase flat, the opening toward her. Snatched up the pillow and pushed her arm along the center to create a fold. Grabbed the pillow at the top and stuffed it into the pillowcase. Ta-da!

Back to start, tag, back again to the pillow, one ruthless yank and it was free of the case. Eugenia looked around, saw she was way ahead of her competition, brushed the palms of her gloves together and strolled back to the start. She passed the boy on the way and gave him another grin.

He called her something she certainly must have misunderstood.

Eugenia accepted the small plastic trophy and swung around to find Harris. When she spotted him she hurried over, brandishing the trophy. "I won!" She threw both arms around him and raised her face for a congratulatory kiss. He reared back and held her away from him.

"What?" She dropped her arms and looked around. The other competitors were giving her a good-natured round of applause. "The winner doesn't deserve a kiss?"

He looked pained. "I didn't mean to give you the wrong impression, Genie. I was just bein' friendly."

"I don't *believe* you. You go back and forth more times than a pendulum." She punched him in the arm and called him the same name the little boy had called her. First he looked shocked, then confused.

"I don't want to be *friends,* Harris." She shoved the trophy at him. When he grabbed it the top, a soccer ball painted yellow in a feeble attempt to disguise it as a happy face, broke off. Eugenia swung out an arm, indicating their audience. "If you'll excuse me, I believe I've met the requirement for public humiliation."

*   *   *

PARKER WATCHED WITH RELIEF as the Catlett sisters and Audrey Tweedy ambled away from the booth, weighted down with half-price plants and their disappointment that MacFarland wouldn't be returning anytime soon.

"Where'd he go?" Nat was just as put out, since she was dying to ask him if he'd meant what he'd said about teaching her to rappel.

"He'll be back. He just needed a break." Parker hooked her thumbs on the straps on her overalls and looked around as discreetly as she could manage. She'd never forget that look on his face after Skullcap's question. The old ladies and their gushing hadn't helped any.

No doubt he'd prefer to be alone, especially after being stuck at her booth for most of the day. But she couldn't bring herself to ignore what had just happened. Not after the way he'd rushed to Nat's defense.

She spotted Eugenia and waved her over. But before she could make her request, the other woman launched into a tirade. Parker caught the words *Harris, prehistoric,* and *lobotomy.* Nat looked on, openmouthed. Finally Eugenia sputtered to a stop, looking exhausted, and Parker hugged her.

"I'm so sorry."

"So am I." Eugenia shook her head, as if to shake off her funk, and her expression turned sheepish. "Did you need something?"

She agreed to stay with Nat, and Parker went looking for MacFarland. She didn't have to look far. He'd found refuge behind the bleachers. He was gripping the back of a metal step, his body slanted forward, his head bowed. His arm muscles bulged, as if the moment he got the go-ahead he'd start pushing the stand into the field.

At that moment Parker accepted the truth she'd been fending off for days. What she'd been too selfish — too frightened — to accept.

She and Natalie weren't the only ones devastated by Tim's death.

And Corporal Reid MacFarland was just as entitled to grieve as she was.

The laughter and music behind her mocked his pain. Pain he obviously didn't want her — or anyone else — to witness. She bit the inside of her lip. She should go.

Then again, she was the one who'd asked him to come today. She was the one who'd put him at the mercy of Thistle Hill. Not intentionally, of course.

She blinked against the heat prickling the backs of her eyes. All those people congratulating him for being a soldier. Thanking him for his efforts in Iraq. Commending his sacrifices. Every comment had felt like a fist pounding against her already battered heart.

So what had it done to him?

She approached him quietly and touched him on the shoulder. It was like touching a piece of granite. "You all right?"

He didn't look up, didn't move a muscle. "I need a moment."

Her palm burned with the need to settle on his back. "If there's anything—"

"Damn it." He jerked upright. "I said I—" He looked away, inhaled and exhaled. "Sorry. That I left you with everything."

"I was worried about you."

"Don't."

"Because you're fine?"

"Look." He put his hands on his hips and she did, admiring the way the pull of his shirt highlighted his muscles. "You don't have to fake an interest in me."

Who was faking? Heat flooded her cheeks and she jerked her gaze up to his. "What?"

"A personal interest. You don't have one. It's understandable."

She frowned. It was also untrue. She just hadn't admitted to one. What kind of fruitcake would he take her for if she started asking about his likes and dislikes and the kind of childhood he had?

Still, guilt wriggled its way under her skin, making her squirm. She didn't appreciate the feeling. At all.

A strangled little laugh came out of her throat. "Guess it would sound kind of twisted if I asked you not to take it personally. That I haven't admitted to an interest, I mean."

"Admitted?"

"I didn't mean that the way it sounded," she said quickly. "I meant I am concerned about you. I'm concerned about all of my employees."

"All two of them?"

"Reid…"

He went still. It took a second to register why, and when it did her blush came back. She shrugged a shoulder. "You ignore me when I use 'MacFarland.'"

"You're not easily ignored, Parker Dean."

She really didn't know how to interpret that comment, so she let it go. "I'd like to apologize. For the ladies. They mean well."

"Most people do." After a pause he said, "They won't understand."

She'd had that same realization. The residents of Thistle Hill wouldn't understand her acceptance of him, considering the tragedy he'd brought about.

"No reason they should find out."

"It's easier for me if they don't."

Um, yeah. But the way he said it... "You say that as if you'd rather they did." When he didn't respond she glanced over her shoulder, at the dozens of townspeople who'd turned out to support their county's rescue services. "They'll learn to deal with it."

"Will you?"

For the longest time she didn't answer. Finally she tipped her head. "I don't have to," she said. "You won't be around much longer." It was true. And something she should be celebrating. Instead a pinch of regret followed the words.

"Word will get out."

She sighed. "Wouldn't the military do everything in its power to keep it confidential?"

"It should be classified, yes. Makes for bad press when one of their own—" He pressed his lips together and shook his head. Shrugged. "Bad press means funding cuts. On the flip side, it's also bad press when one of their multi-million-dollar drones takes out the wrong target."

"But—"

"Exactly. *My* fault, not the drone's. I know it, you sure as hell know it, and two entire goddamned squads know it. But the guys with the green? Not so much. Best way to make sure they find out? Leak it."

"You think your name is out there?"

"I know it is."

A cheer from behind them—the pageant had started. Eugenia hadn't mentioned it, but she was probably involved. Parker struggled to shift mental gears. Neither she nor Reid had any control over who found out what, and Parker had already been away from her booth for too long. Like Harris always said, *Ain't no use puttin' up an umbrella till it rains.*

She touched Reid again, because she could, just the tips of her fingers to his arm. "Thank you. For what you did for Nat."

"I saw your face when I used the word *rappel*. You're thanking me for that?"

"I don't approve of your methods, but I do appreciate your looking out for her."

"It was a juvenile impulse. I don't like to see anyone bullied. Anyway, maybe those boys would benefit from seeing some respect in action. Respect for the environment, for your climbing partner — "

"For gravity?"

His grin made her feel as if she were the one about to walk backward off a mountain. "Hopefully not part of the demonstration."

Another cheer. Parker swung around and started walking. "I have to get back."

"I'll go with you. Wouldn't want to miss the crowning of the pumpkin queen."

"That's the fall festival. In the spring they have the Lilac Queen."

"You mean 'you have.'" He fell into step beside her. "You're part of this community, too."

Parker jerked to a stop. "What is it with people today? What am I supposed to do, throw a party and invite the entire town?"

"If you do, will you make your deviled eggs? And those little pecan tarts?"

"I don't know what people want from me."

"I think they want *you* to want something from *them*."

She caught the note of wistfulness in his voice and resisted the urge to consider its source. Way past time for a subject change. She started moving again, and racked her brain for something to say.

"So. What do you do in Kentucky? When you're not on duty?"

"Don't," he bit out. "Don't feel sorry for me."

Parker winced. That was exactly what she'd been doing. And she understood his objection to pity all too well.

They walked in silence. The next time he spoke his voice had lost its edge. "Lilac. Remind me again?"

"The bush with the cone-shaped flower. Attracts—"

"Butterflies. Got it."

She smiled at him, pleased. "See? We'll make a gardener out of you yet."

His expression turned wry. "That'll prove handy in the desert."

A sudden pang of grief caught her by surprise. Because it had everything to do with fear for a soldier's safety.

And nothing to do with Tim.

*   *   *

NAT SPOTTED THEM AND came running, carrying the geranium she was supposed to bag for a customer. "You really going to teach me how to rappel?"

Parker made a twirling motion with her finger. "Please go give that man his plant before he changes his mind."

Nat ran back to the booth and apologized. Reid watched her, his mouth curving with affection, and Parker stared. Not since Tim had left for Iraq had anyone besides Harris looked at her daughter that way. Nat scurried back and lifted her face to Reid. "So, are you?"

"If your mom says it's all right."

Nat's shoulders slumped. "She won't. She'll think it's too dangerous."

"I'm standing right here, Natalie Claire."

"Doesn't matter, anyway. I have no coordination. I suck at everything."

Reid's expression was as solemn as a prayer meeting but Parker could tell he was trying not to laugh. "That's not true," he said. "I just met you and already I know you're a gardener, and you have a great way with dogs. And you need to be coordinated to ride a bike, don't you? Besides, it takes someone who's patient, detail-oriented and safety conscious to be good at rappelling and you're all of those."

"Really?"

They reached the booth and Parker thanked Eugenia, who shamelessly ignored her so she could listen to what Reid was telling Nat.

"You wear a helmet when you're on your bike, which means you're cautious. You love solving puzzles and mysteries, which means you're detail-oriented. And anybody who's friends with Harris Briggs must have a boatload of patience." Nat giggled and Eugenia offered a loud "Amen." Then Eugenia asked for luck and hurried off to cheer the Lilac Queen contestant she'd signed on to sponsor.

Nat kicked at a tuft of grass. "I wear a helmet 'cause my mom makes me."

"But you wear it. A good leader knows how to take orders as well as he—or she—knows how to give them. Now, why don't you start packing away some of those plants and let me talk to your mom about it." He turned to Parker. "It is time to close up, right? Because of the pageant?"

She nodded, and looked from him to Nat and back again. "You really expect me to let you teach my nine-year-old daughter how to rappel?"

"It'll give her confidence."

"It'll get her killed."

"Give me some credit. I don't plan to take her up to the top of a cell tower and push her off. We'll pick a tree, build a platform. About ten feet up. Do some drops from there."

"How about six feet?"

"Deal." He held out his hand. She took it and squeezed. When he made to let go she held on, and the sudden caution on his face made her feel ashamed.

"She's a great kid," he said. He started to say something else, and the look in his eyes had Parker holding her breath. Then he closed his mouth and moved away to help Nat close up shop.

* * *

"YOU SURE HE'S GONNA be there?" Natalie, perched between Harris and Reid on the sagging bench seat of Harris's tanklike pickup, chewed on a fingernail. She sat with her body angled forward, hair pulled back in a short ponytail, green-eyed gaze focused on the cars ahead of them. Harris had to keep reminding her to sit back.

Reid turned his head to aim his smile at the passenger window. He'd lost count of the number of times Nat had asked that question.

Eagerness pulled her thin body taut. "You *sure?*"

Harris exhaled. "Yes, he'll be there. He's the one who invited you, ain't he? Now sit back and don't make me tell you again."

With a frustrated huff she thumped back against the seat and crossed her arms. "We're gonna be late," she muttered.

"We'll be fine." The brakes rumbled as Harris slowed for a traffic light turned yellow. "Practice doesn't start for another fifteen minutes."

Nat's knee bounced. Again Reid trained his gaze out the window, but this time wistfulness replaced amusement. Parker was concerned her daughter would bond with him? Maybe she needed to worry about him doing the bonding. And anyway, it was Gallahan Nat couldn't wait to see. Although Reid had her pretty excited about learning to rappel.

Unease tightened his jaw and he shifted in his seat. He was jealous, damn it. Over the affection of a kid he'd never see again after a couple of weeks. He swallowed, hard.

Harris steered the truck toward a decades-old building he identified as the high school. Behind the faded brick structure stretched a green expanse of grass, bordered by a chain-link fence splotched with rust. In the center of the field loitered a couple dozen men wearing jeans and numbered jerseys, some sunshine-yellow, the rest sapphire-blue. Reid breathed in the sharp, sweet scent of fresh-cut grass and felt his spirits rise.

Nat slammed the truck door and hovered at his elbow. "I don't see any other kids."

"'Cause this is an adult league." Rounding the front of the truck, Harris zipped up his jacket against the early-evening chill. "Not having second thoughts, are you?"

She didn't answer. "Here comes Joe."

They looked toward the field, saw Gallahan loping toward them, ball cap dangling from his hand. Reid grinned. When Gallahan got within hearing distance, Reid gestured at his jersey.

"Didn't know you were playing for the Canaries."

"Very funny." With a flick of his wrist, Gallahan settled his hat on his head. "We're the Fireballs, thank you very much."

Gaze superglued to Gallahan, Natalie nodded toward the field. "Who're they?"

"The Blue Devils."

"You can take 'em."

Gallahan laughed. "Good to know someone has faith in us. Last season our stats left a lot to be desired. But we're not playing tonight, just sharing a practice field. C'mon, I'll introduce you to the guys."

Natalie walked away with him, toward the ball field. Though she did more bouncing than walking. Annoyance kicked at the center of Reid's chest.

What the hell was the matter with him? The kid needed a man in her life. He should be glad she'd picked someone like Gallahan. Someone dependable. Kid-friendly.

Someone who hadn't killed her father.

He jammed his ball cap on his head and looked around for Harris.

When they caught up, Gallahan was introducing Nat to a lanky set of twins.

"Meet the Williams brothers. Curtis and Jesiah. Guys, Nat here would love some pointers. Maybe teach her a thing or two she can take back to gym class. Show off a little. You understand."

"Sure we do." Jesiah, the twin with the mustache, winked. "Old Mr. Devers still the gym teacher?" At Nat's nod he made a face. "Then you need all the help you can get, little sister. That man doesn't know a softball from a hard-boiled egg."

Nat giggled.

"Yeah." The clean-shaven Curtis thrust his chin in his brother's direction. "Which is why you should ignore everything Jesiah says and pay attention to me."

"Do that and you'll be laughed off the field."

Shaking his head, Gallahan gave both brothers a light shove in the direction of the dugout. "Knock it off, you two."

Jesiah looked over his shoulder and aimed another wink at Nat. "So what do you think? You game?" When she nodded, he stopped and lifted his jersey to reveal another one tucked into his waistband. "Then you'll need this. Might be a little big, but this will show those Devils you're not a free agent. We don't want the other team trying to recruit you, now, do we?"

Eyes wide, Nat shook her head, and Reid vowed then and there to buy the entire team a round at Snoozy's. Too bad Parker couldn't be there to see her daughter's face. Curtis helped her into the jersey and led her away to introduce her to the others.

"Okay, team." Gallahan clapped his hands. "Let's get a move on here. MacFarland," he barked. "Hit the mound."

For the next hour the Fireballs took turns coaching Nat in batting, catching and stealing bases. Reid tried his hand at pitching, delighting in the determination stamped on Nat's face whenever she was up to bat. She seldom got a hit, and once or twice sneaked a scrub at the frustrated tears she couldn't hold back, but never balked at trying whatever the players asked her to.

Damn, she was a trouper.

He was hanging out in the dugout between shifts on the mound, leaning forward into the fence, fingers hooked in the cold metal links, when Harris sidled close. Watched him watching Parker's daughter.

"She's havin' the time of her life." Reid didn't respond. The old man kept talking. "Great group of guys. They'll look out for her. Good idea, to put 'em together."

Reid's grip tightened, the steel pressing into the joints of his fingers.

"It's killin' you, ain't it? Knowin' you won't be around to look after her."

"She's not my responsibility." But she was. Parker, too. For a while, anyway. Then he'd have to trust Harris and Gallahan and Eugenia and the rest of Thistle Hill to pick up where he left off. That had been his plan all along. Apologize, do what he could to help, give as much money as he could scrounge, then get back to the desert and do his goddamned best to keep his brothers safe. And not only from the enemy.

That plan had kept him going. Given him a purpose, while he sat shell-shocked through debriefings and hearings and counseling sessions, then after reality set in and he'd struggled through days so dark he knew he'd never make it to the light. And still he couldn't allow himself to think too far ahead.

So why all of a sudden did it feel like, instead of giving him a purpose, his plan was taking one away?

He kicked at the fence. It gave a muted clang in protest. Harris chuckled and Reid swung around. Time to give the old man a taste of his own medicine.

"So what's the story with Eugenia?"

Harris's innocent look gave way to a glower. Reid saw the pain behind it and his voice gentled. "She seemed pretty upset with you after the festival."

"She had a right to be." Harris slumped back against the wall of the dugout. "She's a good woman. She deserves better than me."

Shit. Reid knew exactly what he meant.

Curtis and Jesiah jogged over to the dugout and he welcomed the distraction. Jesiah took off his hat and slapped it against his thigh. "You sure can toss a ball. Joe said you might come to practice regular while you're around. Give our pitcher some pointers."

Reid gazed at the brothers, twenty-something kids with too much trust. "Look, I'd love to help out. But you guys don't know squat about me."

The twins peered at each other, their expressions comical in their confusion. Curtis scratched his head. "Joe vouches for you. What else do we need?"

"Yeah." Harris joined them at the fence. "What else do they need?"

"C'mon, man. We really could use the help." Jesiah gestured with his cap. "Besides, Harris here's a busy man. How will Nat get to practice if you don't bring her?"

A lame-ass argument if ever he'd heard one. But what could it hurt? For the little while longer he'd be in town, he'd get some exercise and watch Nat gain some sports confidence.

"Right. Count me in."

Curtis nodded, satisfied. "Hey, Nat's looking a little bored out there. You want to join her in left field? Jesiah and me'll make sure you get some action."

Reid grabbed his glove and jogged onto the field. Soon they'd have to call practice. Dusk was coming in quick. Before long the grass would grow too slippery to be safe. Afterward, according to Gallahan, the guys planned to hit the diner for a burger.

Good thing Parker hadn't set a curfew.

He called out to Nat as he approached. "They sent me to tell you to keep an eye out. Should be a few hits coming this way."

She offered up a sage nod and punched her fist into her glove. Swallowing a grin, Reid gave her a thumbs-up and moved several feet to her right. The first ball that came their way was a grounder. She ran up on it, awkwardly scooped it up and tossed it back with a surprisingly strong overhand.

"Way to go, kid."

She shrugged, punched her glove again and sank into her half crouch. "Maybe next time they'll let me pitch."

"Maybe."

They were quiet as they watched the batter hit a foul the catcher managed to snag out of the air. Then a tentative voice from his left. "Will you teach me?"

A sweet, unfamiliar warmth crept into his chest. It took him a moment to find his voice. "Happy to. One thing, though. In this league they pitch underhand."

"I like overhand."

"It's against the rules."

"But I throw better overhand."

He shrugged, then shrugged again, amazed at how light his shoulders felt. "Which means your underhand needs work."

Another foul ball. Nat slapped her glove against her leg and rose out of her crouch. "Reid?"

"Yeah?"

"What's friendly fire?"

10

DESPITE THE LONG SLEEVES of her hoodie, the cool night air made Parker shiver. Or maybe it was the lonely shadows pressing against her back. Whatever the reason, she appreciated the pale yellow glow that filtered through the motel room's blinds.

She frowned at the pockmarked door labeled with a not-quite-straight number six. She tucked her hair back into its clip and knocked again.

No answer. A glance over her shoulder confirmed that Reid's Jeep was parked less than ten feet away. Maybe he'd fallen asleep with the light on. As hard as he worked she wouldn't be surprised.

She looked up the sidewalk toward the dimly lit office. Or maybe he and Joe were hanging out together, playing cards or cheering the sports channel. Her teeth sank into her lower lip as she looked back at the closed door in front of her.

Or maybe he was in the shower.

An unbidden image flashed in her brain. Slick, naked muscles stretching and bulging under a fall of hot water. Strong, beckoning hands and a steamy-eyed invitation. Her breath caught in her throat and her palms got damp. She fell back a step and dragged air into her lungs. Good God, where had that come from? She pressed cold hands to hot cheeks and counted her blessings that he hadn't answered her second knock.

This could wait. Whatever Harris thought Reid needed to tell her, it could darned well wait. She whirled toward the parking lot.

She heard it as she stepped off the curb. A distant clanking sound.

She looked to her left, and spotted a sliver of light in front of the motel's very last room. The door had been left ajar.

Another sweep of the parking lot. Besides her car, Joe's truck and Reid's Jeep, the lot was empty. No other guest, then. Maybe Reid was helping Joe renovate? She hesitated. For some reason she felt unsettled. Maybe she should let well enough alone and wait until tomorrow to find out what it was Reid wanted to see her about.

Then again, Harris had said it was important. And that it had to do with Nat. Which was why he'd offered to stay with Nat while Parker went to see Reid. She sighed, fisted her fingers around her keys, sent a wistful glance toward her car, then headed for the end door.

More clanking sounds, punctuated with the occasional grunt. What the heck? She reached out a finger and pushed at the door to peek inside.

Reid was alone. Dressed in navy sweatpants and a faded gray muscle shirt, he sat on a bench facing a mirrored wall that reflected an impressive array of fitness equipment. His back to the door, his elbow anchored against the inside of his knee, he lifted and lowered a dumbbell with rhythmic precision. Sweat molded his short hair to his scalp and gleamed along his well-developed biceps. The occasional soft grunt signaled the effort each lift was costing him.

Need — immediate, flaming, audacious need — caught Parker by surprise and she gasped. She was halfway to her car when she heard him call out.

"Wait."

She thought about ignoring him. About bursting into a panicked run, locking herself in her car and channeling Danica Patrick. But the reprieve would be temporary. She'd still have to face him in the morning.

Light spilled into the parking lot, chasing away the shadows around her as the door behind her swung wide. She pushed her shoulders back and turned. Reid stood in the doorway.

"You wanted to see me?"

Sooo many ways she could answer that. She decided on the safest one. "Harris said *you* wanted to see *me*."

He angled his head toward the room behind him. She dithered a moment, then slowly retraced her steps. "Sorry to interrupt your workout."

"I was ready for a break." He led her inside. She looked around at the battered paneled walls eclipsed by gym-quality equipment. She eyed the elliptical and felt a twinge of jealousy.

"What a great setup."

"That's what I said."

She lifted her head. Their gazes caught and held in the mirror. Reid gestured at the water cooler.

"Something to drink?"

"Thanks." Her throat was suddenly parched and something wet sounded perfect. Unfortunately that thought brought back the shower image. God in heaven. Worse, she found herself mesmerized by the movement of Reid's throat muscles as he guzzled first one cup and then another. A drop of water slid down his chin and she wanted to touch a fingertip to it.

Seriously? What was *wrong* with her?

Okay, wait. She knew exactly what was wrong with her. But why on God's green earth did Corporal Reid MacFarland have to be the one to resuscitate her sex drive?

"You plan to drink that?"

"What?" She looked down at the untouched paper cup in her hand. "Oh." She swigged the water, wishing it was something stronger. She refilled the cup, and turned to find him eyeing her outfit.

"Do you own any clothes that fit?"

Just in time she stopped herself from volunteering "underwear." "I don't like to feel constricted," she said instead.

He ignored that, as if he'd already known the answer. She burst into speech before he had a chance to tell her why he'd summoned her.

"I want to thank you. When Nat got home from practice tonight I almost didn't recognize her. It's been a long time since I've seen her so excited, especially about playing sports. I appreciate what you're doing for her."

"You're welcome."

"She did get a little sad, though, when she told me you're up for reenlistment."

He nodded. "During my next deployment. Though with stop-loss, it may be a moot point."

Tim had dreaded that, as well — that the Army would extend his contract past his end-of-service date so they could keep him overseas. "She's hoping you won't re-up. She's hoping you'll move to Thistle Hill."

He rested an arm on the treadmill. "Damn."

"Exactly." She sighed. "All I ask is that you help her understand you're not coming back." She stopped, horrified. "I mean — "

"Forget it." He grabbed a towel.

God, she couldn't believe she'd said that. She fought to get her thoughts back in order. "Um, Harris said you had something to tell me?"

He nodded, and took a moment to wipe the towel over his face. A long moment. Her fingers tangled inside her pockets. Whatever he had to say, she had a feeling it wouldn't be good.

He put his hands on his hips. "At practice tonight. Nat asked about friendly fire."

Much worse than not good. Parker sank down onto the weight bench. "What did you tell her?"

"I told her what it meant. The unintentional firing at one's own forces or at allied forces while attempting to engage the enemy."

"Did she understand that?"

"She seemed to."

"Did she say why she asked?"

"Came up at school, apparently. You know what the next thing is that'll come up, right? That that's how her dad died?" She didn't say anything. He didn't get the hint. "Why haven't you told her? Think twice before you say it's none of my business."

"What I do and do not choose to tell my daughter is none of your business."

"She's going to hear it from someone. Wouldn't you rather it be from you?"

Parker was shaking her head. "You have no idea how hard it's been. Not for me, not for her. I will not make it worse by telling her that her father didn't get the chance to die a hero."

"He *did* die a hero. He fought for what he believed in. He put his life on the line for you, for her, for all of us. That makes him a hero. I took his life, but I didn't take his principles."

She couldn't speak. The raw, scalding ache in her throat wouldn't allow it. Slowly, Reid approached and reached for her hand. She kept both tucked firmly in the center pocket of the hoodie. He gripped her forearm instead, and gave it a small shake.

"She's all the family you have. I saw to that. If she hears the truth from someone else, she might not forgive you. Not a good feeling. Trust me. You really want to risk losing what's left of your family?"

She slid down the bench out of his reach and got to her feet. "Good thing I already thanked you. Because I'm all out of gratitude." The last few words were barely more than gurgles. Desperate for the privacy of her car, she still only made it as far as the doorway. Because that's when the shame kicked in.

Since when had running become her first line of defense?

"I'm sorry. I didn't mean that." He was toweling off his neck and arms, and raised an eyebrow. She forged on. "You've done a lot for the company. For Nat. And for me. I'm just...lashing out."

"I get it."

"I—I don't think you do. This isn't me. I'm not usually so abrupt with people."

"Guess I'm the exception."

"In more ways than one," she muttered. She pulled her hands free and smoothed the hair that had escaped from her clip. Reid frowned.

"You're shaking." He tossed the towel in the direction of the weight bench and came closer. Somehow she resisted the urge to retreat. He touched two fingers under her chin and gently lifted. "Shadows under your eyes." His gaze locked on to hers, and she saw a mixture of regret and yearning there.

Yearning for what? She didn't want to care. Still she couldn't help wondering. Was he longing for a way to erase the past? To make up for his mistake? He had no family, no girlfriend. Did he miss having someone to be close to?

Or did he wish he could be close to her?

He dropped his hand and stepped back, and she almost followed him. "You're not sleeping."

She allowed her gaze to rove his face. "Few of us are these days." She breathed in, and regretted it when the smell of male sweat lured her eyes down the length of his body. His muscles tensed under her scrutiny and she wanted to yank him close as much as she wanted to shove him away.

"Remember when I said our arrangement made me feel as if I'm betraying Tim?" She pushed her shoulders back, and looked up. "It's more than the arrangement that's making me feel that way."

His eyes darkened, and his nostrils flared. He moved forward again and this time she did back up, but only because she needed the support of the wall behind her. He braced one hand beside her head. The other toyed with the drawstring on her hoodie. He was breathing quickly again, his heavy-lidded gaze riveted on her mouth. From her throat came a sort of squeaking, gasping sound, and his lips curved. Then he tugged on the drawstring to pull her toward him, and at the same time dipped his head.

He…was about to kiss…her.

"Wait. Wait." She stopped him with a palm to his sweat-soaked chest. When her hand tingled with the urge to stroke him she curled her fingers into a fist. "I—I want this." Her mind skittered away from thoughts of Tim. She licked her lips. "And I'm feeling a little dizzy because you seem to want it, too."

"But." The word came out ragged.

"It's not just a kiss." He was leaving. And he was…who he was.

He closed his eyes and hung his head, then pushed away from the wall. He snatched another paper cup from the stack next to the water cooler. But instead of filling it with water he crumpled it. "Guess I should thank you for being honest. Not sure I'm grateful, though."

Struggling to quiet her panting, she crossed her arms. "You couldn't have missed the way I've been looking at you."

"I put it down to wishful thinking. Looks like I'll have to get used to that." He gave a harsh chuckle. "That's something Thistle Hill *really* wouldn't understand."

"That doesn't have anything to do—"

"I know." He threw the cup into the wastebasket. "I get it." After a charged moment he looked up, jaw tight. "I won't take advantage of this."

"I know," she said, with the faintest of smiles. "I appreciate that." At least a part of her did. Like, maybe the littlest toe on her right foot. The rest of her wished he would lunge at her and take the decision right out of her hands.

She turned in the doorway. "Have you thought about getting out?"

"Only every day since Erbil."

"Which side is winning, Army or civilian?"

He cocked his head and gave her a once-over. "At this point the civilian side has everything going for it."

* * *

PARKER SET DOWN THE bucket with a huff of relief, patted the pockets of her sweatshirt and clicked off the flashlight. The cool spring evening settled in around her. Closing her eyes, she lingered beside the greenhouse and breathed in the comforting smell of wet earth. A torn piece of plastic flapped in the lake-borne breeze. In the distance the raucous song of a bullfrog echoed, long and loud. She rolled her shoulders back. Tried to relax. But the memory of Reid's mouth descending toward hers snapped her eyes wide open again.

And the way he'd looked at her...

She'd wanted that kiss. She'd wanted it bad. Which was why she'd made it clear—to both of them—that it couldn't happen. Still it had made for a long, sleepless night.

Again.

A hank of her hair slipped free and slid down her cheek. Darn it. She peeled off her soiled gloves and trapped them between her knees before shoving her hair back into place. She put her gloves back on and chewed at her lower lip. All day long she'd battled to put those few crazy, heady, completely irresponsible moments behind her. But even while paying bills and filing invoices and counting bags of soil conditioner she found herself dwelling on that near kiss. Completing it in her mind. Dreading and at the same time anticipating her next encounter with Reid MacFarland.

Which, besides being a ridiculous waste of time and energy, had put her behind in her chores. Luckily neither Harris nor Reid had seemed to notice her preoccupation. Or that she'd gone out of her way to avoid Reid the entire day.

She frowned. Then again, maybe he'd been avoiding her.

To borrow Nat's favorite word, *whatever.*

With a flick of her thumb she turned the flashlight back on, hefted the bucket and rounded the hut's corner. Beneath her heavy boots the gravel crunched and scattered. Of all the chores involved in operating a greenhouse, this particular task was her least favorite. But it had to be done.

Let's get some light in here. She turned back toward the greenhouse entrance. The flashlight's beam glanced across a man's face and she shrieked. She stumbled backward and her heel struck the bucket. Warm water sloshed over the rim, soaking the legs of her overalls. Her heart jerked in a pattern as wild as the circle of light bouncing around on the plastic walls.

"Parker. It's me."

She'd have made a smart-aleck response if she hadn't needed all her breath to avoid passing out. She aimed the flashlight at the ground and concentrated on slowing the push and pull of air. How had she missed hearing his footsteps?

"Sorry I scared you. You okay?"

"Fine," she wheezed.

"What are you doing out here in the dark?"

I could ask the same of you. At least she had a flashlight. "Hit that switch to your right," she managed, "and it won't be dark."

He did. She swung a forearm up onto the bridge of her nose, shielding her eyes from the abrupt glare of the overhead lights.

A brief silence, interrupted by the intermittent squeaking of a nearby cricket. Reid gestured at the sodden leg of her overalls.

"Sorry about that."

"It's okay." She peered down into the bucket. Still more than half-full. At least she wouldn't have to make that trip from the house again. When she looked up again Reid was frowning.

"You shouldn't be out here alone."

"I brought protection." She pulled a pair of plastic water guns from the pockets of her sweatshirt and held them up.

He stared. "What the hell were you planning to do with those? Make someone choke on their own laughter?"

She rolled her eyes. "No one bothers us out here."

"No one has yet."

"I have my cell," she said, her voice testier than she intended. But darn it, she couldn't afford to get used to the cozy sense of security she felt whenever he worried about her.

More silence. Then he nodded at the water pistols. "So what are those for?"

"Slugs. Salt water's the only thing that'll get rid of them."

"Sorry I asked." He wandered over to one of the tables and fingered a geranium leaf. She watched, riveted. She'd seen those hands with a hammer, yanking rusted nails out of rotted boards, and she'd seen them stroke Chance's ears. She couldn't help imagining them on her. Rough, soft, and anywhere in between.

Her pulse pounded in her ears and she ventured closer. Had he come to finish what they'd started last night? Because it was late. And it was dark. And they were alone.

And if he touched her, this time she wouldn't be able to back away.

"I've been thinking about your business," he said. "And what we could do to save it."

Her lips stopped tingling. "Things are tough, but I'm not going to lose my business."

"Not as long as you keep producing. But what if one of the greenhouses floods? Or catches fire? What if a…horde of rabbits comes in and eats your entire crop of geraniums? What then?"

"Rabbits don't eat geraniums."

"You know what I mean."

"They are, however, partial to petunias." He cocked an eyebrow. With an impatient sigh she yanked the stopper out of one of the water pistols and dunked the toy into the bucket. "There is no way I can be prepared for every type of emergency."

"Understood. But are you prepared for any?"

"Your point?"

"You don't have a safety net."

She straightened and jammed the stopper back into place. "And you know how I can get one."

"What about your family? Can't they help?" Something of what she was thinking must have shown on her face because he gave a sheepish nod. "Okay, yes, I'm not only trying to lend a hand, I'm curious."

She hesitated, then shrugged. "There isn't any family. Not really. Not on my side, and as for Tim's side, let's just say Nat's better off without them."

"Why?"

"Because." She kicked at a piece of gravel, watched it skitter under a bench, and finally lifted her head. "Because they wanted the death gratuity. They didn't even wait for the funeral to be over before they demanded I turn the money over the moment I received it. I offered to give them a percentage but for them it was all or nothing. It got ugly. I didn't want Nat exposed to that so as soon as I could manage it, we left Virginia." She waved a hand, frustrated to see that it shook.

"We needed to get away from the memories, anyway. And like I told you before, Tim and I...we'd already planned to settle here."

"Why would they think they were entitled to the money?"

"It was more that they didn't want *me* to have it. They always believed I was the reason he enlisted. So when he died..."

"They blamed you." Neither spoke as they considered the irony. Finally Reid exhaled. "Okay. Family's out. That leaves the people of Thistle Hill."

Oh, for heaven's sake. "I refuse to depend on the charity of my neighbors."

"I'm not talking charity. I'm talking business partners." When she banged the water pistol down onto the nearest bench and opened her mouth to protest, he held up a hand. "Hear me out. I've done some research. You could set up a network of growers. You provide the plants, they provide the labor. That lets you offer more product and a bigger variety. And it means you're no longer a single point of failure."

"It would also mean I'm no longer independent."

"But if your independence costs you your business—"

"It's why I'm in business. To be independent."

"Parker." His voice gentled. "You're going to have to make a choice. I'm going to email you some links. If you get a chance, check them out. The headquarters of an established growers' network is only a few hours away, in Darleton—we could set up a meeting, ask some questions." He reached out, as if to touch her, then pulled his hand back and stuffed it in his pocket. "Just think about it. I'd hate to see you lose this place."

She watched him disappear through the doorway. He cared. No matter his reasons, he did care. But she couldn't let that sway her decision. Because keep her business or lose it, Corporal Reid MacFarland wouldn't be around to see it.

Once he left Thistle Hill, he had no reason to come back.

*　*　*

WITH A GRATEFUL SMILE, Eugenia slid the green-and-white-striped bag across the polished surface of the dark cherry sideboard she used as a countertop. "Thank you for coming in. And have a wonderful day." The customer nodded her thanks and hurried her toddler to the door. Home to lunch, no doubt. The bells over the exit jingled a cheery signal that they'd left her alone.

Eugenia mentally tallied her sales for the morning. Not bad. Not bad at all. Word must finally be getting out.

"Now what?" she asked aloud. Lunch, her stomach answered. She thought of the tuna sandwich she'd packed that morning and wished she'd thought to wrap a pickle. Before she made it to the storeroom/office in the back, the bells rang out again. Another customer. Her stomach shimmied at the prospect of making another sale, of having yet another buyer show approval of her taste and style. Every transaction was like a validation.

The tuna could wait.

Her hands smoothing her skirt, her face beaming an authentic welcome, she spun on her high-heeled mules to greet her customer. And came face-to-face with Harris Briggs.

Her smile, her step, her confidence faltered. The hurt and anger she'd thought she'd banished days earlier came scuttling back, pinching and poking at her heart.

He stood just inside the door, a big, robust man backlit by a haze of sunlight, surrounded by racks of flimsy blouses, silky skirts and fragile scarves. He angled his head, as if trying to identify the scent in the air. The source was the dish of lilac-scented potpourri Eugenia had placed in the window behind him.

He looked good. He'd traded his signature plaid shirt for a pale blue dress shirt he'd never be able to button at the neck. Snug khaki trousers replaced his usual overalls. His hands fumbled for his front pockets, then dropped to his sides.

Eugenia struggled to keep a reluctant smile away from her face. If the man had any hair, it probably would have been slicked back.

Yes, he looked good. Better than good, actually. But that didn't change the fact that he'd acted like a jerk. She pushed herself forward, molding her lips into an I-don't-want-to-wait-on-you-but-I-suppose-I-have-to smile.

"May I help you?"

"Hope so."

His steady blue gaze rendered her heartbeat not so steady. Why didn't he just tell her what he wanted? "Are you looking for something in particular?"

"I have this friend — a lady..."

She caught her breath. He'd come to apologize. At least she hoped that's why he was there. If he'd come to buy a gift for a girlfriend, she'd brain him.

"I owe her one hell of an apology."

The tightness between her shoulders eased. Carefully, slowly, she exhaled. And waited. But he didn't say anything more and her backbone stiffened yet again.

For Pete's sake. Did he expect her to make it easy for him? *Dream on, big boy.*

"I'm sorry, sir," she told him in a pleasant, singsong voice. "We're all sold out of apologies. Anything else I can show you?"

He moved farther into the store, his expression pained. "Genie. I apologize. I said some rotten things. That day outside Parker's, and again at the festival. I never meant to hurt your feelings."

It was the most she'd ever heard him say at one time. But it wasn't enough.

"You did mean to hurt my feelings, Harris Briggs, and you know it. At least you did when you accused me of being careless with my money. As for the festival, you knew how I felt about you. Still you led me on. I'd always considered you a straightforward kind of guy. Apparently I was wrong."

He frowned. "You weren't wrong. I've always said, without honesty you've got nothin'. That's why I'm here."

Eugenia's throat tightened and she suddenly found herself unable to utter a word. She looked around wildly for her water bottle while

Harris tried to find something to do with his arms.

"Parker told me about the loan you offered her."

"I didn't offer her a loan. I offered to say yes if she decided to ask me for a loan since I was foolish enough to bet you I wouldn't spend money on other people." Where, oh, where had she left her water bottle?

"She told me she turned you down, but you didn't kick up a fuss about it."

"What did you think I'd do? Sit on her, until she agreed to take it?"

He scowled. "You're not makin' this easy."

"And why in the world would I do that?"

He grinned, and she forgot she was dying of thirst. "You're right. You're as stubborn as I am, which is why —" He cleared his throat. "This money thing. It's important we figure it out. To this day my daughter refuses to talk to me 'cause I won't give her money."

"Really," said Eugenia, her voice as barely there as the lingerie spilling suggestively out of the bureau behind her.

"Sounds bad, I grant you, but she and her husband got involved in an insurance scam and..." His jaw went hard. "Bottom line is, they will never get any more money from me."

Eugenia felt faint. She stumbled over to the nearest clothing rack and started sliding the hangers back and forth. *Squeak. Squeak.*

"You all right?"

"Fine." *Squeak.* "Just fine."

"We can talk about all that money stuff later. There's somethin' else I need to let you know."

"Something —" *squeak* "—else?"

He ran a palm over his head. "I have this condition," he began, and when she froze he took her hand and patted it while he explained the problem with his heart. And as Eugenia listened to him talk, her hopes, her plans and her own heart crumbled.

Even if she'd managed to mimic Harris's bravery by making her own confession, she could never risk his health. And after what she'd just heard, coming clean would pose a definite risk. One not worth the handful of dates they'd enjoy before another dispute pushed them apart again.

Their relationship was destined to be temporary. There were just too many fundamental differences between them.

"I'm so sorry," she said. "Thank you. For telling me."

"I wanted you to know so we'd have everything out in the open. This thing I have. Bad enough I got stuck with it. I didn't want to stick someone else with it."

"I understand."

"But I saw how mad Parker got with Reid, with him makin' business decisions for her and all, and I figured I should give you all the facts and let you make your own decision."

What could she say? "I appreciate that."

Another frown. She wanted to warn him his face could freeze that way.

"What I'm tryin' to say is, life is short. You get sick, you figure out quick what matters. You should see Reid with Nat. He's developed a powerful affection for that girl but chances are he won't see her again. Not for a long while, anyway. Point is, if you think you can deal with it, Genie, I'd like to start datin' again."

Oh, God. She groped at the nearest rack, grabbed a handful of material and squeezed. Hard.

"I'm sorry, Harris. I don't think it would work."

"What?"

"I—I don't think dating is a good idea."

His face turned brick-red. "Why the he—why not?"

She licked her lips, looked around again for her water bottle, shook her head. He drew in a breath so deep she feared for his shirt buttons.

"Is there someone else?"

Another shake of her head. For the first time since he'd walked in, his gaze broke from hers. "You're not the type to hold a grudge. So I can only figure you don't wanna saddle yourself with a sick man. Can't say I blame you." He turned toward the door. "If you ever change your mind, Eugenia Blue, you know where to find me."

This time when the bells over the door jingled, she wanted to tear them down and drop-kick them across the store.

* * *

FRIDAY AFTERNOON. THREE DAYS since Reid had almost kissed Parker—hell, since he'd even talked to her, besides the call he'd received the morning after he'd found her in Hut Three, preparing for the slug fest. She'd told him to go ahead and set up the meeting in Darleton, which had surprised the hell out of him, but he'd done what she'd asked him to do. Now they had a two-hour drive together. Each way.

He felt like a teenage boy wondering how he could manage to impress the girl and at the same time keep from groping her.

He parked the Jeep, hitting the brakes a little too hard. Truth was, he was nervous as hell. In fact, the last time he remembered being this nervous was right before boarding the C-130 that would deliver his unit to Kuwait, where they were scheduled to climatize for several days before finding transport to Iraq. The way his palms were sweating, anyone would think he was taking Parker out on a date instead of picking her up for a business meeting.

Stop right there. No way he could let himself start connecting the word *date* with Parker Dean. They'd agreed. All they had in common was heartbreak. And they'd each had enough of that to last a handful of lifetimes. So why invite more?

He got out of the Jeep, hoping he wasn't overdressed in his oxford shirt and borrowed tie. He was wearing jeans, because he feared that Parker in her overalls might give Mr. Orson the idea that Reid was her boss. Which Parker would *not* appreciate.

Her boss. The erotic possibilities were overwhelming. So overwhelming he had to take several deep breaths and envision a cold shower to calm his body. This was business. Not pleasure. Business.

But he couldn't stop thinking about the stark need that had flared in her eyes when she'd found him in the gym, or the way her eyes and mouth had softened when he'd moved in for a kiss. Couldn't help fantasizing about holding her, tasting her, unfastening her overalls, strap by strap, lowering that ridiculous bib and raising her tee, pulling her hips to his and stroking his palms over her —

Damn it to hell. He leaned back against the Jeep with a groan. Slowly filled and emptied his lungs. Concentrated on the perfume of the fat, ruffly blooms on the bushes that lined the driveway. What were they called? The ones the ants loved so much. He welcomed the distraction as he struggled to remember.

Screw it. Didn't matter. He made a quick zipper check and relaxed. Mission accomplished.

He jogged up the steps to the front door. Too bad he didn't have time to jog around the block. Damn, he was tense. He knocked, rolling his shoulders back. Two hours alone. Each way. Surely he could manage to control his libido that long.

She opened the door and his mind went blank.

11

N O OVERALLS. NO DENIM at all. And nothing that could be considered even remotely baggy. Parker wore a hip-hugging pair of black pants and a green top that clung to breasts she should be arrested for hiding. Her hair swung loose, the way it had after the people at the Cooper's Hardware booth had styled it at the festival. The soft ends grazed her shoulders and Reid had a sudden desire to see them brushing her skin. Hell, he wanted to brush that himself, with his fingers, his lips, his teeth —

Jesus. How would he survive this meeting, or even the drive there, without making a slobbering ass of himself?

"Something wrong?"

He forced his gaze upward. His scrutiny had put color in her cheeks and a rare uncertainty in her eyes. When he didn't — couldn't — say anything, she pressed her lips together and lifted her chin. He read her body language, loud and clear. She'd decided against asking if she looked all right. Once he found his voice he'd make it up to her.

If he found his voice.

With brisk, impatient movements she grabbed up a black leather portfolio, shut the door and stepped out onto the porch. "Ready?"

And how. He suppressed a groan.

They'd reached the Jeep before his throat muscles started working again. He opened the passenger door. "I figured Harris or Nat might be joining us." As much as he looked forward to having Parker to himself, it probably would have been better if they had.

She frowned. "Someone has to stay behind. And Eugenia invited Nat to help her out at the shop. I didn't think Nat would appreciate having to sit in on our meeting, although…"

"Although?"

"She did want to come." Her tone made it clear she wasn't sure what to think about that. But the lack of bitterness alone was reason to celebrate.

She made to step up and hesitated. "I'm not sure about this."

"The meeting? Or being alone with me?"

"Either. Both."

"We're just doing recon here. No commitments. As far as being alone with me…" He closed in on her, right hand on the door, left hand on his ride. She backed away, staring up at him. But there was more curiosity than fear in her eyes and he couldn't hold back a grin. "Anxiety's part of survival," he said. "Keeps you alert."

She smiled back, and her face took on a glow that rivaled a desert sunrise after a sandstorm. A teasing light made her hazel eyes sparkle, and her cheeks recovered some of her earlier blush. God, she was gorgeous. Her lips moved, and she looked up at him, waiting. He blinked.

"Sorry?" He had no idea what the hell she'd just said. All he knew was that she smelled like honeysuckle, and if he didn't get her into the damned Jeep soon he was going on the attack.

And wouldn't that just win him some points.

"I said, are you planning an ambush?"

He reminded himself she couldn't read his mind. Otherwise she'd already be running for the house.

"If I told you ahead of time it wouldn't be an ambush, would it?"

He closed the door behind her and took his time getting to the driver's side. Talk about ambush. He'd told Parker he wouldn't take advantage of their mutual attraction, and he meant it.

But she wasn't making it easy for him.

* * *

WHEN REID TURNED INTO the parking lot of Beryl Growers in

Darleton, Parker blinked in surprise. Once they'd gotten past their initial awkwardness, the two-hour drive had gone faster than she'd imagined. They'd talked about black-and-white movies, investing in the stock market—maybe it was time to give Ivy Millbrook a call—discovered a shared appreciation for office supplies and Greek food—they agreed moussaka was highly underrated. They also discovered they both enjoyed classic rock, and knew all the lyrics to Van Halen's "Jump." Not that the words were challenging.

Reid had made Parker promise not to tell Harris about the singing. She smiled as he put the Jeep in park. He'd be fun to travel with.

And there it was. That wistful feeling again. She pressed her lips together and opened her door. Harris and his big ideas. She was in the middle of a stretch when she recognized the scent that was making her stomach sit up and take notice.

"Basil." Reid came to stand beside her, inhaling with appreciation. Out of the corner of her eye she admired the way he filled out his shirt, and allowed herself a brief fantasy involving his tie. Eventually she forced herself to look away. What had they been talking about?

Of course. She'd forgotten that Beryl Growers specialized in organic culinary herbs. But there was no mistaking the smell of basil.

"And oregano," she said aloud. "And mint."

"Right." He looked at her oddly. Maybe he'd already said that. "Ready to go in?"

"Um, yes." She ducked back into the Jeep for her portfolio. "So, what are the chances that on the way back I can talk you into stopping at an Italian restaurant for lunch?"

"I had peanut butter crackers for breakfast. I'd say the chances are pretty good." He touched a palm to the small of her back, sending a tingling warmth down her spine. "Let's go see if we can find Mr. Orson."

They walked toward a two-story brick house that had been converted into an office building. Just before they reached the front door Reid bent his head. "By the way," he said, his voice pitched low. "You look amazing."

She stopped, and stared up at him. When tears filled her eyes his face went slack. He tugged her off to the side. "Shit. I mean, damn. I mean, I didn't mean to upset you."

Mortified, she pressed her hands to her face. But the tears kept coming. "I'm sorry," she choked out, and vowed to get even with that guy at the Cooper's booth who'd reintroduced her to mascara. "I'm sorry. It's just...not since my husband..."

He gathered her into his arms. "I should have said it sooner."

"It's not your fault." She pushed away, and fumbled in her purse for a tissue. "Go on in," she whispered, dabbing at her eyes. "I'll be right there."

He didn't want to leave her. She could see it in his face. But he was smart enough to sense that if he didn't walk away he might have a full-fledged meltdown on his hands. He stroked a finger along her jawline, then went inside.

Five minutes later she joined him at the reception desk. Thankfully he didn't ask any questions. He peered at her closely and gave an approving nod.

"Orson's waiting in the conference room. Something came up, so we're down to fifteen minutes." Not a hint of reproach in his voice. For some reason that made her want to start crying all over again.

What on earth was wrong with her?

The president of Beryl Growers, Inc., a thin, restless man with lots of black hair and big white teeth, offered them coffee and sat them down at a table Parker would have loved to have in her dining room. He settled across from them and gave Parker an appreciative look, then turned to Reid, all business. Parker caught herself before she rolled her eyes.

Maybe she didn't like the table, after all.

"So, Mr. MacFarland." Mr. Orson tugged at his cuffs and sat back. "You're interested in starting a growers' network?"

"I made the appointment, Mr. Orson, but Mrs. Dean here is the actual business owner."

"I see." He swiveled his chair in her direction and showed his teeth in all of their blinding glory. "What can I do for you, Mrs. Dean?"

"I own Thistle Hill Growers. We supply annuals to supermarkets and independent garden centers. Corporal MacFarland here did some research online and recommended I look into network growing as a way of expanding my business." She fought to keep the skepticism out of her tone. Judging from Reid's wry expression, she didn't quite succeed.

Mr. Orson swung back to Reid and sat forward. "*Corporal* MacFarland. I didn't realize. Army?" Reid nodded and the man slapped the table. "My son and I were just discussing the Army. He wants to enlist. The kid's gung ho on getting to Iraq. Told him he better keep on the straight and narrow or they'd throw him in the brig. You been to Iraq?"

Parker hid a smile. It would be tough for the kid to end up in the brig, unless he joined the Navy instead. Of course, there was a time when she herself hadn't known there was a difference between a post and a base.

Reid gave a curt nod and picked up a company brochure. Mr. Orson didn't get the message.

"Good for you, son. Good for you. What a minute. Corporal?" He squinted at Reid. "Man your age? What are you, thirty? Thirty-one? Got a late start, did you? What's your specialty?"

"I'm a machinist."

The clock was ticking. Parker cleared her throat. "Mr. Orson —"

"So you repair weapons? You build them, too? I bet those generals fall all over themselves, clamoring for limited edition hardware —"

Parker set her coffee cup down on the polished tabletop with a loud *clack*. "About the growers' network, Mr. Orson." When he turned toward her she gave him her best smile, though it was nothing compared to his. "Can you please tell me how that works? How you start one up?"

"Oh, certainly, certainly." He looked back at Reid, drummed his fingers and sighed. "First you have to find associate growers. Decide how many you want to start with, what you want them to produce, then get out there and recruit. Just like the Army." He gave Reid a nod. "Inexperienced operators are a plus because you can teach them to do things the way you want them done. It's perfect for stay-at-home moms."

"What would an associate grower need to get started?"

"A greenhouse, some training and a whole lot of plants. You provide the training and the starter plants. Pot 'em, tag 'em, ship 'em out. Like soldiers headed to the CZ." He leaned toward Parker. "That's 'combat zone.'"

Reid coughed into his fist, but Parker already knew Mr. Orson had pulled that one out of his butt.

"Some of your growers might want to specialize. The more variety, the better—helps you keep up with demand and offer more product options to your customers. Most network leads check in with their growers on a weekly basis. Get sort of a mission status, you might say."

Uh-huh.

"What if there are challenges?" Somehow Reid managed to keep a straight face.

"You mean, what if things go pear-shaped? That's part of the growers' agreement. You're not obligated to buy any substandard product."

Parker set aside her pen. "So we need to find associate growers, set them up with training and product, and work on having an actual market for when that product is ready."

"Bravo Zulu, Mrs. Dean."

No sense in telling the man he'd made another switch from Army to Navy lingo. "Anything else I should know?"

"Bottom line is, with a growers' network, instead of investing in equipment and greenhouses, you're investing in people. Just like—"

"The Army." Parker and Reid finished the sentence together.

"Affirmative." Mr. Orson beamed. He stood, and clapped a hand on Reid's shoulder. "What's it really like over there? My son says you soldiers live in tent cities, with gymnasiums and pools, but I told him it's all sand and diesel and bloo — "

Parker jumped to her feet. "We really appreciate your time, Mr. Orson, but we shouldn't keep you from your next appointment." She bent at the waist and leaned in, careful not to look directly into his teeth. "The corporal doesn't like to talk about his tour. PTSD."

"But — " their host blinked " — surely they wouldn't send him back. Not with PTSD."

"He only thinks he has it."

"I see. Certainly. That's okay, then." He showed off his teeth again. "Thanks for coming by. Happy to help out. Anytime." He shook Parker's hand and saluted Reid. "Fair winds and following seas, soldier."

* * *

THE INSTANT THEY HIT the parking lot Reid yanked at his tie. "Maybe next time you could let me decide what kind of condition I have."

Parker wasn't sure if he was mad at her or Mr. Orson. Or both. "You're angry that I picked PTSD? And to think I was considering syphilis."

He rounded on her, and she froze. Apparently she'd said the wrong thing.

"I get what you wanted to do. I get the guy was being a chauvinistic moron. But PTSD is *not* a joking matter. Soldiers kill themselves over that shit."

He jammed his hand in his pocket, wrenched out his key fob and stalked over to the Jeep. Parker followed, remorse slowing her feet.

"I'm sorry," she said soberly. "I wasn't thinking. I saw your face when he asked about conditions over there and I just wanted to make him stop talking." He reached for the handle and she leaned against the door, blocking him. "You lost someone. To PTSD."

He didn't say anything, but the muscle ticking in his jaw gave him away. After a long while his gaze found hers, and his shoulders relaxed. "I'm sorry, too. You had no way of knowing. And Orson…well, Orson is —"

"Annoying." She hesitated. "Thank you. For setting this up."

"But?"

"This isn't what I wanted. It isn't what Tim wanted."

"He didn't want you to succeed?" She glared, and Reid raised his palms. "Personality disorders aside, Orson is a successful businessman. His advice could mean the difference between keeping your business and losing it."

"In your opinion."

"You're not going to pursue this, are you?"

She pushed away from the Jeep. "Tim and I had a plan. Changing it wouldn't honor his memory."

"Why do you believe you owe him? Because he's dead and you're alive?" He was shaking his head. "Why did you even come with me today?" She dropped her gaze and he grunted. "It was Harris, wasn't it? He guilted you into it."

"He didn't *guilt* me." She bit her lip. "He dared me." She turned away from the frustration on his face and fumbled at the door handle. "We'd better get going."

Reid didn't say anything, just reached around and opened the door for her, then walked around to the driver's side. He hesitated and slid around in his seat to face her, left arm resting on the steering wheel.

"I need to tell you something." He must have seen the guardedness in her face because he set his jaw and added, "About Nat." He tapped the steering wheel. "She wants to be my pen pal."

"She what?"

"She asked if she could write to me. While I'm in theater."

Parker felt an ache, deep in her chest. *Oh, Nat.* "What did you say?"

"That she should check with you."

Parker lifted her gaze from his hand, where it gripped the steering wheel. "Then I'll leave it up to the two of you."

"You'd let her write to me?" She nodded. "Because you don't mind if she keeps in touch? Or because you think she'll eventually get bored and stop?"

No mention of a possibility that he wouldn't be going back overseas in the first place. "The second one," she said.

He nodded once. Then without another word he reached for his seat belt.

* * *

LATE MONDAY AFTERNOON, REID finally tracked Nat down at the picnic table. Or more specifically, at the large oak tree that stood ten yards south of the picnic table. He found her sitting cross-legged behind the oak. And he wouldn't have managed that if he hadn't spotted the tip of a sneaker the color of Pepto Bismol.

He rapped on the bark with his knuckles, clicking his tongue against the roof of his mouth to imitate knocking sounds.

Jesus. No wonder kids thought adults were morons.

She didn't look up from her book. He didn't blame her. But he was under orders.

"Your mom sent me to find you," he said. "Did you forget you'd promised to wash the dog?"

"Do you mind? I'm reading."

"I'm no Ellery Queen, but that much I figured out."

She squinted up at him. "Who's Ellery Queen?"

"Who's—" He stumbled back a few steps, hand over his heart. "I can't believe what I just heard. And you call yourself a mystery fan."

"So who is she?"

"He. And I'll tell you later. Right now your mom's looking for you."

"Whatever."

Okay, so reminding the kid of her responsibilities wasn't going to get her back to the house. Especially when he was the one doing it. He hitched up his jeans and crouched. She gave him a sideways glance but didn't shift away.

"Know one of the best parts about reading a good book?"

"The quiet?"

Smart aleck. "The suspense. And I know you like suspense. Like when you have to put a book down just when someone's about to get coshed on the head or expose the killer. You really want to keep reading but you have to stop because it's time for lunch or you need to go to the bathroom. But then you don't really mind after all because it draws out the anticipation. You get extra time to look forward to finding out what happens next."

"Can I get back to my book now?"

He slapped his palms against his knees and stood. "Let me put it this way. Wouldn't it be better to put that book aside, do your chore and have the freedom to pick the book back up later, rather than have your reading privileges suspended for a week? Again?"

"Who told you?"

"How else would you punish a reader?" She scowled. A lot of that going around. Reid kicked lightly at the bottom of the nearest Pepto-Bismol-colored shoe. "Tell you what. You let me borrow that book when you're done and I'll help you wash the dog."

"For real?"

"Hey. I don't joke about Agatha Christie."

*　*　*

REID HAD PICTURED GIVING Chance a bath in the house. In the bathtub, where the inevitable mess could be contained. But Parker had left strict instructions before heading out with Harris on a delivery—she did not want a waterlogged dog anywhere near bedroom linens or carpets. Or furniture. Or clothing. So Reid positioned a rust-rimmed washtub close to Hut One's water hookup while Nat rounded up towels and a girly shampoo no male dog should have to suffer.

Despite the chill in the air he and Nat both wore shorts, and neither wore shoes. It didn't take long for them to get into the spirit of things. They fashioned Chance a bubble turban, a bubble tutu and a bubble beard, and when the Lab jumped up and down and splashed Reid, making him swallow a mouthful of soapy water, Nat laughed so hard she dropped to the ground and rolled in the grass. That was when Reid made his fatal error. He bent over Nat and tickled her, gave her a minute to catch her breath and tickled again. Meanwhile, neither of them had control of the dog.

So, when Chance spotted a rabbit, there was no one to hold him back. With an eager bark the Lab leaped out of the tub and took off, trailing bubbles. Reid and Nat looked up to see a rabbit zigzagging across the field and Chance in close pursuit.

"Chance! Chance, no!"

They gave chase, but it was ridiculous to try to herd a dog who had more energy than an entire squad carrying two-day passes to a red-light district. Reid stopped running. He sucked air, and when Nat caught up he motioned for a time-out.

"He'll keep running if we keep chasing," he managed. "Let's wait for him to get bored. He'll come back and we'll try again."

They stood in the middle of the yard, soaked to the skin, chests heaving, bits of grass and clover stuck to their bare legs. Then Nat gave a shout and pointed. The rabbit was bouncing across the yard. Chance couldn't be far behind. Then Reid saw something that punched the rest of the air from his lungs.

The rabbit was headed for the greenhouse. Oh, shit. Had he shut the door?

Oh, no. Oh, no, no, no, no, no. *The delivery.* Parker had taken on an extra-large job with the sole intention of paying a fistful of overdue utility bills.

He exploded into a run. Chance burst into view, and with a gleeful howl scrambled after the rabbit into Hut One. Reid ran harder, but he hadn't even hit the door when he heard the first clatter. Followed quickly by a series of thuds.

Son of a *bitch.*

He dashed though the open door and almost fell to his knees. The inside of the greenhouse looked like a tornado had ripped through it.

Damn it. No way in hell they'd make the —

There was a growl, and an ominous ripping sound at the far end of the hut. So much for the new plastic. Reid wiped at the sweat dripping down his face. He inhaled and went after the Lab.

Dog first. Damage assessment later.

After he'd tied Chance up by the tub, awaiting another bath, he and Nat walked the greenhouse from one end to the next. Or maybe "maneuvered" was a better word. Two of the benches had collapsed and flats of geraniums had toppled to the floor. Bright red, pink and purple petals, bits of damp soil and pieces of black plastic littered the concrete. Most of the planters and baskets they'd stacked in the corner in prep for delivery lay on their sides, contents half in and half out.

Reid set his jaw. Some help he'd turned out to be. Once Parker got a look at this catastrophe he'd be lucky if she didn't fire him on the spot.

Did this have to happen now, just when she'd begun to see the benefits of depending on someone else?

Nat turned in a circle, and her sniffling graduated to a full-fledged wail. "My mom is going to kill us!"

"Not you, kid." He put an arm around her shoulders. "This one's on me." All of it. And to fix it he'd have to pull a miracle out of his ass. He blew out a breath. "Okay, time to embrace the suck. Let's get this cleaned up. See how much we can salvage."

They ended up saving a lot more than Reid had expected. Still, half the delivery had been damaged. Along with some of the tubing for the drip irrigation system, and a four-foot section of plastic Reid assumed the rabbit had escaped through. He'd jerry-rigged the two benches Chance had collided with but the fix was only temporary. They'd have to be replaced.

He needed to make another list.

He was on one knee, tying up the last garbage bag, when he called to Natalie, who was double-checking the drip hoses. "Ready to go? I need to get in touch with Gallahan ASAP."

She didn't answer. He followed her stricken gaze to the doorway.

Where her mother stood. Reid got to his feet, but he felt as if his stomach had stayed level with his knees. Parker was paler than any redhead had a right to be and she had that same look on her face, that same devastated mix of anger and loss she'd had when he'd first introduced himself.

Her gaze traveled from him to the corner where the precious delivery had been prepped, to the bare spots on the benches, to where Nat stood wide-eyed and wet cheeked, to the collection of garbage bags gathered around him, and back up to his face. Her expression remained carefully controlled but there was no mistaking the grief and resignation in her eyes. Shame soured his stomach.

Parker held out her arms and Nat scuttled into them. Reid wished he had the freedom to tuck both of them into his own embrace.

"Don't worry," he said. "I'll fix this."

A shuffling sound came from the corner. They all turned, and watched a sleek brown rabbit hop out from under the end bench. He paused, nose quivering, then scooted outside.

12

REID FOUND PARKER BACK at the scene of the crime, in the dark, save for a flashlight she'd tucked into the bib of her overalls. She was kneeling in front of the damaged plastic, a length of duct tape between her teeth. He waited until she'd smoothed it in place before he spoke.

"I plan on replacing that entire section for you."

She stiffened. She stood with extra careful motions and carried the duct tape to an open drawer. She tucked it inside and freed the flashlight from her pocket. Finally she turned to face him, the beam directed at the floor.

"I know. But in the meantime I don't want that rabbit sneaking back in to finish the job."

He winced. "Any particular reason you're doing this in the dark?"

"Harris is up at the house with Nat. He thinks I'm relaxing in the bathtub."

"I'm sorry I took that away from you."

"The bathtub?"

Good try, but her tone was flat. "The ability to relax."

"I'm not sure I ever had it." She rubbed at her arms, as if she were cold. "I'm glad you're back. We need to talk."

She was going to ask him to leave.

His entire body clenched. He stepped closer, the jingle of the truck keys loud in the insulated silence of the hut. "I bought replacement flats back from that supermarket we delivered to on Friday. I knew you wouldn't want to provide any plants for tomorrow's delivery but yours. They said they'd take more when you have them. They were fine with it." He cleared his throat. "I left them on the truck, figured it'd save us time in the morning." No response. "Parker —"

"It's late. Either you drove two miles an hour both ways or you had trouble with the truck."

"I got hold of Pete. He took care of it. We're all set for the morning."

She clicked off the flashlight and set it on the tabletop. The late-night dimness settled back inside the greenhouse. Weak tendrils of moonlight stroked the plants, the floor, her cheek.

"Thank you for doing that," she said. Her voice was tight.

Still angry, then. And why the hell wouldn't she be? The notched edges of the keys bit into his fingers. "It was the least I could do." Where had he heard that before? Maybe it really was time to get his ass back to Kentucky. "I am sorry."

Her hands were restless, dipping into pockets, rubbing her arms, smoothing creases from the worn denim of her overalls. "What happened was an accident," she said.

A surge of relief nearly melted Reid's bones. "It was carelessness. My carelessness. I should have shut the door. Nat's not to blame —"

"No. I'm talking about...what happened to Tim."

He went still. Not angry, then. Hurting. She was in pain. Something crowded the air from his lungs but he didn't really give a damn because he was listening too hard to breathe.

"The m-missile. It was an accident." The rawness in her voice set off an ache, deep in his chest. He moved, and she moved, and his arms went around her and he pulled her close.

"I needed someone to blame," she said, her voice muffled by his shoulder. "I needed it to make sense and —" She pressed her forehead into his neck, her palms curled against his chest. "I'm so sorry. It was an accident. I know it was an accident." As sobs buffeted her body, jagged puffs of breath warmed his skin and he felt the cascading wet of her tears. And as he tightened his hold on her, something inside him loosened.

* * *

PARKER CRIED FOR HERSELF, for Nat, for Tim, and for the man who was comforting her, the man who would soon be heading back into the same hell that had claimed her husband. When her tears slowed she pulled away long enough to wipe her face on her shirtsleeve, then burrowed in again. Without a word he widened his stance and tightened his arms around her. His heat seeped through her clothing and into her skin. It radiated throughout her body, banishing the chill that had long since settled in her bones. Her legs started to hurt after standing for so long on the concrete floor but she didn't want to let go of Reid any more than a four-year-old Nat had wanted to let go of her Winnie the Pooh blanket.

He seemed to sense what she needed. He guided her over to the bench along the wall and sat with his back to the corner, tucking her in beside him.

She didn't have time for this. And she didn't have the energy to deal with the consequences of blubbering all over a man she'd treated like compost since the moment he'd introduced himself. Still she couldn't bring herself to move away from the truest comfort she'd felt in…forever.

"I'm sorry," she choked out. "I'm not usually so pitiful."

"Don't apologize," he said, his voice harsh. "You're the strongest woman I know."

She'd had to be.

Still had to be.

"Nat," she said, and pushed upright. Immediately he let her go and she couldn't help feeling disappointed.

What a hypocrite.

"Feeling better?" he murmured, and the deep timbre of his voice made her shiver. She managed a nod and he stood, a little stiffly. "I'm sure Nat's asleep by now. I'll walk you back to the house."

"I'll be fine. But thank you. For everything."

"You're welcome."

She fiddled with the metal button on one of her straps. "We're not... I'm not..."

"I know," he said quietly. "Understanding is not forgiving."

That wasn't what she'd wanted to say. But his version had the same desired effect—distance. So why did it bother her, that he assumed she still couldn't forgive him? Because she didn't. Forgive him. Despite—or maybe because of—the physical awareness growing between them.

Then again, did any of it really matter? Less than two weeks and he would be gone. Parker bit at the inside of her lip. The problem was it did matter. He was headed back overseas and that bothered her as much as it relieved her.

Yet another reason she really had to get back to the house.

"I'll see you in the morning," she said, then hesitated. "We'll need to do an early inventory, just to make sure we have what we need for the delivery. When you get here come on up to the kitchen. I'll have breakfast ready."

*   *   *

EUGENIA SMOOTHED HER DAMP palms down the sides of her skirt and tried a smile. But her lips were quivering too hard to cooperate. Harris opened the door, and the unabashed welcome in his eyes loosened the tears she'd been fighting all day. Somehow she managed to hold them back.

"Genie." His expression slipped into its usual scowl. "What's going on?"

"I know it's early. I wanted to catch you before you left for work."

He stepped back from the door. "Want some coffee?"

That time she did manage a smile. "No, thanks. Your coffee's not much better than your lemonade."

"I'll ignore that, but only because you look so pretty."

She blinked. Usually getting a compliment out of Harris was as likely as finding Veuve Clicquot at the local Stop & Shop. She murmured a response, and headed for the nearest chair. The thick odor of coffee and something else, something not breakfast-related, did ugly, threatening things to her stomach.

She swallowed, and looked around. "I'm sorry, but what is that *smell?*"

His face went red. "I was cleanin' out the fridge. Hold on a sec."

Eugenia watched as he opened a window. Lord help the woman who took him on. It wouldn't be her, of course. Once she told him what she'd done he'd retract his offer to pick up where they'd left off.

But after what he'd said about honesty, she had no choice.

He sat down across from her. "Now suppose you tell me why you came by this mornin'."

"I have something to tell you and I'm rather nervous about it."

He paled. "Don't tell me you're sick, too."

She shook her head and he sank back against the sofa cushions. "Now I know what Parker went through," he muttered. His gaze sharpened on her face. "If you're plannin' to continue that conversation we had in your shop, there's no need to be nervous."

"That's not it."

He exhaled. Too bad she couldn't take any joy in the disappointment spreading across his face. "Then what is it?" he asked.

"It's about Kerry."

"Kerry? You mean, my daughter Kerry?" She nodded and he frowned. "But you've never even met her."

"We've talked on the phone."

"You called Kerry?"

"She called me."

He was starting to get the picture. Slowly he pushed to his feet. "When?" he barked. His face was stern, his stare merciless. She didn't know what he'd done in the Marines but if he'd been a drill sergeant he'd doubtless been legendary.

"Two or three months ago. You and I had only been out together three or four times."

"How the hell did she get your number?"

Eugenia shrugged. "I assume she looked it up. You must have told her about me."

"Why would I do that?"

Hurt struck, swift and sure. She changed her guess from drill sergeant to Marine sniper.

"Oh, I don't know, Harris. Maybe you called your daughter to say hello or she called her father to say hello and somewhere during the conversation you happened to mention you were dating someone. Someone who at one point in time actually seemed to make you happy. Do you think that's possible?"

His expression relented. "I didn't mean I wouldn't tell anyone about you. I meant I wouldn't mention your name."

"She called me, Harris." Eugenia spoke through gritted teeth. "She knew my name."

"She's a smart kid. Maybe I mentioned you own a store." He grimaced. "I'm sorry, Genie. She hit you up, didn't she?" When she nodded, he dropped back onto the couch. "You shoulda told me."

"She asked me not to. She was embarrassed."

"For Pete's sake, she's a stranger to you. Why would you feel you had to promise her anything?" His head jerked up, and all the color that had left his face earlier surged back. "You didn't give her money, did you?"

"As a matter of fact—" she really could use a bottle of that Veuve Clicquot right about now "—I did."

*   *   *

REID MIGHT NOT HAVE heard the knock if he hadn't already been awake. Who could sleep with all that rain slapping at the windows? He desperately needed some shut-eye, though—after that all-day delivery and then a marathon softball practice, he was bone-tired. Parker had to be feeling worse—he suspected she'd been up baking muffins all night, probably worried they wouldn't make the delivery after all. But they had, and she'd walked away with a good-size check.

Another knock, stronger this time. He tossed aside his book and glanced at the clock beside the bed. Nearly eleven. Had to be Gallahan on the hunt for a drinking buddy. Or maybe he needed a spotter. Either way he was on his own.

He slid on a pair of flip-flops and was shaking his head when he opened the door. "No way I'm going out in this—"

But it wasn't Gallahan who waited on the other side. It was Natalie Dean. She stood huddled on the mat, skinny arms wrapped around her waist, hair plastered to her skull, jeans and pink-striped pajama top soaked through. She was quaking like a Chihuahua caught in a blizzard.

What the hell?

He reached out and tugged her inside. "What's going on?"

"I c-c-can't find Chance," she said, through chattering teeth, and he closed his eyes briefly before shutting the door and guiding her over to the nearest chair. He pulled the top blanket off the bed and wrapped it around her, left her long enough to grab a towel from the bathroom. When he stepped back into the room she was rocking back and forth in the chair, gaze locked on the toes of her sodden sneakers.

"Someone took him," she said, her voice full of anguish. "I know someone took him 'cause he'd never run away."

Reid moved behind her chair. Using the towel, he pressed the wet from the ends of her hair, then fashioned a lopsided turban. Her shoulders shook, and not just from the cold.

He crouched in front of the chair and rearranged the blanket. "He was probably just chasing a rabbit and followed him a little too far from home. When did you last see him?"

"This m-morning. He walked me to the bus, like he always does."

And Parker hadn't been around to notice the Lab missing. "How did you get here?"

"My b-b-bike."

Holy hell. He forced his imagination to shut down, not wanting to dwell on all the horrible things that could have happened to her on the way. He had to ask the question, no matter how stupid. "Your mom know where you are?"

Lips pressed tight, she shook her head.

"Nat, why didn't you tell her?"

"I heard her crying in her room." She ran her hand under her nose. "I didn't want to bother her."

He swore silently. "I need to call her. Let her know where you are. Okay?"

"Ask her if Chance is th-there."

Reid prayed that he would be. He handed Nat a box of tissues and reached for the phone.

Parker answered on the first ring and he could tell from the breathless panic in her voice that she'd already discovered Nat missing.

"She's here," he said.

A pause, and a quavering inhale. "Thank God." Another pause, and a low-pitched *oomph,* and he pictured her sitting on the floor, forehead in her hand. "Is she all right?"

"She's fine. She's cold and wet and missing her dog, but she's okay."

"I swear to God she'll be twenty before I let her back on that bicycle."

Nat stood, and the blanket slipped to the floor. "Is he there?"

Parker must have heard because she sighed. Reid shook his head at Nat. The child collapsed back into the chair with a wail, and the chair groaned right back at her.

"I'm on my way," Parker said. Reid heard the scrape and jingle of snatched-up car keys. "Does she need anything? Ask her if she needs anything."

The kid didn't need anything but her dog, but Reid did as Parker asked. He held the phone away from his mouth. "Do you need anything?"

"Yeeeeees," Nat wailed, knees gathered to her chest. "I need Chaaaaaaance." She dropped her head to her knees and sobbed.

Helpless sympathy clogged Reid's throat so it was just as well Parker repeated that she was on her way and disconnected.

He stood with one hand on the back of his neck, the other on his hip, and watched a little girl's heart breaking. *Damn it.* He swung around and grabbed the single-serving-size pot from the coffeemaker.

"I'll make you some tea."

"R-Reid?" He swung back to her. "W-will you go look for him?" She was leaning forward in the chair, hands clutching at each other in her lap, eyes as big and round as his beret. "Please?"

"It's raining, Nat. Hard."

"He's scared. I know he's scared."

"He's a smart dog. He's probably holed up somewhere safe —"

"I know he isn't!"

" — waiting out the rain. How about in the morning we —"

She jumped up from the chair. "That's too late! He needs me. He'll wander out in the road and he'll get run over and he'll die."

"Nat, calm down."

"I want my dog. I want Chance."

Reid set aside the pot and hugged her close, rubbing his hand up and down her damp back. A distant symphony of drips told him the room was far from weatherproof and he huffed out a soundless laugh.

"I'll look for him," he said. "I'll go as soon as your mom gets here."

"Thank you, Reid." She smiled up at him, her face full of hope and gratitude, and he felt suddenly hollow. She wouldn't look that way after she learned the truth about how her father died.

Headlights flashed through the blinds as a car pulled up outside the room. Reid cleared his throat and stepped out of Nat's embrace, opened the door before Parker had a chance to knock. She rushed past him, shoving back her bright yellow hood. She ran straight to Nat and gathered her into her arms. Reid stepped outside and gently closed the door.

A silvery black curtain of rain waited, just beyond the sidewalk, teasing him with needling sprays of moisture. He rolled his eyes and tried not to think about how wet he was about to get. The kid knew easy prey when she saw it.

He shivered in his short-sleeved T. Then he spotted the bicycle, and drew in a ragged breath. Nat had ridden her bike five miles. In the rain. On a busy road. All the ways that ride could have gone wrong turned his knees to rubber.

The door opened behind him and Parker came out, Natalie wrapped around her in a four-point hug. She hustled Nat into the front passenger seat of her Camry, turned up the heat, then joined Reid under the overhang. Her lips curved but it was a sad excuse for a smile. He could see the panic banked in her eyes, figured once she got Nat tucked up in bed the shakes would start.

"I don't know what to say. Except thank you."

He made do with a nod, since he didn't trust his own voice. She reached for his shoulder, didn't actually touch him but made a face at the condition of his T-shirt.

"Nat said you promised to look for Chance. You don't have to do that."

"I gave my word."

"You'll catch pneumonia," she said, and there was no mistaking the concern in her eyes.

"Nat will need to know her dog is safe."

She started to say something, then stopped and shook her head. "I'll get her bike later. Will you check in with us?"

He said he would and she turned away. He watched until the Toyota's taillights disappeared into the murk, then headed back inside to grab a jacket, a flashlight and his key fob. Outside his room he hesitated. Why suffer alone?

Less than a minute later Gallahan opened the door in boxers and a tee, a newspaper in one hand, a glass of what looked like low-fat milk in the other. A pair of reading glasses was perched on his nose. Reid grinned. "Did I wake you up, Grandpa?"

"Why are you at my door, MacFarland?"

"I need your help."

"Loan shark, jealous husband, or dead body?"

Reid suppressed a flinch. "Missing dog."

"Just as bad." Gallahan turned from the door, gulping his milk with one hand and reaching for his jeans with the other.

Their strategy was to Jeep-creep three klicks north of Parker's house, then three south, calling Chance's name and hoping they could hear barking over the pounding of the rain and the growl of the engine. If they didn't find him they'd go for five klicks.

Reid spent the first five minutes after they started their search defending his use of the term *klick*. Gallahan conceded only after pulling out his cell and doing an internet search.

No luck north. While Reid maneuvered a U-turn Gallahan sat back from the window and ran both hands through his damp hair.

"Tell me again why you promised you'd find this dog?"

"I didn't. I promised I'd look for him."

Gallahan grunted. "Something going on between you and Parker Dean?" Reid shot him a look and Gallahan held up his hands. "Just checking. Didn't figure there could be, after that 'Mrs. Dean' bit at the bar." Reid didn't comment and Gallahan sighed. "At least tell me how many beers I'm earning."

"Help me find the dog and I'll buy you a damned keg."

Gallahan shot up in his seat and Reid shook his head. "Seriously? Ever consider AA?"

"Go fuck yourself. Hear that?"

Reid braked and listened. A faint yapping over the drum of rain. He squinted into the darkness.

Gallahan pointed. "It's coming from that abandoned house."

"Or the woods behind it." Reid pulled off the road and grabbed his flashlight. "Let's find out."

"I know this is a hell of a time to bring this up —" Gallahan pressed a button and his window whirred upward " —but please tell me this dog doesn't bite."

They tramped through a field of tall grass — no way they could find what used to be the driveway. The dark and the rain hid the ruts and the groundhog holes — they took turns stumbling and cursing. The closer they got to the house, the louder the barking. And the more insistent.

"At least we don't have to go traipsing through the woods." Gallahan picked himself up after tripping over a limb and landing on one knee. He shook his head at the mud that caked his palms and wiped his hands on his jeans. "Not sure we'd survive it."

But the Lab wasn't in the house after all. They found him in the side yard, in a crater left by the root-ball of a downed tree. A stray root had threaded through Chance's collar, holding him prisoner. When Reid and Gallahan walked up on him, his tail wagged so hard his entire body vibrated.

"I'll do it. Can't get any dirtier." Gallahan clambered down into the hole, worked the collar—and a wet, wriggling Chance—free and passed the dog up to Reid.

Reid struggled with the sudden weight, wondering what the hell Parker had been feeding the pooch. "He's lucky he didn't choke himself."

"What makes him lucky is two brainless chumps willing to sacrifice their warm, dry beds and the Playboy Channel just to find his happy doggy ass."

Back at the Jeep Reid handed Chance over. Mud went everywhere as Gallahan shifted the squirming dog in his arms. Reid grimaced and shut the door. Guess he'd spend an hour or so the next day scraping mud out of the passenger seat. Considering what Nat had gone through, a little vacuuming wouldn't kill him.

He settled in behind the wheel, started the Jeep, then looked over and grinned at the sloppy pink tongue that wasn't missing an inch of Gallahan's face. "By the way, you ever gonna tell me your story?"

Gallahan shot him an incredulous look as he dodged Chance's kisses. "You gotta be kidding me, man." He clamped a hand around the Lab's muzzle. "How about I give you a rain check?"

Reid laughed and slapped on the wipers.

It was going on one o'clock in the morning by the time they got to Parker's. She met them at the front door, and Reid knew he wouldn't ever forget the look of relief and delight on her face when she realized what Gallahan had in his arms.

"Chance," she cried, and laughed when the mass of dirt and dog hair launched itself toward her fluffy yellow robe.

Gallahan fought to keep him off her but the Lab refused to cooperate. "He'll be okay. Got his collar snagged on a tree root."

Parker struggled to keep Chance from barreling past her into the house. "Nat will be so excited. And grateful. I know she'll want to thank you both in person, but it'll have to wait. I gave her a hot bath and put her to bed as soon as we got home."

Reid wondered how many washings it would take to put the yellow back into Parker's robe. "Can we help you get him inside?"

"Thanks, I've got him. Just let me stash him in the laundry room and I'll be right back."

She disappeared down the hallway, a bedraggled Chance in tow. Rain thudded against the boards on the porch, and from the waterlogged ditches bordering the road a family of frogs sang their low-pitched song.

"I've had worse dates," Gallahan said, and despite Reid's glare launched into an account of a blind date with a woman who refused to eat anything except rice cakes and cheddar cheese and kept her toenail clippings in a jewelry box on her nightstand. No matter what Reid threatened, he wouldn't shut up.

When Parker reappeared she'd exchanged her mud-streaked robe for a pair of striped pajamas, oversize and perfectly respectable but made of some slinky material that had Reid's fingers itching. Gallahan must have decided Reid needed more exposure to women's nightwear than he did. Or maybe he didn't care for stripes. Or possibly Reid's threats had finally started to register, because the motel owner backed up and worked his way down the steps.

"Listen, it's cold out here. I'm going to go sit in the Jeep. Probably turn the radio on. Loud. So loud I'll never be able to hear —"

Reid swung around. Gallahan disappeared. Reid turned back. On the other side of the screen door, Parker had her arms crossed, and she couldn't seem to find a place to rest her gaze.

"You all right?" he asked.

"Thanks to you."

"And Gallahan."

"And Joe."

"How about Nat?"

"So far so good. I'll check on her through the night." She started to blink, and then sniffle. When she swiped at her nose with the back of her hand he opened the screen door, kept it open with his foot.

"What can I do?" he murmured. He longed to hold her, but she'd have to make the first move.

* * *

PARKER DIDN'T KNOW HOW to answer him. She wanted...heck, she didn't know what she wanted. Okay, wait, what she wanted was someone to hold her—no, she wanted *Reid* to hold her, because he'd done it so well before. But that wasn't an option. Simply not something she could consider. At all.

Ever.

So she gave a tight shrug. "It's just...she's lost so much already. I was afraid we'd have to add Chance to the list." She looked down, but not staring at his chest didn't stop her from thinking about it. Stepping into his arms wouldn't be difficult. He stood less than two feet away, and he was holding the screen door at an inviting angle, with just enough space for her to squeeze through... .

Don't be an idiot, Parker Anne.

She choked out a laugh. "I'm okay."

"Sure?"

She forced a slow nod. Then her gaze met his. God in heaven. Why did he have to look so worried? Her chin wobbled. She told herself she swayed forward only because she wanted to hide her face. But then he reached out and she reached out and he was holding her.

And it was lovely.

She flattened first her palms, then her cheek, against his rain-soaked shirt, and closed her eyes. For several moments they stood like that, with the screen door half-open, Nat sleeping above their heads and Joe waiting in the Jeep. But those thoughts barely took shape before they vanished. His warmth surrounded her and soothed her, like a blanket fresh from the dryer. It was wrong, she knew it was wrong, to find solace in this soldier's embrace. But it felt so darned good to be tucked into the safety of a man's strength.

From a distance she heard Chance whine. Reluctantly she stirred and opened her eyes. Her teeth pinched at her lower lip. As hard as it had been to seek Reid's comfort, it would be that much harder to face him now that she'd pushed her way into his arms. Then she shook off the thought.

She had more urgent things to worry about.

When had the rise and fall of his chest quickened beneath her cheek? Her hands curled into fists as she registered the tension in his muscles. Felt the scorch of his hands on her shoulder blades, pressing her into him.

Her nipples bloomed into awareness. Or maybe it was the damp cold of his thin jacket, soaking her pajamas.

Or maybe she should stop kidding herself.

Desire stroked at the pit of her belly, tempting her hips forward. She fought the temptation, and moved slowly away from his heat.

He let her step back but kept his hands on her arms. "Feel better?" His voice sounded frayed.

She nodded, quivered, fought the impulse to burrow once more into his arms.

"The hug helped?"

She nodded again. If he didn't let go of her soon, she'd end up plastered against him a second time. Like a giant, needy, extra sticky Band-Aid.

"Glad to be of service." Out of the gloom, a flash of white teeth. "But I can do better."

Her belly tingled, and she held her breath as his hands stroked up her arms and over her shoulders to her neck. He tugged her close again and cupped the back of her head. His thumbs stroked her jaw line, and she could do nothing more than return his focused gaze and shudder.

This was so not a good idea.

"What do you think?" he husked. "Try for better?"

Try for sanity, Parker Anne. Sanity. She palmed his impressive biceps and braced herself to push away. Then he dipped his head, and his warm, firm lips replaced the fingers exploring the hollow behind her ear. The touch of his mouth fueled the need that simmered in her belly. Her head fell back, and her fingers curled into the damp sleeves of his jacket. The pounding of the rain echoed the mad beating of her heart.

His lips moved from her ear to her jaw to her cheek. The word *no* hovered on her tongue. Where was her self-respect? Hadn't she just lectured herself about this very thing? Then he murmured something, and the sexy rasp of his voice sent heat zinging to her core. She wet her lips, licking the unspoken rejection away, and turned her head. Their mouths collided. She parted her lips and his tongue found hers and her knees turned to melted butter.

She'd been craving this for days. Night after night she'd imagined kissing him, tasting him, surrendering to a hunger she'd never welcomed but couldn't wait to satisfy. Her fantasies hadn't involved the front porch. Or the rain. Or her faded striped pajamas.

Nor had she imagined how special she'd feel, how feminine and powerful.

Their tongues tangled as his hands skimmed up over the material covering her hips and rib cage, and trailed inward to cup her aching breasts. The sensation robbed her of breath. She wrenched her mouth from his and buried her face in his neck, panting. His thumbs scooted upward, and her nipples tightened with need.

A high-pitched, yipping sound forced its way into her consciousness. Parker was busy licking raindrops from Reid's neck so she didn't think she was responsible for the noise and didn't care, anyway. And since Reid had his mouth full of shoulder she knew he hadn't made it. When she heard it again, she recognized Chance's whine.

And thinking of Chance made her think of her daughter.

And her husband.

"Wait," she gasped. She twisted away from his mouth and grabbed at his hands. "Wait."

He froze, then dropped his forehead onto hers, his breathing labored. "I'm beginning to hate that word."

She wrapped her arms around her waist and stepped away, her breathing as ragged as his. She'd let him kiss her. She'd let *him* kiss her.

"I wasn't thinking."

"You're not supposed to."

"Someone has to. That can't happen again."

"I'm still here. Which means it can." He reached for her and she evaded him, pressing herself against the house. Rainwater soaked into the back of her pajama top. Desperation gave voice to her truest fear.

"I loved and lost one soldier. I won't do it again."

Reid paused. "I must have missed something. Did we just jump straight from lust to love?"

How ridiculous, the bleakness that followed his words. "We already established this. There's to be no jumping at all."

"'Jumping' being a euphemism for..."

"Sex."

He scrubbed a palm over his hair and exhaled. "It's not because I'm a soldier, is it? It's because I'm *that* soldier."

"It's both."

"So this was a literal kiss-off." He laughed sharply. It wasn't a pleasant sound. Then he laughed again.

Parker gritted her teeth. "Care to share?"

"Yeah. I can't screw you because I screwed you."

One step forward and she slapped him. Hard. She felt the impact in her bones from her wrist to her shoulder. The *thwack* echoed in the dark.

Immediately a nauseating shame writhed in her belly. What had she done?

He hadn't moved, hadn't flinched. But his breathing grew harsh, and his eyes glittered through the gloom.

"I deserved that. And worse. I hope you'll forgive my poor choice of words."

"This isn't a bar," she managed to say. "You can't run a tab." Her palm stung as she spun and groped for the handle to the screen door, and let herself quietly into the house.

13

PARKER LAY ON TOP of the covers on Nat's bed, with Nat snuggled up against her. She replayed the scene with Reid over and over. Her stomach churned with regret at slapping him. Her only consolation was the knowledge that he'd behaved almost as badly as she had. Once they'd stopped kissing, anyway. Before that he'd been good. Very, very good.

She sighed and cradled her aching hand to her chest. He'd spent a solid ninety minutes in a torrential downpour searching for her daughter's pet and Parker had repaid him by smacking the stuffing out of him. Though he certainly had asked for it.

When her cell rang, playing the default ring tone, she knew who was calling. She scooped her phone off the nightstand.

"I can't sleep," Reid said.

"Not my problem," she responded, and disconnected. She shoved the phone under her pillow and lay back down. Five seconds later it rang again. This time when she answered, no one spoke. A glance at Nat showed she was still deeply asleep. Parker carried the phone — and her pillow — back across the hall and into her own bedroom.

"Are you planning on actually saying anything," she said into the phone, "or are you just looking for an excuse to do some heavy breathing?"

"I was waiting for you to hang up."

"Well, I wouldn't want to disappoint you." She disconnected again. *Take that, Reid MacFarland.* With a small, satisfied smile she climbed onto her bed and settled against the headboard. This time ten seconds went by before he called back. She let it ring. When the phone fell silent she picked it up, determined to turn it off. But it rang again and she answered before she could stop herself.

"You don't sound any more sleepy than I am," he said.

"What do you want, MacFarland?"

He sighed. "To apologize."

"You and I spend a lot of time saying 'I'm sorry.'" No response. "Aren't you going to ask why I need to apologize?"

"The entire left side of my face is on fire. I know why."

"I am sorry for hitting you."

"What I said was inexcusable. I deserved it."

"I think we both know there was more behind that slap than anger over ugly words. And I'm ashamed that I resorted to violence."

"You're being too hard on yourself."

"So are you. You were frustrated. Your reaction was understandable. Juvenile, but understandable."

"I don't think you know what 'inexcusable' means."

"I know what 'lonely' means."

"We're getting a little off topic here."

She leaned forward and frowned at the unpainted state of her toenails. "I should be more mad at you."

"Why aren't you?"

She bit her lip. "Your comment about screwing me over. Despite what I said the other night you yourself don't accept that what happened defending that outpost was an accident."

"It wasn't. I made a conscious decision."

"A decision you thought would protect other soldiers." He didn't say anything. She pulled her knees up to her chest. "Can I ask you something?"

"I'm afraid of you. I have to say yes."

"Mr. Orson said you should be a higher rank. They took it from you, didn't they?" Silence. "What did they do to you?"

"Not enough."

"I'd like to know."

A much longer silence this time, and Parker wondered if he'd refuse to answer. Finally he exhaled. "I received an Article 15. They stripped me down from staff sergeant to corporal, docked my pay, assigned me extra duty and mandated extended counseling."

Article 15. Nonjudicial punishment. He made it sound as if he thought he'd deserved a court martial. And as cavalier as he was about the pay issue, a corporal was only one step up from a private. Which meant he'd taken a sizable cut in pay.

Yet he'd put a lot of money into her business.

Had he taken out a loan?

She decided to save that question for another occasion. "Did it help? The counseling?" She'd been offered counseling as well. But no way she could have handled sitting in a room with other bereaved wives. At that point in time she hadn't even wanted to be with herself.

"I'd rather have been with my unit."

"So you're looking forward to going back."

"I was."

Okay, enough. She was starting to feel like a high-school girl afraid a less-than-desirable guy might actually ask her to go steady. And half hoping he would.

Yet less than an hour earlier she'd declared she'd never kiss him again. *Parker Anne, you are one fickle female.*

And it was way past time to end the conversation.

"Think you can sleep now?"

"Maybe if I had an ice pack."

She smiled. "You've suffered worse." Then she thought of his scars and stopped smiling. With a press of her thumb she ended the call, and set the alarm so she could check on Nat in an hour.

The next time the phone rang Parker felt like she'd managed maybe ten minutes of sleep. But a one-eyed squint at the clock showed it was six in the morning. Which meant she should have been up an hour ago. She fumbled for the phone.

"Hello?"

"Parker?"

Eugenia. She'd been crying. Parker struggled to sit up. "Is

everything all right?"

"I'm sorry for calling so early. I figured you'd be up and I just…I don't have anyone else to talk to."

"I didn't get to bed until late last night. Did something happen with Harris?"

"He didn't say anything?"

"I was out on a delivery with Reid most of the day." Parker raked a hand through her hair. Poor Eugenia sounded miserable. "What happened?"

"I finally told him something I should have told him a long time ago. About his daughter."

"Let me guess. You gave her money."

"I only wanted to help. I figured she was calling me instead of her father because he couldn't afford to give her a loan."

"And he's holding you responsible for something you weren't even aware of?"

"He kept ranting about my lack of financial savvy."

"Oh, and he's Warren Buffet's long-lost twin."

Eugenia's chuckle sounded strangled. "This money thing. It's a huge issue and I just don't think we can get past it. And I wish we could. I'd really like to be part of his life."

"Give him some time. Harris isn't known for being levelheaded." And speaking of Harris, no doubt he would soon be banging on the kitchen door demanding his early-morning muffin. In fact she was surprised he hadn't already come upstairs and hauled her out of bed. She really did need to get a move on.

They talked for another few minutes, but after they hung up Parker wasn't convinced she'd been much help. She lay back and stared at the ceiling. When she finally rolled out of bed, she stumbled over to her desk. She opened her laptop and smothered a yawn in the crook of her elbow. Once it booted up, she typed "how to forgive" into her browser.

Much of the advice didn't apply to her situation. *Do not allow yourself to be victimized again.* Parker clicked away from that link. She didn't have any more husbands to sacrifice to friendly fire. *Q: How do I know when I've forgiven someone? A: When you can laugh at the things that once hurt.* Obviously she'd never be able to laugh about Tim's death.

Those links made for painful reading, but then she found something that got her thinking. *If you want to be happy, forgive your enemy. No matter what evil has been done, no matter what misery your enemy delighted in bringing about, the only way to be truly free of the pain is to forgive the unforgivable.*

She drew her legs up onto the chair and hugged her knees to her chest. *Evil. Enemy. Unforgivable.* If she continued in her refusal to forgive Reid, did it mean she considered him her enemy? That she thought him evil?

Of course neither was true. And the idea that Reid found any delight in Tim's death was not only ludicrous, it was offensive.

Maybe she'd been looking at this the wrong way. Maybe instead of focusing on the reasons she shouldn't forgive him, she should be figuring out what it meant if she didn't.

And maybe if she managed to forgive him, he'd be able to forgive himself.

Her cell rang again. Her belly gave a hop, skip and a jump before she recognized Harris's ring tone. She moved back to the bed, scooped up the phone and waited for a lecture on tardiness. Sixty seconds later she was scrambling for her clothes.

*   *   *

REID FELT LIKE A high school boy, hoping to catch a glimpse of his crush in the hall between classes. He'd been running late, but not even Chance had been around to greet him. So he'd made his own coffee — the advantage to beating Harris in, who seemed to be running even later than he was — put on his gloves, and got back to emptying the outbuildings of years of accumulated junk.

Although he'd snagged only a couple of hours of sleep, he'd

awakened feeling more at peace than he had in over a year. Guilt clamored for its usual spot in the front row but for once, something else took precedence. When he'd talked to Parker the night before, to apologize for acting like an ass after they'd kissed, she'd actually defended him. And though he still considered his conduct inexcusable, the fact that she could forgive him for it gave him hope like he'd never had before.

It also gave him ideas. Big, crazy, wonderful ideas.

Of course, he should know better. Especially after being told point-blank that as a soldier — and as *that* soldier — he had no chance of any kind of relationship with her.

He heard the school bus come and go. He stopped what he was doing and took a swig of coffee, and at the same time eyed a tangled mess of barbed wire he'd have to figure a way to get outside without dragging half the building along with him. What the hell had they needed barbed wire for?

"Reid."

He swung around, and when he saw Parker's face he shoved his cup at the nearest flat surface and met her halfway.

"What? What is it?" Oh, shit. Oh, no. He gripped her shoulders. "Nat?"

She shook her head. Her lips were quivering. He tore off his gloves and pulled her close, rubbed his palm up and down her back. "Tell me."

"H-Harris," she said. "They took him to the hospital. I didn't want Nat to know. I've been waiting for her to leave."

He was already urging her toward the house. "What happened?"

"Chest pains." Her breath hitched. "He called nine-one-one."

He guided her across the yard and up the steps of the farmhouse. "Who called you from the hospital?"

"He did."

Reid stopped, his hand on the front door. "*He* called you?"

"From a regular room, not ICU. He's under observation."

Reid exhaled. "Good. That's very good." Jesus, he'd pictured the old man on his deathbed. He ushered her inside and helped her find her purse. "I don't think anyone in Thistle Hill will suffer if they can't buy a plant for the next few hours. I'll drive, you navigate." She was in no shape to get behind the wheel.

She picked up a sweater and a packet of tissues and gave him a watery smile. They headed for his Jeep and Reid sent up a prayer.

What would Parker do without Harris?

* * *

THEY FOUND HARRIS IN room 304. He was watching a cold-case show on TV with the volume turned up way too high. A middle-age nurse stood beside his bed, wearing navy scrubs and a tired smile.

"All right, Mr. Briggs. As soon as the doctor's available he'll be in to sign your release papers. It may be a while, so just sit tight."

Harris spotted his visitors and tried to scowl but it didn't quite come off. While Parker leaned over and gave him a hug, Reid found the remote and adjusted the volume.

"You scared us," Parker said when she let go.

"I scared myself."

Reid reached across the bed and shook Harris's hand. "Sounds like you just got good news. So what happened?"

Harris ignored him and narrowed his gaze at Parker. "Did you call Eugenia?"

"You asked me not to." His face didn't change and Parker relented. "Okay, I did."

"Well, you can call her back and tell her not to come." He adjusted his blanket. "It was the chili."

"The what?"

"I had some of Snoozy's chili, all right? It gave me heartburn."

Parker breathed a mental sigh of relief and patted him on the shoulder. "Don't look so guilty. We all give in to temptation now and then."

Reid handed the remote to Harris. "I'll go downstairs and call

Eugenia. Give you two a minute to visit."

After Reid left, Parker settled in the chair next to the bed. "She was very upset. She thought her confession had something to do with this."

"Guess I got some thinking to do."

A cart trundled past the door. A remote, droning voice paged a Dr. Yates.

"About Eugenia?"

"And other things." He looked at her, his expression crafty. "You, too." He poked a finger at her. "Remember when you asked me how long the rest of my life would be? And I said ten years or ten days?"

"I remember." Of course she remembered. And she didn't need Harris's not-so-subtle hints to get her thinking.

Opportunity was knocking. Maybe she should open her bedroom door and let it in.

* * *

THERE HADN'T BEEN MUCH conversation between Parker and Reid when he'd rushed them to the hospital to see Harris. Worry had shoved aside every other emotion. And on the way back, with Harris in the Jeep, Reid sure as hell couldn't broach the subject of The Kiss. They'd dropped Harris off at his house and headed back to Parker's. Reid had cleared his throat and opened his mouth. Only to spot Nat's bus.

The last grain of sand had dropped to the bottom of the hourglass. Part Two of his apology would have to wait.

They stood beside the Jeep while the school bus squealed to a halt at the bottom of the driveway. Nat performed her usual stop, drop and roll with Chance, then jumped to her feet and came barreling toward Reid. When he realized she didn't intend to slow down he braced himself, and caught seventy pounds of nine-year-old in his arms. She hugged his waist hard, and looked up at him with a smile that took up half her face.

"Thank you for saving Chance."

He stared down at her freckled face and a sudden fierce surge of affection jammed up his throat. He leaned down and hugged her back, swallowing hard.

"You're welcome, kid. But I didn't do it alone."

"I know," she said, her cheeks suddenly as pink as her mom's. "I'm making Joe a card."

"He'll appreciate that. So you're feeling all right today?" Her head went up and down. "No headache or stuffy nose?" Her head went side to side. "How about Chance? How's he doing?"

"Annoyed. Mom gave him a shower." She let go of his waist. "You promised to teach me how to rappel. When can we start?"

He blinked at the sudden subject change. "Uh." He looked at Parker, who mimicked Nat by crossing her arms and tipping her head. He smiled, relieved to see the fear for Harris had faded from her eyes. "We need a platform first. Why don't I go ahead and get started on that?"

"Right now?"

"Right now."

Nat bounced on her toes and clapped her hands. "And I'll go start my card for Joe." She took off for the house and Parker called after her to take her backpack. Nat changed course and Parker turned back to Reid. She dropped her arms.

"After the day we just had, you have to be exhausted. Are you sure you want to do this?"

"What can I say? I'm a sucker for freckles."

She hesitated, and her own freckles suddenly got lost in a sea of pink. He couldn't stop his grin. It widened when she frowned. She toyed with the strap on her purse. "I have to start dinner and help with homework. Can we talk later?"

"Roger that. Meanwhile I'll go find a sturdy tree."

"The sturdier the better," she said, and made a beeline for the house.

It took him an hour to gather everything he needed because Nat kept running back and forth between the tree and the house, asking questions, giving opinions and making a general nuisance of herself. When she brought him a peanut-butter-and-jelly-sandwich she'd made herself he felt guilty, but only until she started asking him what Joe's favorite colors were and did he think Joe liked butterflies. Reid couldn't help wondering why *he* didn't rate a homemade card.

Then the great Joe himself showed up and Nat threw herself at him, forcing Reid to acknowledge that maybe Nat's attentions hadn't been that irritating, after all. Before long Parker called her inside, and though Reid was disappointed he hadn't received an invitation to dinner, he was glad for the chance to find out why the hell Gallahan had been giving him the eye since the moment he'd arrived. He asked him as soon as the kitchen door closed behind Nat.

"Want to tell me what's up?"

Gallahan took his time examining the "steps" Reid had fastened to the tree with drywall screws. Finally he turned, and shrugged. "I don't know what else to do but put it right out there. Word is you're responsible for Tim Dean's death."

Talk about a punch to the gut. But he'd known it could happen. All it took was two words typed into a search engine. It had only been a matter of time.

Parker.

Oh, Jesus. *Nat.*

He jerked a nod. "Word's right." He looked at Gallahan, and the lack of censure on the other man's face eased the tension that gripped Reid's muscles. Carefully he packed up Harris's battery-operated screwdriver. "What are they saying?"

"They're trashing you at Snoozy's. Saying you took the man's life and now you're trying to take his family."

Oh, shit. Reid fell back a step and Gallahan held up a hand. "I disagree and I made that clear. I've seen what you've done for this family. You had a bad break and —"

"It wasn't a bad break. It was an error in judgment and it cost a man's life."

"Okay. But we all make mistakes —"

"Killed anyone lately?"

"Chill, man, all right?" Gallahan blew out a breath. "All I'm trying to say is — hell, I don't know what I'm trying to say. Except I know a good man when I see one."

For the first time in a long time, Reid's inner voice didn't immediately snap back with a self-deprecating, smart-ass comment. The realization gave him a certain sense of freedom. And responsibility.

He looked toward the house. Had he heard a door open? He turned back, and gathered the rest of the tools. "Thanks for telling me."

Gallahan picked up a hammer and placed it in the bucket Reid had used to tote supplies. "You're headed for Snoozy's. Sure that's a good idea?"

"You make a mistake, you gotta take the consequences."

"Noble Johnson's one mother of a consequence."

Reid winced. He might get that broken rib after all.

"Don't think I'm not going with you, man." Gallahan flexed his hands. "Been a while since Snoozy rearranged the furniture."

*   *   *

NAT SAT HUNCHED OVER the table, a squeezable foil container of fruit punch in one hand and a balled-up napkin in the other. She'd tucked her hair behind her ears to give her mother a clear view of the disappointment on her face. "I still don't get why they couldn't stay."

Parker frowned down at her own plate, which held the remnants of a rapidly cooling slice of store-bought pizza she'd been ecstatic to find in the freezer. It wasn't the lackluster meal she was serving that had prevented her from asking the guys to join them.

It was The Kiss. Every time she remembered how it felt to have Reid's hands on her, his mouth on her, his breath against her neck and his body pushed up against hers, she flushed from the inside out and her pulse pounded like a hard rain on pavement.

No way she could sit across the table from him without letting on. Without fantasizing about where the next kiss might lead. Without wondering if he was thinking the same.

It'd be bad enough if Joe caught on. But if Nat figured something was up she'd get ideas. Family-type ideas. And she was already way too attached to him.

Parker bit her lip. Nat wasn't the only one.

"Mom. Did you hear me? *Why* couldn't they stay?"

She sighed and shoved at her plate. "I already told you. I'm too tired to be decent company, and I'm sure Reid feels the same. Plus I have extra work to do in the morning since we spent so much time at the hospital."

Nat pushed back from the table. "That's another thing. You should have taken me with you."

"You know very well you couldn't miss your math test. And anyway, Joe and Reid seemed to be in a hurry when they left, so I doubt they would have stayed for dinner."

"Reid said he was going to Snoozy's. Joe said he didn't think that was a good idea."

Parker blinked. Why not? Reid certainly deserved some downtime. Only...was he planning on coming back? Her stomach twisted. Maybe he'd changed his mind, figuring he'd get slapped again. Or maybe he was killing time, until he knew Nat would be asleep —

"...instead of redecorating."

Parker finally registered her daughter's disapproving tone. "I'm sorry?"

"Reid," Nat said with exaggerated patience. "It sucks — I mean — it's not fair that he had to leave. Why can't Snoozy move his own stuff around?"

"What on earth makes you think Reid is helping Snoozy redecorate?"

"Because he and Joe were talking about Noble Johnson, and how he was saying stuff about Reid, and that they'd all be rearranging the furniture."

Oh, God. "What kind of stuff?" she asked carefully.

Nat shrugged. Parker exhaled, squeezed her eyes shut for a moment, then jumped up.

"Change of plans, sweetie." She reached for the phone. "Mind if I drop you off at Eugenia's for a while?"

"Why? What's wrong?"

"Not a thing." Parker managed a smile. "I just think that Snoozy's will survive the, uh, sprucing up a lot better if I'm there to offer my input."

"Can't I go?"

"It's a *bar*."

Nat threw her empty juice box into the trash. "I never have any fun."

* * *

SNOOZY'S WAS BUSIER THAN usual for a Wednesday night — busy enough that no one paid attention when Reid and Gallahan walked in. Those who weren't parked in front of the flat-screen TV in the corner were either playing pool or watching Liz Early threaten to dump a pitcher of beer on a man sitting at a table with three grinning buddies.

"Touch me again and you'll not only be wearing this, you'll be picking plastic out of your skull for a week."

The man held up his hands in surrender and Liz set the pitcher on the table. When she turned around she spotted Reid, and froze.

Anger, disappointment, curiosity, speculation. They paraded across Liz's face and Reid felt a chill, deep inside. This is what Parker would have to deal with. Every time she went to the store, the library, the gas station on the corner.

He should have let her know. Before coming here, he should have told her that everyone knew.

The place had gone quiet. Except for the crowd going wild on the television, you could have heard a grenade pin drop.

"Soldier boy." A bearded man in grease-stained work clothes got to his feet. "You got some nerve showing your face in here."

The other man at his table followed suit. "What's the Army thinking, letting a killer go free?"

Gallahan stepped forward. "Wait just a minute —"

Reid blocked him. "It was an accident."

A woman with a voice like a dog's squeaky toy called out, "Like that hit-and-run a few months back was an accident?"

Grease-stained guy tipped his head. "Least that asshole had the excuse of being drunk."

"Why don't you go back to where you came from, soldier boy?"

"Hell, no, man, don't send him back. I got a cousin over there. I'd kinda like to see him again."

Rough, expectant laughter. Then Noble Johnson pushed his way to the front of the crowd and Reid rolled his shoulders up and back. *Here we go.*

The pale-haired giant set aside a half-empty mug of beer, licked his thumb and bounced twice on the balls of his feet.

"Too bad I never collected on that keg," Gallahan muttered.

"We survive this and I'll throw in an autographed poster of Halle Berry."

"In her James Bond bikini?"

"Nothing but."

"Deal."

Noble's glare was hot enough to be a fire hazard. "What the hell were you thinking, sport? Letting us all believe you were a friend of Parker Dean's."

"He is her friend," Gallahan said.

"Some friend. He blew up her husband."

"Can it, Noble." Snoozy leaned against the bar, not looking as worried as Reid would have expected. "You know you got no beef. You're just looking for an excuse to break something."

"And you're just defending him because you don't want to heft a broom."

Reid looked Noble in the eye. "I wouldn't be here if she didn't want me to stay." Which was mostly true.

"You expect a grieving woman to have her head on straight?" Noble shook his head. "And to think I trusted your ass with a library card."

Someone let loose a beer bottle. Someone with shitty aim. The bottle sailed over Reid's head and smashed into the gilt-framed mirror.

Bits and pieces of glass clattered and tinkled to the floor. The room went silent. With a display of more liveliness than Reid could have guessed he'd had in him, Snoozy scrambled over the bar and stomped into the center of the room.

"Who threw that?" he demanded. "Who threw that bottle?" No one spoke. Someone belched and someone else gave a muffled laugh. Snoozy's face went as bright pink as the chair facing the shattered mirror. He wrenched off his apron, tossed it to the floor and gave it a kick. "I swear to God, I find out who threw that bottle and they'll never set foot in here again!" He gave the apron another kick and somewhere a beer bottle tipped over, rolled heavily across a table and hit the floor with a liquid crash.

And that's when all hell broke loose.

* * *

PARKER'S FIRST CLUE THAT all was not well inside Snoozy's was when a chair leg punched through the front window. She scurried away, sidestepping the broken glass, and fumbled for her cell phone. After disconnecting from the sheriff's office, she peered through the shattered pane of glass in time to see her plumber punch Reid in the face.

She wrenched open the door and started yelling. "Stop this! Stop it right *now!*"

No one paid attention. She stepped over bottle bits and puddles of beer, dodging bodies and furniture as she made her way to Reid and

Joe. The two men stood back-to-back in front of the bar, warding off blows and shot glasses. Before Parker could reach them an arm came out of nowhere, catching her in the chin. She went down hard. Her palms slammed down onto broken glass and that's when she went back to screaming.

It took some time, and a few well-aimed missiles of her own, but eventually she became the center of a concerned circle. The circle broke when Reid pushed through with a stack of towels. He crouched beside her and lifted each hand, carefully brushed off the glass and pressed a towel to her palm.

"We need to get you up and over to the sink," he said, his voice tight. "Anything else hurt?"

"My butt," she muttered.

"I can take a look at that for you." Joe appeared on her other side. He was probably grinning but it was hard to tell with all that blood smeared across his mouth. Then she got a good look at Reid and her stomach churned. He had a seeping cut above one eye, the left side of his jaw was bruised, and the rest of his face was covered with scrapes and scratches.

She closed her eyes. "I need a ginger ale."

The two men helped her to her feet. Liz grabbed a towel and started swatting glass off her butt and Snoozy offered a glass of seltzer water. Reid took it and pressed it to her lips. The owner of the arm that had knocked her down had both hands fisted in his hair. "I'm so sorry. I didn't see you. It was an accident."

"That's right. It was. What is wrong with you people?" Parker pulled away from Joe and Reid and glared at the bunch of barflies gathered around her, none of whom would look her in the eye. "My husband died. *Mine.* If I can forgive Corporal MacFarland for that then why can't you?"

Parker took a huge gulp of seltzer water, gave a tiny burp and resumed her rant. "You've all been such a huge help to me and my family. Do you remember how that started? When our delivery truck broke down, do you remember who recruited you? The same guy who made me accept your help because I was too stubborn to realize I couldn't do it all myself. Well, if this is the price I have to pay for your help then I don't want it."

She slammed the glass down onto the bar. "Let's go, guys."

Reid balked. "First we need to get you cleaned —"

"I need to leave. Now." She accepted her purse, which Liz had brushed off and then thrust at her.

"Hold on." Joe hustled back behind the bar, dumped a bowl of potato chips and scooped up a supply of ice. "We'll need this."

Outside Parker sacrificed the seltzer water and her dinner to the gods of the parking lot. Unmindful of the blood dripping down the side of his face, Reid handed her a box of tissues, then helped her to the Jeep. She'd have to come back and get her car later.

By the time they got to the motel, her stomach had settled but her palms were on fire. Reid parked outside his room and the three of them got out. Joe motioned with his chin toward the office.

"Anything else you need besides peroxide and bandages?"

Reid swiped at the blood on his chin. "A couple of beers would be nice."

"Whiskey would be better. Be right back."

Parker followed Reid into the room. He tossed his key card on the table while she closed the door.

"What I'd really like is a shower." She spread her arms and surveyed the splotches of blood and beer that stained her overalls. Even her face felt sticky.

"Right. We can handle that." He pulled an Army tee and a pair of running shorts from a drawer, then snagged his flip-flops. "Once we get your boots off you need to wear these. In case we didn't brush all the glass off our clothes."

He sat her down in one of the lawn chairs and knelt at her feet. She felt more than awkward, having him unlace her boots, but she was grateful not to have to fumble through it on her own. He slid the flip-flops onto her feet, then stood and considered her hands.

"Let's wash your palms first, get all the bits of glass out. We'll put on some bandages after your shower."

She followed him into the bathroom. He turned on the faucet, adjusted the temperature carefully and gently grasped her left hand.

"This is going to hurt," he murmured.

Water hit raw flesh and she hissed in a breath. Considering the state of Reid's knuckles his own hands had to hurt like heck but he never even flinched. When she tried to jerk her hand away, he held fast, stroking his thumb across her palm as he searched for grit and glass. Despite the discomfort, his touch sparked a thudding warmth that traveled up her arm to her chest and pulsed through her body.

She was suddenly, intensely aware that she and Reid were crowded into a bathroom the size of a broom closet. And that her cheek hovered close to a rather impressive bicep. And that the owner of that bicep smelled like sweat and beer and Snoozy's French fries and she was more turned-on that she ever remembered being. Her gaze sneaked upward and settled on his profile.

She wanted to press her mouth to the five-o'clock shadow that had sprouted along his jaw. *Not the time, Parker.* Not when Joe could walk in at any moment. Reid's jaw flexed and she let out a tiny moan. He looked up.

"Stings, I know. Sorry." She bit her lip and lowered her gaze. He patted her palm dry with a towel, then reached for her other hand.

"Thank you," she said quietly.

"Thank *you*."

"For what?"

"For what you said at the bar. About forgiving me. You didn't have to say that."

"Yes, I did. Because it's true." She ignored the tumble in her belly and took the towel he offered. "I should have said something sooner. This was always more about me than you. About…trying to hang on to something that was long gone. I'm sorry for what I put you through, I— What? What is it?"

"You're sorry for what you put *me* through?" He straightened. "How can you forgive me? How can you say what I did is okay?"

"I knew it," she whispered. "I knew you couldn't forgive yourself." She leaned against the sink, searching for the words that would make him understand. "I'm not saying what you did is okay. I'm saying I know you didn't mean to do it. I said that before but the difference is that now I can say it without feeling I'm betraying my husband. I've been holding on to a grudge that stopped being a grudge a long time ago because it turned into a...sort of friend. It was familiar."

She swallowed the thickness in her throat. "What happened to Tim doesn't make you a bad person. It makes you a person who made a bad choice. You've struggled so much because you're a good person. A good man. A good soldier."

He went rigid and she gave him a little shake. "You know what? It doesn't matter that I forgive you. What matters is that you forgive yourself."

He looked down at the ugly tiled floor, and when he looked back up his eyes were damp. He took the step that brought them thigh to thigh and cupped her elbows. "Parker—"

"I'm ba-ack." Joe made the announcement as if he thought they needed time to put their clothes back on. Five more minutes and he might have been right. "I have peroxide, Band-Aids, three cold beers, and though you didn't ask for it—" he stepped into the bathroom doorway and rattled a small plastic bottle " —aspirin."

"And what's that?" Parker nodded at the bottle tucked under his arm.

"That, my sweet, is single-malt whisky. Only for those among us who kicked ass tonight. Oh, wait." He grabbed the bottle by the neck and toasted her with it. "That would be everyone here." He winced, switched the bottle to the other hand and peered at a slash across the insides of his fingers. "I think I need a Band-Aid."

"You'll have to wait. Parker wants a shower."

"Wait a minute, I don't need to take it right now. You two need attention first."

"Two against one. You're outvoted." Reid reached into the shower and turned on the water. Then he nodded at her hands. "They're going to hurt like hell all over again."

Joe spoke from the doorway. "We could wrap plastic bags around them."

"That's okay. I'll be careful."

Reid held the curtain open and tipped his head toward the spray of water. "Stick your elbow in. See if the temp's right."

There was barely enough room in the bathroom for one adult, let alone two. In order to put her elbow under the spray of water while Reid held open the curtain, Parker would have to bend down, grab something for support — like the waistband of his jeans — and lean in.

Not a good idea.

So of course she went for it.

She took a step forward, which brought her up against him and, without breaking eye contact, poked out her elbow. "I'll have to hold on to something," she said softly.

One eyebrow quirked. He grasped her upper arm. "I've got you."

Slowly she tipped to the side, the bib of her overalls rubbing across his chest. Her gaze never left his. The spray hit her elbow and she shuddered. His jaw muscles tightened.

"It's just right," she breathed. He pulled her upright and her gaze dropped to his chest, which was noticeably rising and falling. "In fact, it's perfect."

Speculation narrowed his gaze and his fingers tightened on her arm. A sudden fantasy flashed — him thrusting her against the wall and then thrusting into her and she shuddered again. He let go abruptly.

"Right. We'll leave you alone." He turned, but Joe was blocking the doorway.

"She might need help. I could hold the washcloth for her."

While Parker fumbled with the straps on her overalls Reid muttered something rude and pushed Joe out of the way. When the door closed behind them Parker sagged against it.

He'd let go of her so quickly. Almost pushing her away. Did he think she was teasing him? Hopefully she'd be able to convince him that she'd changed her mind once they were alone.

And then maybe they could pick up where they left off after that kiss on her front porch. Eugenia had offered to keep Nat overnight. Parker planned to take her up on that.

Ten minutes later she opened the bathroom door again. She probably didn't look much better than she had in her overalls, considering the size of Reid's T-shirt and running shorts, but she felt refreshed. Her getup wasn't sexy, but then again, neither were the jammies she'd been wearing the night of The Kiss.

She gave her hair one last comb-through and picked up her hair clip. Reid's flip-flops slapped against her heels as she left the bathroom in search of a plastic bag to hold her dirty overalls.

"Okay, guys," she said. "Bandage time."

They'd opened two of the beers. They stopped mid-conversation and looked up. Joe whistled and Reid stood.

"Bet that T-shirt never looked so good," Joe said.

"You'd win that bet." But Reid's face was grim as he spoke. She'd done something wrong.

As soon as she had the thought she wanted to slap herself. The man had just taken a beating. No doubt he'd given as good as he'd gotten, but still. He was in pain. And he'd been raked over the coals by people he'd considered friends. Why wouldn't he be grim?

It's not always about you, Parker Anne.

He picked up the peroxide and bandages Joe had brought and led her back into the bathroom. He nodded at the toilet. "Sit."

The three of them took turns patching each other up. After politely refusing Joe's offer of a butt bandage, Parker ended up with gauze wrapped around both hands. Reid had a butterfly bandage over his left eye and another along the ridge of his right cheek—no sense in trying to bandage his split lip or the cuts on his knuckles. Joe had sustained the most damage. Besides cuts and bruises to his face and hands, he also had a loose tooth and two black eyes. He accused Parker of being too stingy with her sympathy but kissed her on the cheek anyway, and cautiously shook Reid's hand on the way out.

"Can't remember when I enjoyed an evening more."

They bumped knuckles and Reid gave him the Army sign of approval. "Hooah."

Parker rolled her eyes. "Lots of luck, you two, getting Snoozy to let you back into the bar."

Joe's eyes went as wide as they could go, which, considering his injuries, wasn't very wide. "We didn't start it," he said.

Reid followed him to the door. "You don't want to finish your beer?"

"Nah. If I stayed I'd have to share. So I think I'll just take my Glenlivet and go find some gratuitous violence to watch."

Reid frowned. "I thought your set was on the blink."

"Who said anything about TV? I'm going back to Snoozy's."

"Joe." Parker slapped her hands on her hips and yelped. She cradled her bandaged palms to her chest. "For God's sake, you can hardly see. Go home."

"Maybe." He sighed. "Guess they'd make me share at Snoozy's, too."

Parker watched him walk a mostly straight line to the motel office. "Think he'll be okay?"

"He'll be fine." Reid shut the door. His gaze went sharp. "Why? How worried are you?"

She felt a little thrill. "No more worried than you are."

He grunted. "How'd you end up at Snoozy's tonight, anyway?"

"Nat heard you and Joe talking." He stilled and she shook her head. "She didn't understand. But once I realized what it was she'd overheard I dropped her off at Eugenia's and went straight to Snoozy's."

"I wish you hadn't. You could have been seriously hurt."

She moved closer, and lightly stroked a finger along the gauze on his cheek. "So could you."

"How about a beer?" He reached for the unopened bottle. She stopped him with a hand on his forearm.

"Back to what we were talking about before. In the bathroom. I

209

want to know if you think you can. Forgive yourself."

"I don't know." He held her gaze. "But I appreciate that you can."

Parker swayed toward him. He twisted away and used Joe's opener to lift the cap off the third beer and handed it over. He clinked his bottle against hers. "To battle scars."

"Battle scars." She dutifully took a sip, and swallowed her disappointment along with the ale. Reid wasn't interested. Maybe not anymore, or maybe just not for the night. She knew she should respect that.

She also knew she probably wouldn't have the courage to put herself out there again.

Now or never, Parker Anne. Her pulse picked up speed, as if she were a long-distance runner who'd spotted the finish line.

"I don't really want this," she said, and put her beer back on the table. "But I do want you."

He froze, the bottle halfway to his mouth. Then he blindly set it aside and reached.

"Thank God you changed your mind."

She gave a husky laugh. "Thank God you didn't change yours." She slid her bandaged palms up to his shoulders and around to the back of his neck, where she interlocked her fingers. She licked his chin, and he swooped in.

His mouth covered hers in a hard, fierce kiss that must have hurt because he grunted and eased up on the pressure. He raised his hands and tunneled his fingers into her hair, holding her head captive as his tongue traced the seam of her lips. She opened for him, he groaned, and her knees went liquid.

The kiss was as delicious as the first. Only better, because this time she knew exactly where she wanted it to lead. This time, she knew she deserved it.

His fingers slid across her shoulders and down her back. Then his hands found her butt and she must have made a sound because he froze. He let go and stepped away.

"Come back," she murmured, tugging at his shirtsleeve. "It didn't hurt." He cocked an eyebrow. "Okay, it did, but not much."

He was breathing heavily as he stroked a finger across her forehead, shifting the hair out of her eyes. His own eyes were guarded. "This doesn't have anything to do with sympathy, does it? I mean, considering my face will never be the same."

She knew exactly what he meant. It had nothing to do with his face and everything to do with his own struggle to forgive. She fought back a tangled surge of compassion, indignation and self-reproach — none of which he'd appreciate — and thrust back her shoulders.

Time to break out the visual.

"Sympathy?" With one swift motion she pulled the Army tee over her head, revealing her lacy, sapphire-blue bra. Thanks to the miracle of online shopping, she'd recently scored some come-hither lingerie and a few other small but mandatory items without alerting any Thistle Hill residents.

"Try seduction." She leaned forward, giving him a better view of breasts that wouldn't win any wet T-shirt contests but weren't undersize, either. "The panties match," she whispered, and her own boldness made her stomach tumble.

His dark eyes smoldered. He pulled her close, pinning her hips against his. When he spoke, his voice was guttural. "I'd have settled for pity."

She didn't believe him. But with his erection pressing against the juncture between her thighs, she also didn't care. The hard, intimate heat scorched a path straight to the tips of her breasts. As if following that unseen trail his hands traveled up to her bra. His thumbs flicked at the lace covering her nipples and she moaned. How long had it been since she'd been touched this way? She could remember if she concentrated, but she didn't want to.

This was Reid. This was new.

He dipped his head and pressed openmouthed kisses to the hollow between her neck and her shoulder. She started to shudder and couldn't stop.

"Your hair smells like rain," he muttered.

There was a rumbling sound, and it took Parker a few seconds to realize it wasn't Reid purring his approval. Bright light from a pair of headlights squeezed through the blinds and arced across the paneled walls. Parker and Reid went still, waiting for the slam of a car door, followed by a knock. They heard neither.

"She'd have called my cell," she whispered, mostly to herself. "If something was up with Nat, Eugenia would have called."

Outside the room someone yelled that the motel was closed, and the headlights reversed their arc across the dim room. Simultaneously Parker and Reid sighed with relief. She tipped her head, exposing the neglected side of her neck, and nudged him. "Carry on, soldier."

"Damn, you're adorable."

"I don't want to be adorable. I want to be irresistible."

He let loose a soft bark of laughter and dipped his head. "You are. Which reminds me." He stroked his tongue along the ridge of her collarbone. "I forgot to mention you look damned good with my shorts on." His hands skimmed down her back, and his clever fingers slid beneath the waistband of her panties. "Why don't we see how you look with them *off?*"

14

A N ABRUPT CASE OF nerves took Parker's voice. She wanted to protest, wanted to demand Reid lose his clothes first, but if this was a test she had every intention of passing it. His ragged breath warmed the nape of her neck and boosted her courage.

Along with the rest of her clothes, she would shed the specter of her only other lover.

Her gaze locked onto his, she took a step back. She grabbed the waistband of the shorts she'd borrowed and pulled them down past her hips, where a languid heaviness had already settled. She raised her hands to lift her hair off her neck, mostly to hide the shaking in her hands, partly to lift her breasts, and let the shorts slither to the floor.

The stark desire in Reid's face sent need rocketing through her. She stepped out of the shorts and kicked them away. Unfortunately she kicked off a flip-flop as well and it smacked Reid in the shin.

He looked down, as if he couldn't believe what had happened, and she clapped her hands to her mouth.

"Sorry," she gasped, and laughed as he kicked the offending sandal out of the way.

"Yeah?" He hauled her close. "How sorry?"

Her fingers found the hem of his shirt and raised it past his stomach. "Very —" she bent her knees and pressed a kiss to the hard muscles quivering above his belly button " — very —" she lifted the shirt higher, pressed a kiss to his sternum " — sorry." She closed her lips around a nipple and he sucked in a breath. An instant later his shirt joined hers on the floor and his hands were at the clasp of her bra. A flick of his fingers and her breasts were freed. He stared down at her, and it was all she could do not to cross her arms. He made a gruff noise at the back of his throat and traced the curve of her left breast with his forefinger.

"Perfect," he murmured. He lowered his head, swept his tongue over her nipple and followed that with a scrape of his teeth. The sensation seared a path all the way to her womb. She cried out and yanked his mouth back up to hers. He hissed in a breath. *His cuts.* She jerked away with an apologetic whimper but he held her tight. Her breasts flattened against his torso and the friction of tender skin against hard chest made her moan.

He ran his hands down and up her arms, across her back and along her ribs, soothing her at the same time he aroused her. She wriggled against him, needing to press every inch of her body to his, frustrated he wasn't naked. She fumbled for his zipper. He broke off their kiss, breath rasping in and out.

"I'm going to take you to bed now." He nipped at her earlobe. "Do me a favor."

"Anything."

"I'm taking cover. You get rid of the other flip-flop."

She gasped and bit his shoulder, and it was his turn to suck air.

He turned her and backed her to the bed, eased her down and straddled her, knees on either side of her hips. With one hand at her shoulder blades and the other under her butt, he positioned her so her legs didn't dangle over the edge of the mattress. She winced at the pressure against the cuts on her backside, and he lowered his forehead to hers.

"Don't worry," he said. "I'll kiss it and make it better. But first we need to get rid of these." His fingers curled under the waistband of her panties and she lifted eager hips. Then his grin vanished, and his body went rigid.

"What? What's wrong?"

He swallowed. "Condoms. I don't have any."

"I do," she breathed.

He groaned and tipped his head back, gulping in air. "Oh, thank you," he said, and his tone was so heartfelt she wanted to laugh. He stood and unzipped his jeans. "How about you get the condoms and I'll get naked."

Easier said than done, especially when she was intent on watching him strip while rummaging in her purse and at the same time trying not to be too modest about her own near-nudity. But once he'd turned to face her, she forgot all about being self-conscious.

Her gaze dropped, and she felt a hot, wet rush of need between her thighs. She forced her eyes back up to his face. "I feel like I should salute."

He laughed out loud, snatched the box from her hands and laid her back down on the bed. "Now where were we?" He eased off her brand-new sapphire-blue panties.

* * *

REID'S BRAIN REELED FROM sensory overload. Parker's honeysuckle scent, her velvet mouth, the silky sounds of her pleasure all shoved him to the brink. It had been a long time, and he couldn't remember ever wanting a woman the way he wanted her. He kneaded her thighs and nibbled at her belly, and her sigh shimmered through him. Inspired him. Challenged him.

Made him hard enough to shoot pool.

He lifted up and stared down at her, his body coiled like a giant spring, his gut clenched with the wonder of having her in his bed. She gazed up at him, her eyes blazing with expectation, her breasts rising and falling with the strength of her desire. Her teeth grazed her lower lip in an unwitting display of nerves.

A powerful shudder rippled along his spine. He lowered his head and took her mouth. Her kiss was frantic, her tongue imploring, as if she feared he'd change his mind. No way in hell that was going to happen.

Her fingers clutched at his back as he skimmed his lips away from her mouth and along her jawline, to her ear —

"Oh, my God."

He froze. The horror in her voice was like a bucketful of cold water. He shook his head against the haze in his brain. "What'd I do?"

"That ceiling," she said. "It's hideous."

"Seriously? I have my tongue in your ear and you're noticing the paint job?"

"I can't help it. It's right above me. Who paints a ceiling turquoise?"

He reached out and clicked off the light. "You can't see it now." He pressed his hips to hers. "And in case you haven't noticed, *I'm* right above you."

"I'm ready to pay attention now," she whispered. She reared up and kissed him with an intensity he wasn't sure he deserved. She broke off the kiss and whispered into his cheek. "Please." She raised her hips and he groaned, on the cusp of surging forward. But she deserved better. And they had all night.

"What's the rush?" He lifted away and she growled.

"What happened to 'Yes, ma'am'?"

"I think you'll like this better." He bent his head to her breast, and she whimpered in agreement. Her bandaged hands clutched at his hair.

Warm. Scented. Sensitive as hell. And so many delicious freckles. She moaned his name as his teeth grazed a nipple. He smiled and exchanged the tight nub for its twin. He wanted to worship a little, felt the topography demanded it. But then she scooted down and wrapped her fingers around his cock and he forgot his plan of attack.

"We can explore later," she said. "I look forward to exploring later. But I need you inside me. Now."

He snatched up the box of condoms, ripped it open and did what he needed to do. Then he positioned himself between her legs and eased forward. Their bodies joined in one smooth, wet glide.

She cried out and arched her back. He paused, pulsing inside her, struggling to catch his breath. He meant to give her time. Time to adjust to the feel of him, the size of him. But she had other ideas.

She dug her fingers into his biceps and wriggled beneath him. Waves of electric pleasure set his hips in motion. He pulled away and plunged again, growling deep in his throat as she sank her teeth into his shoulder.

Her husky cries of pleasure spurred him on. Faster and faster he pumped, driving her into the mattress, frantic to slake the hunger she'd aroused the moment he'd met her. The rippling heat of release grew insistent. He tried to slow, tried to change his rhythm, but with Parker's thighs holding him prisoner and her nails digging into his back, he found himself close to the point of no return. And despite her wild response her face told him that unless he did something different he'd end up there alone.

With a monumental effort, he forced his hips to stop moving. He pressed his mouth to her ear. "Talk to me, Parker." He nipped at her earlobe. "Tell me what you need."

Eyes shut tight, she shook her head. Damn. First he'd lost her, then he'd embarrassed her.

Or maybe she was having regrets.

Jaw clenched tight as he fought the burning need to finish what they'd started, he cradled her face and passed his thumb over her lips. "Do you want to stop?"

She opened her eyes. "No," she whispered fiercely. "*No.* It's just…never been easy for me. You finish." She cracked a smile. "Save yourself."

God, he loved this woman. He brushed his lips over hers. "I think there's room in the lifeboat for both of us. Let's try this." He shifted to his side and turned her so her back was against his chest. Maybe if she wasn't facing him she'd find it easier to relax. He lifted her leg and positioned it over his thigh, and eased back inside her. He heard her breath catch, and she gasped even louder when he slid his hand to where their bodies were joined.

He took his time, moving slowly in and out, stroking her lightly with his fingers, whispering to her, caressing her shoulder with his mouth. When she began to thrash and he felt her inner muscles tighten around him, he picked up the pace. Just as she stiffened and cried out, his own explosion ripped through him and his mind went blank. Spasm after spasm held his muscles prisoner as he came. A droplet of sweat skated down his forehead and he squeezed his eyes tight against the salty sting.

Unbelievable. He let his chin fall to her shoulder. The tremors lessened but he held on tight, keeping his hips pressed against her. He swept his hand up over her belly and cupped her breast. She quivered and he smiled.

*   *   *

PARKER COULDN'T STOP TREMBLING. She felt like her body wasn't her own. A warm lassitude had seeped into her muscles. She remembered how she'd shuddered and screamed and figured she should be embarrassed, but though she barely had the strength to shift position, all she could think about was trying for another orgasm.

With him.

It had been incredible. He'd made it incredible.

"You're incredible," she said.

He laughed soundlessly, huffing air against her shoulder. "You're pretty amazing yourself." Slowly he pulled out of her, and she couldn't hold back a disappointed groan. "I won't be long," he said, and the bed dipped as he got to his feet. He made his way through the shadows to the bathroom, and closed the door before turning on the light.

The man was as considerate as he was sexy.

While he was gone she managed to roll over. She stretched, and reveled in the tingling pull of her muscles. When he came back, he left the light on and the door ajar.

"Can't have you tripping in the middle of the night," he said as the bed dipped again. She felt a little thrill at his words, pleased that he expected her to stay. Too bad she couldn't. He leaned over her, his expression intent, and traced a lazy finger from her forehead down the length of her nose, past her lips to her chin. "You look a little shell-shocked."

"For good reason. I can't remember when I've been so very…"

"Impressed?"

"I was going to say relaxed. But your word will work, too." She captured his hand and he allowed her to pull him down beside her. He propped his head in his hand.

"No regrets?"

She shook her head and continued to play with his fingers, tangling and untangling their hands. After a long while she said what was on her mind. "My husband didn't deserve to die," she whispered. "And you didn't deserve to be the one who pushed that button. And my daughter doesn't deserve a mother who can't let the resentment go only because it means letting her dead husband go." She looked at him then. "Thank you for helping me let go." She managed a grin. "In more ways than one."

"Is that what this was?"

"Partly. Another part was, I wanted to show you I forgive you."

"You're killing me here. Please tell me there was a third part and it was blind lust."

"I can't." When he stiffened, she shifted to face him, and pressed a palm to his heart. "I mean, yes, there was lust. But it wasn't blind."

He stared at her, then reached for her, burying his fingers in her hair and lifting her face to his. He kissed her deeply, despite the cuts on his lips, and she pressed up against him, sliding her leg between his and caressing his back. She trailed her hand down his side, and felt the ridges of his scars. She pulled away from the kiss, still stroking his ribs.

"May I ask how this happened?"

He didn't answer right away, instead struggled to control his breathing. Then he rolled onto his back with a sigh, one arm bent behind his head. "My first deployment. Kandahar. A roadside bomb. Wasn't even our patrol who ran it over, it was a farm tractor. Carrying women and children. Most of our guys were wearing armor. The civilians never had a chance."

"Does it hurt?" she asked. He shook his head. "How long were you in the hospital?"

"Couple of weeks."

"Then they sent you back."

"Not right away. I had a year between deployments."

"How many times have you been over there?"

"Three."

"Is there a limit?"

"No limit." He turned his face toward hers. "You didn't know that?"

"No. It was Tim's first tour." She shifted her gaze to the ceiling. "So this will be number four for you."

"It would have been."

Her heart bounced. "Does that mean..." She couldn't say the words.

He reached out and tugged her up against him, her back to his chest. "Let's wait and see what the Army says, okay?"

She nodded, and he pressed a kiss to her shoulder. "Parker?"

"Hmm?"

"I'm worried about you. About the greenhouses."

She sighed. Her legs grew restless, and she pulled her knees up to her belly. She was trying to absorb his comment about his upcoming tour. "Can we talk about it some other time?"

"Yeah. Okay." He pressed a kiss to the top of her head, smoothed a hand down her arm and tangled his fingers with hers. She was thinking about setting the alarm on her phone when she fell asleep.

Her empty stomach woke her sometime later. She lay unmoving, eyes closed against the dark, reveling in the sensation of Reid and his soothing heat wrapped around her. She didn't want to open her eyes, didn't want to break the spell. But she had to. She had a daughter to think of. A dog to look after.

And she had to pee.

She carefully disengaged herself from Reid and scooted to the bathroom. When she came back out the light was on and Reid was sitting with his back against the headboard, the sheet gathered at his waist. She stared at the sculpted lines of his chest and the tips of her breasts tingled.

"Responsibility bites," she grumbled, and reached for her underwear.

"Guess that means I can't sweet-talk you back into bed." He threw back the covers, standing to pull on his jeans.

"I have to pick Nat up in the morning and take her to school. I suppose I should get *some* sleep." She froze. "My car. It's still at Snoozy's."

"I'll drive you over, then follow you home." She opened her mouth to protest and he leaned in to silence her with a kiss. When he drew back, she placed a palm on his chest.

"How about dinner Saturday? I'll cook. And I'll take advantage of Eugenia again, if Nat's up for another sleepover."

"Does that mean I get to have a sleepover, too?"

"Roger that," she said. She nipped at his chin and pressed a kiss to his throat. He made a rumbling sound and her thighs quivered. She leaned around him and grabbed her cell. A peek at the time and she set it back down with a grin. Then she grabbed his hand and led him back to bed.

* * *

PARKER HADN'T MANAGED MUCH sleep after finally making it into her own bed. After dragging herself out of Reid's arms the second time, she'd gotten dressed but it had taken longer than it should have, probably because he insisted on playing keep-away with her bra. Then after they'd picked her car up from Snoozy's and Reid had followed her home, they'd spent half an hour making out on her front porch. And once she'd collapsed onto her bed, she'd spent the rest of the night reliving the time she'd spent with Reid and smiling up at her ceiling like a nutcake.

But she wasn't tired. After removing her bandages, so she wouldn't scare Nat, Parker had surprised her daughter with French toast and fresh-squeezed orange juice for breakfast, made Nat's lunch, cleaned out the refrigerator and even finished her to-do list for Saturday night's dinner. All while keeping an ear open for the sound of Reid's Jeep.

He arrived just before she had to put Nat on the bus. A little later than usual, but who could blame him? It was just as well he didn't come up to the house, since his face was even scarier than Parker's bandages had been.

After Nat left, Parker stood in the middle of the kitchen, hands fisted around the straps of her overalls. She wanted to run out and greet Reid, and at the same time she didn't want to appear overly anxious. Which was ridiculous. The man would be leaving in a week. She should take advantage of the time they had left. Besides, he and Harris had a delivery to make, which meant they'd be gone most of the day. She grabbed the muffins she'd arranged on a plate and headed for the potting shed.

And tried not to be too disappointed when she found Reid drinking coffee with Harris.

"Good morning." She set the plate down and slid her hands into her pockets. Barely glanced at Reid and smiled at Harris. "Everything all set for today?"

Harris looked from Parker to Reid and back again. "What's going on?"

Parker's high-pitched "What do you mean?" couldn't have made her sound more guilty.

"What do I mean? Reid's actually drinkin' my coffee and you're supposed to be roamin' the greenhouse with those bud thingies stuck in your ears. Anything either of you want to tell me?" Parker shrugged and kept her gaze on Harris's face, not trusting herself to look at Reid. Harris squinted, then broke into a smile. "I'll be damned."

Perfect. She'd never hear the end of it now. "What you'll be is late if you two don't get a move on. Let me know when you get back."

"Oh, we will," Harris sang out. "We will." As she started down the path toward Hut Three, she heard him making kissing sounds. She swung around, opened her mouth to shout something about cutting off his carrot cake supply, then gave a dismissive wave. It wasn't worth the trouble. But as she continued on her way to Hut Three, she couldn't stop smiling.

By the time three-thirty rolled around, Parker had stopped smiling because her face had started to ache. She got up off her knees and stretched. Three hours weeding around her strawberry plants and she was ready for a break. Which was just as well, because Nat should be home at any moment.

Reid and Harris, too.

She caught herself smiling again, and rolled her eyes.

Ten minutes later the delivery truck had returned and Reid was walking toward her. No sign of Harris, bless his bald head. Parker tugged off her gloves, mainly to give her hands something to do as she watched him approach, looking tired but sexy as ever in his rumpled jeans and T-shirt. He fit, she realized. He'd become part of her world.

She opened her mouth to say hello but he spoke first. "I missed you," he said, and kissed her. When he lifted his head he smiled at her expression. "You don't believe me?"

"I believe you, I just…it's nice to hear."

"I'm sure it is."

Her cheeks heated. "I missed you, too."

The arrival of Nat's bus had them backing away from each other. Parker shaded her eyes with one hand and waved with the other. She stopped mid-wave when she saw the way Nat stumbled down the steps and toward the house, head down, completely ignoring a frantic Chance.

"Something's wrong," Reid murmured.

Parker started to hurry over but then Nat looked up, spotted them, dropped her backpack and charged. Parker could hear her sobs all the way across the yard.

What on earth had happened?

Nat threw herself at Parker and Parker wrapped her arms tight around her daughter. "What's wrong? Sweetie, what's going on?" She hadn't spotted any injuries, thank God. But Nat was crying as hard as she had the night Parker had broken the news about Tim.

She sank to her knees and looked up at Reid, who stood beside her looking as helpless as she felt. She gave him a shrug and hugged her daughter harder.

"Is it true?" Nat choked.

"Is what true?" A very bad feeling started to burn behind her breastbone, as if she'd eaten half a dozen of Eugenia Blue's famous char-broiled cookies.

"Everyone was talking about it at school today. Everyone knew about it. Everyone but *me*."

"Knew what, sweetie?"

Nat disentangled herself and scrubbed at her eyes. Her cherry-red face was streaked with tears and grime. "That Daddy died," she sobbed, "because of *him*." She pointed at Reid, who went white.

15

O H, NO. OH, GOD. Dread iced Parker's insides and her heart gave a violent shiver. The agony in Nat's voice sapped the strength from her legs and she nearly crumpled to the ground.

Nat whirled away from Reid and buried her face in her mother's neck. "A-are they right?" she hiccupped. "Was it h-his fault?"

The symmetry wasn't lost on Parker. They weren't more than twenty feet away from the strawberry patch, where she herself had learned of Reid's role in Tim's death.

She hugged her daughter close and laid her cheek on her hair. "Yes," she said. "Reid made a mistake, and because of that Daddy died."

"I hate Reid. I hate him, I hate him, I *hate* him."

Parker looked up at Reid, helpless to stop her tears. *I'm sorry,* she mouthed. He shook his head.

"I'll just—" He swallowed and turned his face away. Then without looking back at her, he jerked a thumb over his shoulder, in the direction of his Jeep, and walked off.

* * *

HOURS PASSED BEFORE NAT was ready to talk. They'd snuggled up on the couch to watch a movie, sharing a bowl of popcorn—the only thing Nat would consider for dinner. After that Parker had read from *Little Women,* and though Nat sniffled once or twice, she seemed recovered from the shock. But once she'd taken her bath and curled up in bed, with Parker perched on the mattress beside her, the questions started.

"What kind of mistake was it? That Reid made?"

At that moment Parker realized she was her own worst enemy. She should have told Nat sooner. She also should have given some thought to the kinds of questions her daughter might ask. Because she had no clue how to respond.

"He was…protecting some soldiers. He spotted someone he thought was the enemy, and—" *How do I say this to my little girl?* "— he arranged for the enemy to be fired upon. Only it wasn't just the enemy."

Nat's face collapsed. "It was Daddy too," she managed, her voice high-pitched and breathy.

"Yes," Parker whispered. She clasped Nat's hands and squeezed. "It was Daddy."

"Why'd he come here?" She sniffed, and her eyes seemed to take over her face. "Was it to say he's sorry?"

"That's right."

"So he didn't care about us at all. He just wanted to make up for what he did to Daddy."

"That was true at first. Then you came to mean so much to him. Look at how he rescued Chance for you. And just the other day he asked about being your pen pal."

"I changed my mind." Nat pulled away and crossed her arms. "I won't write to him. I won't. He doesn't care about me. If he did he wouldn't have lied."

"He didn't lie, Nat. It was my decision not to tell you."

"Why?"

"Because you were already hurting enough. I didn't expect him to stay but then Harris wasn't feeling well and there was no one else to help and I—I guess deep down I knew we all needed each other." She picked up a teddy bear, and carefully straightened the lapel of its flannel shirt. "But I was also very angry with him. And I didn't want you to have to deal with that, too."

"Mom. I'm not a baby anymore."

"I know you're not, kiddo. And I'm sorry. I wish I could fix this for you."

Nat took the teddy bear and hugged it to her chest. "Don't you care?" she whispered. "Don't you care what he did to Daddy?"

"Of course I do. I'm very sad that Daddy died. But Reid is, too. And if we keep blaming him, then our hearts will be so full of anger that we won't have room for anything else. Like happiness. We deserve to be happy, don't you think?"

"Reid, too?"

"Reid, too." Parker stood, kissed her daughter on the forehead. "Think about it, okay?" Nat nodded, and Parker kissed her again. "Sleep tight. I love you."

She had her hand on the light switch when Nat spoke through a yawn. "Mom? I love you, too."

* * *

FRIDAY MORNING CAME AND Reid had no idea what to do about Natalie. He'd known her less than three weeks but still he mourned the loss of her affection almost as deeply as he'd mourned her father.

He'd let the kid down. And it ripped at him, the knowledge that his actions were changing who she was and who she would grow up to be.

His weight shifted as he leaned harder on the rake in his right hand and frowned at the bright green apple in his left. The agonized betrayal in Nat's wide, innocent eyes would haunt him forever.

Why had he thought that an apology would suffice? That forgiveness would be enough? He'd burdened the wrong person with his need for absolution.

He had to go back to where it all began.

He had to try like hell to save a life in exchange for the one he'd taken.

He took the last bite of his apple and heaved the core at the nearest outbuilding, where he'd spotted a groundhog. Whatever sound the core made as it struck the clapboard couldn't be heard over the grinding wheeze of the school bus as it pulled away. The coast was clear. He'd take a few minutes to find out if dinner with Parker was still on the agenda for tomorrow night.

And even if it wasn't, he'd let her know they needed to talk.

* * *

IN THE SPACE OF two hours Friday morning Parker had managed to break their only coffeepot by dropping it on the concrete floor, hang up twice on a potential client from a large-name gardening center, and leave bloody handprints all over the day's paperwork when a cut in her left palm opened up again. By eleven o'clock she was ready to burrow into the compost pile. She left a sorrowful-looking Harris in charge, after promising him he'd find macaroni salad and sliced ham in the fridge for him and Reid, and for the first time in a long time, she took an extended lunch break.

She found herself standing on the sidewalk outside Eugenia's dress shop. She was tempted to go inside and see if she could find something stylish to wear for her dinner date. But she wasn't sure how Eugenia felt about Reid and the revelation she must surely have heard by now. Besides, Parker didn't feel up to answering questions.

Which meant that driving into town had been a bad idea. She'd already collected more than one curious stare.

She turned away from the window, but not quickly enough.

"Parker." Eugenia stood in the open doorway. "You coming in?"

An easy-listening radio station played in the background, the air smelled of potpourri, and the rich colors and fabrics of the merchandise made the store a feel-good place.

But there was no disguising the vacant atmosphere.

Eugenia led her to a wrought-iron bench outside the changing rooms. "You're my first customer of the day. As sad as I am to say it, if business doesn't pick up I won't last the year."

"I'm sorry to hear that."

"I'm the one who should apologize. I may not have had much traffic in here today, but I still heard about what happened at Snoozy's the other night." She gave an uneasy laugh. "I mean, there I was, making all these suggestions and innuendos, thinking you and Reid MacFarland would make a perfect couple, and the whole time he's the one who —" She grimaced. "No wonder you needed me to watch Nat. You had a lot on your mind, plus being injured." She picked up one of Parker's hands and made a sympathetic noise. "And there I was thinking you and Reid planned to get romantic."

"He's a good man. A good man who made a bad mistake."

"I see." Eugenia uncrossed her legs. "You forgave him."

"Do you find that so hard to believe?"

"No, I find it...splendid." She choked on the word, and waved a hand in front of her face as if to fan away the tears. Parker leaned forward to give her a hug.

"I'm sorry." The next time she saw Harris she was going to thump him on the head. "I didn't mean to upset you."

"You're not the reason I'm upset," she said wryly, and swiped the heel of a palm under her eye. "But enough about me. Tell me more about Reid. Does this mean he's planning to stick around?"

"I'm going to ask him to."

"What about the Army?"

"He's getting out."

"Oh, Parker. I'm so happy for you." Eugenia patted Parker's knee. "Everyone else who knows you will be, too. They'll be curious, maybe even judgmental, but in the end they'll take their cue from you."

"Things didn't go so well at Snoozy's."

"You don't think those guys were just looking for an excuse to fight? But enough of that. You said you plan to ask Reid to stay. I have no doubt he'll say yes. However —" she stood, and moved to a nearby display rack " — how about we stack the odds in your favor?"

*   *   *

229

PARKER HAD A DELIVERY due late Saturday morning. Although Harris offered to watch Nat, Parker decided to give him a much-needed break and take Nat with her instead. Which meant that Saturday afternoon, after she and Nat got home, they spent a whirlwind hour getting Nat ready for her sleepover. And all the while Parker fretted about hers.

He'd said they needed to talk. He hadn't said it with a smile, but he hadn't been frowning, either. Maybe he was considering moving to Thistle Hill. Maybe he wasn't sure how Parker would take it.

She'd need to make sure he understood she would take it very well indeed.

Okay, wait, she was getting ahead of herself. He'd said he could get caught up in stop-loss, which meant he might end up spending another year or so with the Army. But that didn't necessarily mean he'd be deployed. It could mean nothing more than extra duty in Kentucky.

They could handle a long-distance relationship, couldn't they? Take their time, see if it might lead to something more? Assuming Reid was interested.

Which was what Parker had to find out. And explained why her stomach continued to flutter like a tissue in a wind tunnel.

She'd asked him to come at seven, and at five minutes to she heard him on the front porch. She wanted to fling open the door and throw herself at him. But they'd had an emotional few days. Some decorum was probably called for.

So she pulled him inside and instead of a lip-lock greeted him with a fervent hug. He wrapped one arm around her, the other holding a bottle of red wine, and squeezed back. She buried her face in his neck, breathing in the familiar smell of soap and fresh-cut grass. A sudden heaviness settled between her hips.

The heck with decorum.

She bit him.

He jerked and hissed in a breath. He pulled back to stare down at her, dark eyes heavy-lidded and gleaming, then looked away just long enough to set the bottle on the nearest flat surface. She caught a glimpse of raw need on his face before he slid his fingers into her hair and his mouth claimed hers.

He swung her around and backed her up, hips pinning her to the wall, and deepened the kiss. His hands slid from her head to her shoulders, past her waist and around to her butt. He squeezed, lowered one hand and urged her leg upward. She wrapped her thigh around his hip and the skirt of her dress scooted back. When his hand encountered bare skin he stopped. She moaned in protest but he dragged his mouth from hers. Panting, he lowered his head to her shoulder.

"Wait," he said raggedly.

She tightened her leg and squeezed him in closer. "I thought you didn't like that word."

"I didn't even say hello." He raised his head and gave her a quick, breathless kiss. "Hello."

"Hello, yourself."

"Your cuts healing all right?"

She pressed the backs of her hands to the wall above her head, her breathing as labored as his. His gaze dropped to the less-than-modest neckline of her wrap dress and he groaned.

"My palms are up here," she teased, and smiled when he had to force his gaze up. She stopped smiling as she scanned his bruises. "And they're in better shape than your face."

"Thanks a lot."

"Want to inspect my other injuries?"

He caught her hands and kissed them. "We need to talk first."

"I know." She backed away, and straightened her dress. "I'm sorry about the way Nat behaved. It was my fault. You were right when you said I should have told her." She laid a palm on his chest, and gave him a beseeching look. "We just need to give her some time. She loves you. She'll come around."

"Parker." He rubbed a hand over his mouth. "I don't have time. I'm leaving in a week."

"I know, but you can arrange for leave to come back and see us. How long could out processing take? A couple of weeks? A month?" When he didn't say anything she took another step back, and added softly, "Or am I assuming too much?"

He shook his head, but something in his eyes worried her. "I won't be able to visit anytime soon. I'm headed back to the sandbox."

No. He had to go *back*? She wrapped her arms around her waist and held on tight. "You already found out you're being extended? I was hoping you wouldn't get caught up in that."

"I didn't."

"I—I don't understand."

"When my contract's up, I'm signing on for another three years."

Her stomach dropped, and she sagged against the wall. "But you said… You led me to believe that…"

"I know. And I'm sorry. But after you forgave me, and once I saw Nat's reaction to finding out the truth, I realized I had no option. I have to go back. I owe it to my unit. I owe it to you and Nat. And Tim."

"What are you talking about? You don't owe us anything."

One step brought him within touching distance and he cupped her elbow. "Please try to understand. How can I ask you to respect me when I don't respect myself? I want to deserve you. And for that I have to go back."

"*No.* You don't. I respect you now. I can't respect you if you're dead."

"Parker—"

She shook him off, blinking away furious tears. "I won't do it. I won't put my life on hold again. I don't want to spend every minute of every hour of every day worrying about ambushes and IEDs and suicide bombers and—"

"Friendly fire?"

"I won't put Nat through that again," she choked. "I can't go through that again."

"One tour. One more tour and I'll leave the Army."

"You say that now. Just like you said the other day that you were looking forward to being a civilian."

"I am looking forward to that. To being with you. But I have to pay my debt."

"What can I do?" she whispered. She grabbed his hand with both of hers and held it to her chest, squeezing hard. "I'll do anything to change your mind."

He pulled her against him, and with his free hand stroked the hair away from her face. "If anyone could change my mind it would be you. But it would change things between us."

"You've already changed everything."

"Don't say that. I love you."

Grief rolled through her veins like newly poured concrete, weighing down her limbs and hardening her heart. She pushed free. "I think you'd better leave. And I—I don't just mean the house."

"Did you hear me, Parker Dean? I said I love you."

"And I asked you to leave." *Go. Please, please go.*

"I have seven more days. I was hoping to spend them with you."

"And I was hoping to spend them with the man I knew yesterday. But he's not here anymore."

He flinched, then with his forefinger made a *you and me* gesture. "You and I both know what this really is. It's a defense mechanism."

"You won't talk me out of what I'm feeling."

"I'm getting ready to deploy. Soldiers and their families often distance themselves from each other right before a deployment. It helps them handle the separation."

"Only that doesn't apply in this case, does it? *We're* not family. Nat is my family. She's all the family I'll ever need."

His face tightened. "I know you love me."

And the hits just kept on coming. She shook her head. "I told you. I told you I could never love another soldier. I don't love you. I can't."

"Parker—"

"I *trusted* you."

"You can still trust me. Nothing's changed."

"Everything's changed." She jolted into motion, somehow seeing well enough through her tears to stumble past him and wrench open the front door. "Goodbye, Corporal. I wish you the best with your career."

Slowly he turned, his gaze moving from her to the open door. The reined-in pain and remorse she'd seen on his face the day they'd met was back again, and it was killing her.

But once was enough. One soldier was enough. Reid had made his choice. And she'd made hers. *Please, please, please, please go.*

"So that's it?" he asked, his voice strained. "You won't even consider giving us a try?"

"You belong to the Army. There is no *us*."

He slid his hands into his pockets and walked to the door. Stopped, and stared straight ahead. "I need to let you know I talked to a few people. About the co-op." She gasped, but he didn't react. "There's some definite interest. Gallahan can give you the names."

He shrugged. "Maybe you didn't like the idea because it was mine. Or maybe you're not deep enough in the hole yet to realize what a godsend it could be. It's admirable that you want to honor Tim's memory." He turned and looked at her then, his expression more stark than the Arctic skyline. "But what good will that do when you've lost everything?"

She already had, damn him. "Get out."

His gaze shifted forward again. "Looking back on it, I can't believe I was arrogant enough to come find you. It was unfair and it was cruel. I put you and Nat through a lot." He paused. "I'll never forget what you did for me. You forgave me. And if you can manage it, maybe there's hope I can manage it, too."

A moment later he was gone.

She shut the door, and leaned back against it. After she heard the Jeep start up she pushed herself upright, stumbled into the kitchen, and turned off the oven.

16

REID DIDN'T INTEND TO leave Thistle Hill right away. He figured he'd give Parker a few days to think about things, then go back and…well, beg. It was a plan, anyway. After she kicked him out he drove for hours along Lake Erie, rehearsing his arguments, wondering if he should buy a ring.

If only he hadn't opened his mouth about the co-op.

When he got tired of driving, he headed back to the motel and Gallahan's office. At that point he was more interested in booze than company, but Gallahan insisted he stay and talk. Over whiskey and microwave popcorn he told Reid that the growers' network idea seemed to be gaining in popularity and Reid perked up.

"Maybe that's what it'll take," he muttered. "A full company assault." He eyed Gallahan. "Think the people on your list would be willing to talk to Parker about it?"

"Yeah, man." Gallahan poured two more shots. "But whether she goes for the idea or not, she's still got her own greenhouses. Where does that leave you?"

"Meaning?"

"You're giving the Army another three years. What were you planning to do, commute to Fort Knox every day?"

Shit. Reid collapsed against the back of his chair. Why hadn't he thought that far ahead? Being an Army wife meant being mobile. Didn't matter if it was just for one stint. Even if she *had* been okay with his reenlisting, she'd never have been okay with leaving Thistle Hill.

Especially if she set up a growers' network and the damned thing took off. She'd have that much more reason to stay put.

He'd screwed himself but good.

"Excellent point," he said, as much to himself as to Gallahan. He tossed back his whiskey, then slammed the glass down onto the table. The motion felt good but the sound effects left a lot to be desired since the tabletop was padded.

His host gave a rather unsteady nod of approval and tipped the bottle again.

Reid squinted at his glass. If he didn't reenlist, Parker and Nat could be his family. But then they'd have this horrendous thing he'd done hanging over their heads. Parker may have forgiven him, but until he'd forgiven himself he'd be his family's own worst enemy.

And in order to forgive himself, he had to go back.

Maybe she'd wait for him. *Right.* He shoved his glass across the table. And maybe Harris would give up chewing gum.

Besides, he couldn't help remembering what the old man had said about Eugenia. *She's a good woman. She deserves better than me.*

Different woman, same truth.

It was what had made Reid decide to reenlist in the first place.

He considered another drink or two but as much as he craved oblivion, he needed to slow down if he wanted to get on the road first thing in the morning. The faster he got out of Parker's way, the better.

He peered over at Gallahan, decided to linger a minute more. "You owe me a story."

Gallahan shook the empty bottle, and looked around as if he'd somehow misplaced the whiskey that was supposed to be inside. "Forget it, man. You've sucked down enough of my booze to get to sleep without a bedtime story."

Reid cocked his head, and Gallahan shrugged. "Fine. You love someone. Mother, father, sweetheart, child. One of you screws the other over. The end."

Reid grunted. "Guess that means it's time to pack up." He pushed to his feet and scrubbed a hand over his face. "Do me a favor?"

"Name it."

"Let me crash here for the night. Doesn't matter how much

whiskey I drank. No way in hell I'll get any sleep if I have to lie under that ugly-ass turquoise ceiling."

*   *   *

REID STOPPED TO GAS up in Cincinnati. He was just pulling away from the pump when his cell rang. He checked the number and jerked the wheel so he could park, raising a hand in apology to the guy he'd just cut off.

"Parker?"

"No, i-it's me."

"Nat." He winced. Had his disappointment come through in his voice? He was only a couple of hours away from Fort Knox but he'd have turned around in a heartbeat if Parker had asked him to.

"It's good to hear from you, kid. I didn't think you'd want to talk to me."

A pause. Then a sniffle.

"Reid?"

"Yeah?"

"I don't hate you. I know I said it, but I didn't mean it."

"Don't worry about it. We all say things we don't mean. But thank you for telling me."

"So...will you come back?"

Aw, hell. "I can't do that."

"Is it my fault?"

He dropped his head back and it thumped against the headrest. "No, Nat. It could never be you. It's time for me to rejoin my unit, is all."

"You wouldn't have to if you didn't reenlist."

"Look, I know it's hard to understand, and I hope you know it's the most difficult thing I've ever had to do, leaving you and your mom—" he held the phone away from his ear and took a second to steady his voice " —but I have to go back."

"Because of Daddy?"

"Partly. I just...need to do it to feel good about myself."

"Like when I had to apologize to the teacher because I broke her favorite umbrella?"

"Just like that."

She sighed. "Softball practice won't be the same without you."

"With you pitching, they won't need me."

"Guess I'll never learn to rappel."

"I'm sorry I didn't follow through on that. But I did talk to Gallahan. Joe, I mean. He'll teach you."

"He knows how to rappel?"

"Yep. And it'll be more fun learning from him, don't you think?"

"No."

He couldn't help but laugh. "I'll miss you, Nat."

"I know. I'll miss you, too."

"You're a real charmer, kid."

"I know that, too."

*   *   *

EUGENIA STARED AT THE stack of unopened boxes in front of her and then she stared at the fabric steamer in her hand. When had unwrapping and arranging new stock come to feel less like Christmas morning and more like a chore? She sagged down onto the nearest chair. Maybe it was time for a full-fledged mope. À la mode.

Of course she'd have to go home for the ice cream. But considering how slow business had been, no one would notice if she closed early.

She was contemplating garnishing her pity party with hot-fudge sauce and sprinkles when Harris appeared in the storeroom doorway. She jumped and slapped a hand to her heart.

"I called out, but I guess you didn't hear me. What happened to the bells?"

"They met with an untimely death." He looked confused and she waved a hand. "Never mind."

He came into the room, eyes on her face. "You been cryin'?"

238

"Dust," she said, knowing he wouldn't believe her and not caring. "There's a lot of dust in here."

"Should I come back later?" His voice was gentle, which put her in very real danger of starting to cry again. She cleared her throat and started fiddling with the steamer.

"If you're here to help me unpack, then no. If you're here to lecture me, then yes."

"What if it's neither?"

"Then you can help me unpack while you tell me why you are here."

He picked up the box cutter. "How about I help you unpack and you tell me why you're upset."

She was too surprised *not* to answer. "The shop's not doing well. I know it's been less than six months, but if things don't change soon I'll have to give it up."

He lifted a coral-colored silk dress out of the box without a word and she reached for a hanger.

"I could dip into my savings, and keep things going for a while. But why prolong the inevitable? I just don't know how much to put into this."

She spread her arms and Harris draped a pair of leggings over her wrist.

"Everything," he said. "You put in everything."

"Easy for you to say."

"No, it's not. That's the point. When you care enough about somethin' — or someone — you have to be willing to give it your all. Well, without bankrupting yourself. But as scary as it is to put yourself out there, the payoff will make it all worthwhile."

Eugenia blinked. "You sound like an online dating commercial." Then she frowned. "And you're assuming there is a payoff."

"True. But meanwhile you're livin' life. And if it doesn't work out then at least you have the comfort of knowing you tried." He gestured at the clothes she'd put on hangers. "I'm hopin' by now you've figured out I'm not talking about dresses."

"Harris, I can't…I can't do this again."

"This is the last time."

"You didn't even want Parker to call me when you were in the hospital."

"I was embarrassed. So sue me."

She dropped back into the chair. "This back and forth—I feel like the last designer purse two women are fighting over on Black Friday."

"O-kay. But I want you to know something. I'm sorry I got upset about Kerry. You have to, I mean, I *hope* you understand how rotten I feel about not being able to help my own daughter. Not just with money but with gettin' her to see she deserves better than that deadbeat she married. Anyway, the guilt's been eatin' at me and I think I used that thing with Kerry to punish myself."

"What are you talking about?"

He set the box cutter aside and bent toward her, hands gripping the arms of her chair. He smelled like cinnamon, and his face was as red as the wrapper on the pack of chewing gum sticking out of his shirt pocket.

She'd done her best to keep hope shut away. Apparently the little son of a gun had learned to pick locks.

"I failed as a father," he said. "Followin' that tradition means I deserve to fail as a lover, too."

"Oh, Harris." She cupped his face with her palm.

"That's not all I want to say. You have a big heart. It's one of the things I love about you. So why in hell would I want to change that?"

She wanted to kiss him. His face hovered less than six inches away and she wanted to close the gap and lay one on him. Wait a minute. Did he say love?

"Did you say you love me?"

"I did." He bridged those six inches and kissed her lightly. Then he pulled her upright and kissed her deeply and thoroughly, his large hands sliding down her back and lower. And Eugenia had solid proof of what she'd always suspected—Harris Briggs was as passionate as he was stubborn.

She stared at him in wonder, her cheeks as red as his, and he smiled. "Does this mean you can forgive an old man?"

"I'm not sure about that, but I do forgive you."

"So sweet." He pulled her close again, and it was long moments before he let her come up for air. She rested her head on his shoulder.

"Can I ask what brought this on?"

"Common sense. Parker can forgive Reid for the death of her husband but I can't forgive you for bein' generous to my daughter? That's not something I'm proud of."

"How are they doing?"

"Reid went back to Kentucky this morning. And Parker looks as sad as I've ever seen her."

"What happened?"

Harris sighed. "He told her he planned to reenlist."

Eugenia winced. Poor Parker. "So much for her plans to talk him into staying. I'm sorry it didn't work out. She seemed to really care about him."

"I know what you're thinkin'. They've known each other less than a month." He shrugged. "But whenever I saw 'em together it was like they were two halves of a whole." He squeezed her shoulder. "Like us."

"Is there any hope at all for them?"

"Beats me. They're stuck, until one of them gives in. All I know is, I don't want us to be stuck. Not anymore."

"So we're taking it to the next level?"

"I'm all over the next level. But there's one last thing I need to tell you."

Oh, no. Not again. Drawing in a deep breath, Eugenia backed away. "What is it, Harris?"

He gave her a sheepish grin. "Thing is, my middle name really is Marion."

*   *   *

NUMBER OF DAYS SINCE Reid filed his retention forms? Three. Number of days till his unit deployed? Twenty. Number of days since Parker Dean had kicked his ass out of Thistle Hill? Six. But who was counting?

"Corporal?"

Reid jerked his attention back to where it belonged — with the clinical psychologist they'd assigned him for stateside treatment. Damn it. If he wanted to be cleared for combat he'd better get his ass in line and focus.

"Sir?"

"I asked about your leave."

"Yes, sir." Reid was sitting in a well-padded armchair, one hand gripping his thigh, the other hanging over the end of the chair's right arm. Needless to say, he was finding it hard to relax. "It was tough. Tougher than I expected."

"You look like you came through it okay."

"I meant it was tough on her."

"The widow of Timothy Dean."

"Yes, sir. It was also hard on her daughter."

"Yet you stayed."

"I felt I had to. She — they — needed help."

"What kind of help?"

"Physical. And financial." Blood rushed into Reid's face and he shifted in the chair. "By physical I mean manual labor."

The doctor nodded. "Did you become close?"

"This is the first time I've ever resented having to return to my unit."

"Trust me, Corporal. It won't be the last."

"That would be true if they were my family. But they're not."

"You'd like them to be?" Reid couldn't answer. The doctor made a note on his pad. "This is a clichéd question, but I'm interested in the answer. The fact that Mrs. Dean and her daughter aren't your family. How does that make you feel?"

"Sad. Lonely. Frustrated. But those feelings won't affect my duties, sir."

"Corporal, if we kept every sad, lonely or frustrated soldier from combat we'd have no Army. And that includes commanding officers."

"Yes, sir."

Dr. Robbins opened a file folder and paged through the contents. "The last time we talked you said you were feeling 'guilty as hell,' and that you'd 'let everyone down.' Tim Dean, his family, your unit, the Army, yourself. Has any of that changed?"

Reid straightened his spine. "No, sir. I did let them — and myself — down. That won't change. The difference is that Mrs. Dean forgave me. She also helped me realize I need to forgive myself."

"And have you?"

"Working on it, sir."

"And the nightmares?"

"Less frequent."

"Do you feel you're ready to return to combat?"

"That's not my decision to make."

"Still, I'd like to hear what you have to say."

Reid hesitated. "I don't feel ready," he said. "But I didn't feel ready before my first tour, either. I can tell you I will support my unit. Any time, any way, any how. I won't make the same mistakes. I admit I worry I'll be trigger-shy. But if it happens, I'll deal with it. I won't let my squad down again. And I know they'll have my back."

"I see." The doctor didn't look up as he spoke but continued to write in his notebook. Reid waited. What the hell would he do with himself if he didn't deploy with his unit?

Kentucky wasn't far enough away from Pennsylvania. If he had any hope at all of putting Parker behind him, he needed at least half a world between them.

*   *   *

FRIDAY AFTERNOON. NEARLY A week since she'd sent Reid away.

Seven days of sad silences and damp pillows and frozen pizzas in the Dean household. It reminded Parker of the days following Tim's funeral. Which was ridiculous. Reid hadn't died.

But he wasn't coming back.

For Nat's benefit, Parker struggled to return their world to normal. To get things back on schedule. But she didn't have the energy to cook or bake or clean—it was all she could do to help Nat with her homework. Not that Nat could concentrate, either.

Parker stood in the center of the potting shed, staring at the mug of coffee that reeked of scorch. Drinking that concentrated sludge would no doubt get her through the rest of the day. But she doubted her stomach would survive it.

She slumped down onto the edge of her desk. Which should she tackle first—her proposal for landscaping Joe's motel, or preparing the delivery for her newest client? Either prospect should have her tingling with glee.

Ten tingle-free seconds later, she sighed. She'd lost her appetite, and she'd lost sleep. She'd also lost her joy. She knew it was temporary. It just didn't *feel* temporary.

Outside the door a boot scraped over gravel, and she grabbed up some papers and pinned a smile on her face. Harris appeared in the doorway and scowled.

"Don't bother," he said, and she rolled her eyes.

"You're one to talk, acting all grumpy," she muttered. "At the post office yesterday Hazel Catlett told me she'd spotted your pickup outside Eugenia's house every morning for the past week."

He blushed, and Parker relented. "I'm happy for you both."

"Have you heard from him?"

Instantly her eyes filled. Blinking against the dampness, she rounded her desk and collapsed into the chair. She'd known this conversation was coming. Might as well get it over with.

"Last night. He texted to let us know he's headed overseas in three weeks."

"Did you text him back?"

"Nat did."

He frowned. "You know, my girl, I want to be happy for you, too."

"You can be. I forgave him. It's what you wanted from the beginning."

"You know what I mean."

"Be happy I had the strength to do what I had to do."

"Who'd you do it for?"

"Who do you think? Nat and me."

"Yeah?" His gaze narrowed. "You did it for Nat? What do you think the kid needs more, a bunch of flowering plants or a father?"

She would have jumped to her feet if she'd thought her knees could support her. "That's a low blow, Harris Briggs. Think about what happened the last time she had a father on deployment. And while you're thinking about it go away and pretend you work for me."

"Now, don't go gettin' your dress over your head." He settled on a stool in the corner, letting her know he wasn't going anywhere anytime soon. Perfect. Where the heck were her earbuds when she needed them?

"I'm thinkin' you did it for Tim. To protect his dream."

She blinked. "Yes, well, it's my dream, too." He looked skeptical and she pitched forward in her chair. "Okay, you know what? Maybe I do feel guilty. Maybe I am punishing myself. In less than three weeks, I fell in love with a man I shouldn't even want to be around. But the bottom line is he lied to me. He led me to believe he wasn't planning to reenlist. Now he is. End of story."

"You trusted him."

"And look where it got me."

"Let me finish. You trusted him with your daughter, with your business and if he hadn't decided to join up again you would have trusted him with your future. So why can't you trust him when he says just one more tour?"

She didn't bother to respond. Harris didn't get it. Another tour would lead to an Army career. She just knew it. And she didn't want that. Not for Nat, not for herself. More than that, she couldn't bear it.

Harris spread his hands. "You waiting to see if he survives his stint? What if he doesn't?"

"That's the whole point."

"You need to think about it, my girl. No matter what, if he gets killed it'll devastate you. That bridge has been crossed. So why not step up and grab some happiness while you can? You need him, and he can't be here for you. But he needs you, too, and you *can* be there for him."

Her throat burned. She snatched a tissue from the box on her desk. "Whose side are you on, anyway?"

"The same side I've always been on." He stood. "Question is, whose side are *you* on?"

The tissue crumpled between her fingers as she watched him amble out of the shed. Eugenia Blue had a lot to answer for. Parker had liked the old man a heck of a lot better when he was tight-lipped and crabby.

17

NAT HAD TAKEN TO carrying around Parker's cell phone from the moment she got home from school. She wanted to be able to text Reid back as soon as he texted her. They'd only communicated four or five times but Parker didn't have the heart to reclaim her phone. Besides, she was hoping it would help Nat deal with Reid's leaving.

And if she didn't have her phone, she didn't have temptation at her fingertips.

After her conversation with Harris, Parker was feeling especially drained. She wanted nothing more than to throw together a meal of soup and salad, walk Chance and go to bed. Of course, they had homework to power through, but Nat took care of the Chance issue by playing an extended game of tag with him after dinner. By the time Parker called her in to start getting ready for bed, Nat was exhausted and Parker was delighted.

She tucked Nat in, washed the dishes, tended to some paperwork and finally changed into her nightgown. Although her bed was calling her name, she wanted to charge her cell phone so Nat could start her marathon monitoring all over again without any issues. And Parker knew exactly where to find the dumb thing.

After turning on the hall light she crept into her daughter's bedroom and checked the nightstand. Nothing. She checked the floor by the bed, the bureau and even rifled through Nat's backpack. Where the heck was it?

Oh. Her stomach sank as she tiptoed over to the bed. Sure enough, on the pillow beside Nat's head lay Parker's phone. With a misty-eyed glance at the sleeping nine-year-old, Parker leaned over and picked it up. Then she made the mistake of turning it off. The phone sounded its sign-off tones and her daughter's eyes fluttered open.

"Mom?"

"I'm sorry, sweetie. Go back to sleep."

"Will we ever see Reid again?"

Parker inhaled — *in, two-three-four-five-six-seven* — and wondered the exact same thing. *Out, two-three-four-five-six-seven*. She sat on the edge of the bed.

"Aren't you keeping in touch now?" she asked. "And when he goes overseas you'll be exchanging letters, right? You'll be pen pals."

"It's not the same. I need him here so he can help me with my pitching."

"Nat, even if we became a family we wouldn't see him. He's in the Army. His job is in another country."

"But if we were his family, one day he'd come home."

Parker fought to push the words past the lump in her throat. "And he'd leave again, to go to his next post."

"Couldn't we go with him?"

"Maybe. But what if we couldn't? Wouldn't that make you sad?"

Nat shrugged. "I'm sad now."

Parker bent forward to hide her face. Eyes squeezed shut, she pressed a kiss to her daughter's forehead.

So am I, kiddo. So am I.

* * *

THE PHONE RANG SIX times before Harris picked up. "Is there even such a thing as a greenhouse emergency?" he growled.

Parker continued to shove handfuls of her best underwear into an overnight bag. "You're right. I'm a coward. But Nat and I belong with Reid. So I'm going to Kentucky."

"About damned time."

Parker heard Eugenia say "Harris Briggs" and deliver a smack.

"Tell me you're not thinkin' the same thing," Harris muttered.

Parker drew in a shaky breath. "What can I say, I'm a late bloomer. Takes me longer to figure these things out. Anyway, I'm glad you approve because I need you to come stay with Nat."

"Now? It's three in the morning."

"Be proud of me. I'm asking for help."

"Could you call back and ask again in about five hours?"

Another smack. Parker found herself smiling.

"I'll put my best sheets on the bed. Five hundred thread count percale."

In the background Eugenia offered an appreciative "ooh." Harris shushed her.

"How you gonna get there?" he asked Parker.

"Drive."

"Your Camry? I don't think so. I wouldn't trust that thing as far as the liquor store."

Eugenia said something about a new car and Harris shushed her again.

"What did she say?"

"She said you can take her car. And the sooner we hang up the sooner we can get there. Bye."

"That's not what she said."

He sighed. "Reid was gonna get you a new car."

Of course he was. Because he hadn't already done enough. She struggled to stay upright despite the sadness that wanted to pull her to the bedroom floor.

Reid MacFarland was a good man. And she'd been too caught up in her own self-pity to appreciate it. She blinked away tears she'd had plenty of practice keeping at bay.

"I already have enough guilt to deal with. Anyway, after the way I acted I don't blame him for changing his mind about the car."

"You know him better than that. He was smart enough to realize, what with you bein' so independent and all, that you'd want to pick out your own vehicle. So he left you the money instead."

Parker pulled the phone away from her ear and stared at it.

"Said to give it to you once he was gone."

"I don't want any more of his money."

"Not sure why you're tellin' me."

She heard a scuffle, then Eugenia came on the phone. "Is that why you're going to Kentucky? To tell him you don't want his money?"

"No." Parker closed up her bag with a loud *zip*. "To tell him I want *him*."

"Oh, good."

Harris yelled in the background, "We're on our way."

"Thank you both." As she disconnected she heard Eugenia ask, "What if it's too late?"

Parker snapped her phone shut. Maybe she would be too late.

But she had nothing left to lose.

*   *   *

"HEY, MAC! I THOUGHT we were grabbing breakfast at the mess hall."

Reid stopped in the middle of the sidewalk and waited for his squad mate to catch up. "Bosco. Sorry, man, I forgot. I had an appointment at the medical center this morning and I guess I got worked up about it." That, and other things he was trying damned hard not to think about.

"How'd that go?"

"Good. Cleared for combat. 'Course, now your ass outranks me."

"They're not reassigning you?"

"Not yet. The doc said they'd be keeping tabs on me and the whole squad."

"Welcome back, brother." Bosco held out his fist and they exchanged knucks, and Reid flashed to Nat at her first softball practice, her face beaming with happiness and pride.

Damn, he missed that kid.

"Mac?" Bosco said it as if he'd already called him, maybe more than once.

"Sorry. What's up?"

"You know, you really shouldn't skip breakfast. You just got back and already you look like you lost weight. That thing Master Sergeant got you working on that important?"

"What are you, my mother? Kincannon's got me working the lathes. He's all hot and bothered about cutting production time."

Bosco rolled his eyes. "He's going for the quarterly award."

"Yeah, well, he can have it. Hey, I found out I don't have to move. Not till we get stateside again, anyway. But once my tour's done I'm off-post."

"I know. Sucks. You could stay if you got married." Bosco snapped his fingers, thankfully not noticing Reid's flinch. "I almost forgot. They want you over at Human Resources."

"What for?"

Bosco raised jet-black eyebrows. "Does it look like I'm packing my crystal ball?"

Reid grunted. "We got two balls between us and they're both mine."

"Screw you." Reid grinned and walked away. Bosco hollered after him. "You stood me up, asshole. That means you're springing for lunch."

Reid yelled back without turning around. "Roger that."

Fifteen minutes later, he walked into the hulking white building that housed the personnel department. Reception directed him to records, which was actually a corner office divided into three cubicles. He stopped at the first cubicle, and a woman with gray hair cut almost as short as his peered at him over a pair of reading glasses with bright orange frames.

"May I help you?"

"Corporal Reid MacFarland, ma'am. I was told to report."

"Yes. Corporal MacFarland." She poked at her keyboard. "You're with the 1st Infantry?"

"Yes, ma'am."

More poking. "Here we are. Your record was flagged. Ah, I see why. Next of kin."

"Excuse me?"

She rapped at the screen with a white-tipped fingernail. "The 'next of kin' field. It says 'not applicable.'"

"That's because it doesn't apply."

"In what way?"

"In the way that I have no next of kin."

Frowning, she yanked off her glasses. "You have no family?"

Wasn't like I didn't try, lady. He gritted his teeth. "Not living."

"I see. Then whom shall we notify in the event of your death?"

"I'd say the Army, but I suspect they'll already know."

Another tap at the screen. "I have to put something there."

"There is something there. 'Not applicable.'" Jesus, how many times would he have to go through this?

"We can't notify 'Not applicable,'" she snapped.

He shrugged. "Then I guess I'd better not die."

* * *

AN HOUR AWAY FROM Fort Knox, Parker stopped to call home. She chatted with Harris, then asked him to put her daughter on the phone.

"Nat. I'm so sorry I didn't tell you I was leaving."

"That's okay, Mom, I got your note. We're doing great. Harris made pancakes with chocolate chips *and* marshmallows for breakfast. But first we had to clean up after Eugenia set off the smoke alarm. So is Reid going to marry us?"

Parker's stomach was one big, hot ball of uncertainty. "I'm not there yet, sweetie. And once I get there I may not find him right away. But I'll check in with you in a few hours, all right?"

"All right."

"I just wanted to make sure you're okay with all this."

"If I say yes, can I have a hamster? Ruthanne has one called Peanut and he feels really soft when you hold him up against your cheek."

"Who cleans out Peanut's cage, Ruthanne or her mom?"

Nat gave a long-suffering sigh. "Never mind. If Reid comes back do you think he'll bring me a present?"

The knots in Parker's stomach tightened. "If he does, it won't be a hamster."

A pause. "Harris says they have famous horses in Kentucky."

Parker laughed despite herself. "I wouldn't count on that, either." Or on anything. What if she had left it too late? "Nat, I have to go now. I love you."

"I love you, too, Mom." She spoke in a rush. "He knows I like pink, right?"

Parker closed her eyes and leaned her head against the window. "Don't worry. He knows."

*   *   *

REID WAS HEADED BACK to the machine shop when his cell rang. He looked at the caller ID and couldn't help a smile. He'd texted Nat, challenging her to read an Ellery Queen. If she met the challenge he promised he'd send her a gift card to Dairy Queen.

Apparently she was anxious to deliver her book report.

"Hey, kid. So, which one did you read?"

"It's me."

For the second time that day, he stopped short in the middle of the sidewalk. He reminded himself to breathe, and leaned against a signpost. His fingers tightened around the phone. "Parker."

"I want to apologize. For the way we left things."

"That's not necessary."

"I—I didn't really give you a chance to… I didn't listen very well."

"We both know it wouldn't have changed anything." He pushed away from the metal post. "Look. I get it. You and Nat went through hell when Tim was deployed and then you went through worse when he didn't come back. You don't want to go through that again. Especially with me." He exhaled. "But I never set out to lie to you."

"I know."

"You had your revelation after Harris ended up in the hospital and I had mine after — well, after I saw the look on Nat's face when she found out the truth."

"Reid —"

"I accept your apology. But I owe you one, too. I never should have made the decision to re-up without including you."

"But you still would have made it."

He couldn't deny it. "You're an extraordinary woman, Parker Dean. I wish you the best." He swallowed hard. "I have to sign off now."

"Wait."

That word again. It made him ache for a life he could never have. He couldn't speak, but he didn't hang up, either.

"I have more to say but I'd rather say it in person. Could you come off-post?"

"Could I what?"

"They won't let me on-post."

"You're here? At Fort Knox?" Shit. He knew exactly why she'd come. And he didn't think he could do it. Didn't think he could see her in person and let her go away again. Not without begging her to give them another chance.

He stared down at the phone in his hand, his thumb hovering over the End button.

*　*　*

PARKER PULLED IN A strangled breath. "Yes," she managed, resisting the urge to add, *And I need you out here. Now.* "Reid?" Nothing. She bit her lip and ended the call, then settled in to wait. She'd give him fifteen minutes. If he didn't show, she'd have to assume she was too late.

She tipped her head back. Above her the sky was the color of a blue jay's crest, the sun a perfect circle of yellow flame. Still the day felt cold and gray. She wrapped her arms around her waist and leaned back against the car.

Please don't let it be too late.

Ten minutes later, she spotted his Jeep exiting the gate. Her heart began to pound in anticipation. He pulled into the visitors' lot, and she smoothed her hands over the snug plum-colored sweater she wore with her jeans, and did a quick fluff of her hair.

But when Reid stepped out onto the pavement, she saw that he was scowling.

He wasn't pleased to see her.

He strode over, and instead of reaching for her he clasped his hands behind his back. In his ACUs and black beret and with that wide-legged stance of his, he looked like he was reporting for duty. The backs of her eyes burned.

"It's good to see you," he said.

Okay, well obviously that wasn't true.

"Reid." She put her own hands behind her back.

"You're a long way from Thistle Hill." He sounded terse and impatient. Her hands shook and she was glad he couldn't see them. She shouldn't have come. He was a soldier. Not only did he have a tour to prepare for, but he knew how to compartmentalize. He'd already put Parker and Nat and Thistle Hill behind him. He'd had to. It was one of those self-defense mechanisms he'd talked about.

But she'd traveled nearly five hundred miles to say her piece. She might as well say it.

"I had to see you." She struggled to keep her tone as devoid of emotion as his, but she must not have managed it because his frown deepened.

"Is something wrong?" When she didn't answer he gave a tight nod. "It's the money."

"What?"

"You need a car. I don't need the cash. Keep it." He looked away, then back. "It's what I'll get for reenlisting."

She choked out a laugh. "That's...ironic." A breeze pushed through

255

the parking lot and she combed unsteady fingers through her hair. "It's not the money."

His hands came to his sides. "Then why are you here?"

"To apologize."

"You did that over the phone."

She dragged in a breath. "I also need to tell you that you were right."

"About what?"

"About why I picked a fight."

"Why did you?" he asked, his voice gruff.

She lifted her head, and the grim desperation in his eyes made her want to laugh and cry at the same time. A stinging flood of guilt rose in her cheeks and she closed the distance between them.

"I love you," she said. "I couldn't let you go without telling you. I love you."

He stared down at her, the muscles in his jaw working. But he didn't touch her. "You couldn't let me go on deployment? Or you couldn't let me go, period?"

She fisted her hands in his jacket. "Both. Either. You made a decision once, one that you'll regret the rest of your life. I'm here because I made that same kind of decision when I sent you away." Her voice broke and she gave him a shake. "I love you and I'm desperate to know if you still love me because I can't imagine living the rest of my life without you."

He gripped her upper arms and bent his head, and she licked her lips. Then he hesitated, his thumbs caressing her arms, his mouth hovering a torturous inch above her own. "I'm still a soldier."

"Which is one reason I love you. You're an honorable man with an incredible sense of duty. I was wrong to try to take that away."

He wrapped his arms around her and held on tight, his face buried in her hair. "What're the other reasons?" he murmured.

"We can go into all that later." She wreathed her arms around his neck and pressed her mouth to his throat. "Right now I want to know why you haven't kissed me."

"Maybe because I can't find your face."

She choked out a laugh and lifted her head. He smoothed the pad of his thumb over her lips and she started to tremble.

"I love you," he said.

"I love you, too."

He dipped his head and kissed her gently, nibbling at her lips. Then his mouth grew fierce and demanding, his tongue insistent and sensual, and his passion left her sagging against him. When he finally gave her the chance to pull in sweet, sweet oxygen, he rested his forehead on hers, his own breathing hard and fast.

"So." His hands followed the line of her arms, and closed around her wrists at the nape of his neck. "You'll wait for me?"

"To come back from your tour? What then?"

"Then I want to be with my wife and child. If that means weekends only, so be it."

"Wife?" she whispered.

"And child." He unlocked her hands from behind his neck and lowered them to his mouth. "A wedding would make a hell of a send-off for me, don't you think?"

Everything went soft. Her throat, her knees, her heart.

His dark eyes gleamed with heartfelt promises. "Will you marry me, Parker Anne?" His thumb brushed away the tears that spilled down her cheek.

"I'd be honored," she said huskily, and lifted her face. Long moments later she choked out a laugh. "You do remember you're leaving in less than three weeks."

"All the more reason not to waste any time."

"But Nat...and the greenhouse..."

He released her hands and tucked her in close. "You know as well as I do that the kid will be delighted. Especially if I can fit in a rappelling lesson before I go. The rest we'll work out." He leaned away and smiled down into her eyes. "We will make this work."

"Roger that," she whispered, and raised her mouth for another kiss.

EPILOGUE

SURROUNDED BY THE EAGER families of the soldiers returning stateside, Parker and Nat waited inside the Godman Army Airfield hangar. An excited swell of voices drew them up onto their toes and they craned their necks, desperate for a glimpse of the first bus. When a garbage truck lumbered past the entrance, a collective groan rose among the rafters of the huge space, and Parker and Nat settled back onto their heels.

Parker smoothed her palms over the flirty skirt of her sundress, hoping it wouldn't take long for the damp spots to fade. Fourteen months. Fourteen months since she'd kissed her husband of two weeks goodbye. She swallowed against a rising tide of emotion that threatened to become humiliating, reached out and hugged her daughter close.

If those idiot buses didn't arrive soon, she'd recruit a scouting party.

Behind them someone laughed loud enough to create an echo, and a baby started to cry. A whiff of tuna and onion — someone must have unwrapped a sandwich. She winced and guided Nat away from the smell. Nat patted her shoulder, the small flag she carried brushing against Parker's arm.

"Don't worry, Mom. He'll be here soon."

Parker pressed a kiss to the top of her daughter's head. When had she grown so mature?

"It never gets any easier, does it?" A petite, dark-haired woman with a young child in her arms moved closer to Parker and smiled ruefully. "No matter how many times we wait to welcome our sweethearts home, each time is as grueling as the first."

Parker murmured her agreement. No sense in trying to explain this was the second time she'd awaited a soldier's return, and the first time he wouldn't be coming home in a coffin.

Please. *Please.* When was the last time she'd talked to Reid? She suddenly couldn't remember. Three days ago? Four? Her knees started to shake. *What if he didn't get off the bus?*

Beside her the young mother was still talking. "...longest months of my life." She patted her baby's back and swayed.

Parker focused on Nat, who was making kissing noises at the baby and playing with his toes. She inhaled and tried to smile. "Your son is adorable. How old is he?"

"Eighteen months. When his daddy finally shows up, we'll have a lot to catch up on." She tickled her baby under his chin. "Won't we, Scotty?"

He giggled and so did Nat. Parker had just started to feel the first stirrings of maternal temptation when her cell rang. *Saved by the bell.* She excused herself and pressed the phone to her ear.

"Harris. What's up?"

"Is he there yet?"

She turned and rolled her eyes at Nat. "If he were, do you think I'd be answering the phone?"

"Call us as soon as he gets in."

"I'll call you the minute I get a chance, Harris."

"Mom." Nat tugged at the skirt of her sundress. Parker held up a forefinger.

"And listen, my girl, don't be thinkin' you need to tell him right away about that truck engine." His voice dropped to a mumble. "Still can't believe I forgot to put oil in the damned thing."

"How about I let you tell him?"

"*Mom.*"

"Have a heart, Parker Anne—"

259

"Mom!"

Parker turned the phone away from her mouth. "What is it, Natalie Claire?"

"They're coming."

Harris was still grousing when Parker disconnected and thrust her phone into her purse. She looked up, saw the first bus parked at the entrance to the hangar, and groped for Nat's hand.

He's home.

Shouts, whistles, applause and a rollicking sea of flapping American flags greeted the first troops off the bus. They marched into the hangar and lined up in formation, their grins and sidelong glances making it clear they were just as anxious as their families to get on with the hunt-and-hug. But tradition demanded that everyone stand by until all of the buses were unloaded and the unit commander had said a few words.

As if they hadn't already waited long enough.

The first bus took its time moving away, and the crowd began to chant.

"Move that bus. Move that bus. Move that bus."

Parker's chest hurt. And no wonder, since she'd stopped breathing. She dragged in a breath as Nat bounced and fidgeted beside her, and anxiously scanned the faces under the black berets.

Nat was literally humming with anticipation. "Do you see him? Do you see Reid?"

"Not yet, sweetie."

Where are you?

The faces and the uniforms became a blur of olive-green and in some remote section of her brain she registered that the droning noise in the background must be the commander's address. Then the buzzing stopped and the cheers rose again, floating like helium balloons to nudge the ceiling. Someone beside her started to sob, and she found herself jostled from every angle by overexcited relatives. Sweat prickled her scalp, and panic sidled in.

Nat yanked on her hand. "There he is! I see him! Reid! Over

here!" She yanked harder. "C'mon, Mom. *This* way."

But Parker couldn't move. Even if she somehow managed to pick up feet that weighed as much as a pair of armored tanks, she couldn't see through the abrupt flood of dumb, stupid, ridiculous tears. She pulled away from Nat and pressed her hands to her face.

Seconds—minutes?—passed. Tears trickled down her wrists and pooled in the creases of her elbows and her body shook with the strain of keeping her emotions close. And then he was there, standing in front of her. She could *feel* him.

"Parker." His breath drifted across her fingers, and he stroked a hand down her bare arm. But she couldn't move. It was as if her hands were holding back a year's worth of worry, and if she let go...well, it wouldn't be pretty.

"Parker," he said again, more gently. Then her body was pressed to his and his arms were around her and his face was burrowed in the curve between her shoulder and her neck. She shuddered, and eventually worked her hands around so her palms were flat against his chest. She lifted her head and pressed a kiss to his jaw, and they shook together. Nat launched herself at them and wrapped her arms around their waists. Parker leaned back a few inches and stared up into her husband's gorgeous maple-syrup eyes.

"Thank you," she choked out. "For coming back."

His jaw muscles worked as he thumbed the tears from her cheeks. "I had to," he said solemnly. "I forgot my wallet."

She sucked in a breath but never managed the laugh because his mouth was suddenly covering hers. The kiss was long and hard and deep, and life couldn't get much sweeter.

Gradually she registered the insistent pats on her arm. She slid her mouth away from Reid's and reluctantly settled back down onto her heels. He lifted his head and inhaled, moved his hands up to her shoulders and mumbled, "Two minutes. Give me two minutes before you step away."

"Jeez." Nat made a face. "How do you breathe when you do that?" Then her expression turned hopeful, and she stared up at

Reid. "Do you have it?"

"How could you even ask me that?" But he didn't move.

A laugh scraped out of Parker's throat as she swabbed at her face with a handful of tissues. "You all right?"

"Just about. You?"

She grinned. "Never better."

He gave her a wink. Another deep breath, and he let go. "C'mere, kid." He bent and lifted Nat, hugged her tight and swung her around in a circle. She squealed with delight but refused to be distracted. When he set her down she yanked at his sleeve.

"Let me see."

"Roger that." He fished in his breast pocket and pulled out her Hello Kitty watch. "Thanks for the loan. Not only did it bring me luck but it kept excellent time, and it kept me company, too. And it made all the other guys in the squad jealous. Except for the three other guys carrying their kids' watches. We had Spiderman —" he ticked them off on his fingers " — Cinderella, and SpongeBob."

Nat hugged the watch to her cheek and Parker felt an aching swell of love for her little family. Reid smoothed a hand over Nat's head and raised his eyebrows at Parker. "I need to hang around for a few days, for medical checks, then I'm all yours for a month. Think we can get Noble settled in as head honcho of the greenhouse in that amount of time?"

She nodded. "We've already started breaking him in. Though he did buy a round of drinks at Snoozy's when he found out I'd be handling the paperwork from here. He's a little intimidated by the idea of managing our three huts and six growers, too, but Liz offered to help out."

"Good. She's used to working under pressure." His lips twisted. "We've come a long way."

She knew he was referring to Liz's and Noble's initial reactions when they'd learned of Reid's role in her husband's death.

"Don't," she said softly. "That was a long time ago, and everyone is so relieved you're stateside for good."

He inhaled, then with a nod bent to help Nat put her watch back on her wrist. "So you okay with this, kid? Moving to Kentucky? Living here on post?"

"Mom said it was only temporary."

"And she's right. A year and a half and we'll be back in Thistle Hill."

"But meanwhile we'll be back to visit, right?"

"At least once a month."

Parker grimaced. "If only to make sure Harris and Noble haven't buried each other in the compost pile."

"Gross." Nat wrinkled her nose, then tipped her head. "Did you bring me anything else?"

Reid snorted. Nat showed him her teeth and he shook his head, then nudged his duffel bag with the toe of his boot. "You find it, you can have it."

She dropped to her knees, used both hands to work the zipper, and started digging. And Parker moved back into Reid's arms.

"I missed you so much," she whispered.

"How much?"

"I'll show you. Later."

"Not if I show you first." He kissed her lightly and stroked a finger down her cheek. "I know this was hard for you. Harder than I'll ever be able to imagine. But you need to know that your support...it's meant the world to me."

Her eyes took on that familiar wet burn and she blinked impatiently. "In a year and a half, you're leaving the Army and moving to Pennsylvania. You'll be taking on a greenhouse that's still in business thanks to you and a half dozen growers determined to make Thistle Hill the geranium capital of the world. You've agreed to help out Pete Lowry at his garage so he can spend more time with his brand-new grandchild, and you'll have two women, a dog and a cranky old man all clamoring for your attention. I think that qualifies as returning the favor." Her lips shook, and she pressed them to the corner of his mouth. "I love you."

"I love you, too. And I plan to spend the rest of my life showing you just how much."

"Steady, soldier. How about we take it one night at a time?"

"Yes, ma'am." He nuzzled her cheek. "Mrs. MacFarland, ma'am."

"Hey." They both jumped, and looked down at Nat, who sat on the floor surrounded by piles of T-shirts, boxers and socks. She scowled up at them, her arms buried up to the elbows in Reid's bag. "Is there really a present in here or did you just want an excuse to kiss?"

"Yes, there is," Reid said. "And yes, I did." He dropped into a crouch and started stuffing his gear back into the bag. "How about we go back to the town house and find it together?"

"Wait." She was shaking her head, slapping at his hands as he shoved in fistfuls of clothes while she tried to arrange them in neat rows. "You're messing it all up. *Wait.*"

He glanced up at Parker, grinned, then kissed Nat's cheek. "No more waiting, Nat." He zipped up the bag and pulled her to her feet. "C'mon, kid. We have a life to start."

*   *   *

Thank you for reading THE LONG WAY HOME! I hope that Parker and Reid kept you entertained. :-)

Have a sweet tooth? Subscribe to my mailing list and get instant access to an exclusive collection of recipes for the sweet treats featured in the Thistle Hill series. Cupcakes, muffins, cookies and more—inside THE SWEET STUFF you'll find a baker's dozen of recipes and story snippets guaranteed to whet your [romantic] appetite. :-)

You can subscribe on my website (www.kathyaltman.com) for access to the download (ebook only), or scan this handy dandy QR code:

Interested in helping other readers find this book while earning my endless gratitude? Please consider leaving a review. I would love it so much if you did. Thank you!

To find out about upcoming releases, including the next book in the Thistle Hill series, check out my website at www.kathyaltman.com.

ABOUT THE AUTHOR

Author, wife, cat mom, hardcore chocolate chip cookie fan, Kathy Altman prefers her chocolate with nuts, her Friday afternoons with wine and her love stories with happy ever afters. Her contemporary romance and romantic suspense books are an award-winning, feel-good blend of the heartfelt, the humorous, and the seriously sexy.